THE GREAT UKRAINIAN
PARTISAN MOVEMENT

CHARLES MERRILL

The Great Ukrainian Partisan Movement

and Other Tales of the Eisenhower Years

1983

WILLIAM L. BAUHAN, PUBLISHER
DUBLIN, NEW HAMPSHIRE

Library of Congress Cataloguing in Publication data:
Merrill, Charles, 1920–
The great Ukrainian partisan movement and other tales of the Eisenhower years
I. Title.
PS3563.E745165G7   1983   813'.54   83-11758
ISBN 0-87233-071-0

Four stories, *The Garden, A Simple Soul, Freedom* and *The Prophet* were originally published in German by Leykam Verlag, Graz, Austria, 1963.

Charles Merrill is also the author of *The Walled Garden: The Story of a School,* 1982

Printed in the United States of America

For
Catherine and Amy
Bruce, David, Paul

CONTENTS

The Great Ukrainian Partisan Movement   1

The Pursuit of Happiness   36

A Simple Soul   51

A Glass of Mandarin   77

Freedom   86

The Garden   115

O Canada   137

Return and Time   144

The Vortex   160

The Stone Guest   170

Paris in the Spring   211

The Prophet   222

The Honor of the Home   236

I

THE GREAT UKRAINIAN
PARTISAN MOVEMENT

AFTER TWO WEEKS of rain the café was trying to win back profits by jamming the tables so close that when the woman on my left rose suddenly my Dubonnet toppled over onto the lap of the Colonel, on my right. He was a tall, domineering man in his late forties with a face too harsh and muscled for a café, too long and bony for a Frenchman, though he wore the usual red ribbon in his buttonhole, and I feared trouble out of the accident. However, he accepted my apologies with a surprising reasonableness, first in French and then in English, both strongly accented, as he ascertained my nationality. To stir up a little conversation, I expounded briefly upon the lipstick shades promenading by, from Prussian blue to lemon yellow, for I am fascinated by the extremes of French makeup, which either applies rouge with the handle of a toothbrush and leaves the woman's face the glowing pink you find in a mortician's display room or else aims for a maximum effect of decay by the use of eye shadow solely. This subject, however, did not interest the Colonel.

"Freedom is strange thing," he remarked in English with a heavy accent that I now placed as Russian

"Freedom is for the strong," I replied promptly.

"It is a longing of the spirit."

"Yes, indeed."

"It is casting off chains of convention and tradition."

"And the chains of one's own personality."

He raised his eyebrows. I was clearly not an ordinary American.

"What would Kafka have been able to reach had he known the liberty of Paris?"

"Rilke found that liberation, though he paid for it, a high price."

We were even.

"Of course the search for freedom in literature expresses itself in different ways." Slowly, obscurely, this talk was headed in some direction beyond mere esthetics. "And the responsibility is as much to the reader as to the author."

"What do you have in mind?"

In reply, he picked up a heavy paper package from the sidewalk and set it upon his table.

"The Marquis de Sade."

"My!"

"Complete."

"Fascinating."

"One hundred thousand francs."

"Fantastic."

"Morocco. Gold tops. Ninety-eight percent in English."
A pause. "Illustrated."

"Nevertheless."

"The second volume alone, if you have friends—if you are trying to establish a certain relationship——" I checked him, I understood—"will repay the entire cost."

"My hundred thousand francs goes for food, lodging, and Metro tickets."

He turned his dignified, reserved face, tinged with sadness, with incredulity, toward me. This navy blue suit of mine is deceptive.

"A gentleman knows where to choose within the hierarchy of values."

The control of the man, the skill, the daring, began to

recall an old dream that I had let drift away into a mist of speculation. I handed him my card. From an old pigskin wallet he presented me his own: Colonel Porphyry Filipovich Fewchuk. I regarded him sharply. He was too young to belong to the generation of czarist refugees, and he showed an alertness that those gentry have lost.

"From the Ukraine?"

That sort of name is not uncommon, and in the army I had known Ukrainians from the anthracite towns.

"From the greater Ukraine, though I carry, like yourself, I may presume, monsieur, an American passport."

"Czernowitz?"

"Kishinev."

"Pushkin's city of exile?"

"Yes, unhappy years for him, I am afraid. I see you know well our sad old continent, monsieur. Once I was citizen of the kingdom of Romania, but it is as Ukrainian I have always considered myself, when I served in the army of General Vlassov and when I was able to serve the army of your, or may I say, our own country, for which I was rewarded with my green passport."

"Paris is your home?"

"My business skills were inadequate in the febrile world of New York. Paris"—he extended his hands reflectively— "releases my soul."

It was my turn now to direct the conversation.

"Certain forms of business activity which demand courage, individuality, and if I may say so, spiritual control, and which repay the exceptional man with exceptional returns, retaining more the quality of the rapier than that of the club or the screwdriver—as distasteful, I hasten to assure you, to me as to you—still offer special challenges in America."

"As God wills."

The first phase of our association could not have finished more appropriately. I invited him for dinner with me the next evening at a restaurant I knew, so slovenly, so expensive (though the food is not bad) that its clientele is so naive you can speak quite freely. Even if you are overheard you will not be understood.

We separated and I strolled thoughtfully along the Champs Elysées, all my dabbling in lip shades forgotten. Vast risks, a lonely boldness that leads, as Shakespeare expressed it forcefully, to sleeplessness—but I had been to my last PTA meeting, and a steak dinner on an expense account with a hatcheck girl had lost interest for me.

II

Colonel Fewchuk obviously did not eat at many places where he did not have to pay the bill. He sat wordless for ten minutes as he studied the menu; but the thoroughness with which he then commanded herring, soup, salmon, duck, Châteaubriand, string beans, salad, chocolate cake, and camembert, with vodka, wines, and brandies, delighted me. I was seeking a man of appetite, energy, and administrative skill.

I asked him about Vlassov's army, a melancholy outfit which had always interested me, the force of Soviet prisoners under a turncoat Red Army general which might have been a decisive ally to the Wehrmacht in the Ukraine had not Hitler's distrust of all Slavs thrown away its possibilities. The Colonel spoke with force and even a certain humor about the organization, which he had joined from the other direction. When the Russians seized Bessarabia in 1940, he had fled Kishinev (I never pinned down his original trade—timber, journalism, theater, finance: it varied), but more inclined toward the capital of his country's enemy, Budapest, than toward Bucharest to recoup his fortune, he came east again as an interpreter with a Hungarian railway division, and as Vlassov's army began to form early in '42 he became involved in that. Fewchuk, more aware of the ways of the world than the other Ukrainians who had known only Soviet customs, rose to the rank of colonel. As the German lines shrank westward, he moved with them, putting himself safely into Salzburg at the end of the war, a Romanian in theory so that the Russians could not demand his repatriation, a Soviet expert when this became useful, an officer of Vlassov's army, that tempting example to the bright young men of the State Department and the New York magazines of how the Soviet Union would collapse if intelligent violence were applied. He had lived in New York and written for magazines himself, but his value as an expert fell, and eventually he found himself in Paris, which gave a living haphazard and skimpy yet offered the boulevards he did not find in America.

By the time we reached coffee I felt sure enough of his value to change our line of discussion.

"You sell only the marquis?"

"I do not compete with postcard vendors," he stated. "Any man of culture knows that Sade is top. Casanova, Boccaccio, Balzac—if well illustrated they make tasteful gifts, but in my days as New York businessman I learned respect for what you Americans call class."

"This trade should grant you a wide knowledge of human nature, as Chekhov, for instance, found in medicine."

"Quite correct. Again I return to the word class. One hundred thousand francs demands respect. Twenty thousand francs, what the books cost, is ordinary. I sell to foreigners. They expect this in Paris. They are disappointed, and become cynical and end up at the Opéra in outright acceptance of mediocrity. But they carry their money with them in large amounts. For real value, they are willing to spend heavily. My only misfortune with you, dear sir, was in finding a man less rich and more cultured than I had expected."

I ignored the compliment. My voice sank to a whisper.

"Yet, retaining the Morocco binding, a certain type of salesman might sell even the New Testament at the same disquieting price."

"It could be done. But it would be harder."

"You are a man of understanding, Colonel Fewchuk, the man, perhaps, I have been looking for."

He bowed respectfully but without conviction. I am, despite my vocabulary and my expensive suit, a nonimpressive person. You would not look at me and rush up with your life's savings to invest.

"Colonel, from your experience with Americans, what are they interested in?"

He smiled deprecatingly.

"But in what else?"

"Communism."

How hard I was trying to disguise my excitement!

"Really? Not in their gleaming bathrooms, their intricate little gadgets?"

"No. Europeans like to think so, but they are twenty years too late. The Americans take that for granted. If the toilet does not flush, they become distraught, but technology is no longer a challenge to them."

"Communism is?"

"The American is upset, he is fascinated. Communism denies his entire contribution to the world. Between the Communist and the American exists the same relationship as between the heroes of the Marquis de Sade and the unfortunate prudes who fall across their path."

"Go on."

"Again, the security of the Americans' lives makes them relish the violence and cunning imperative for survival in Communist society. Like sex, it is the last frontier."

"Colonel Fewchuk," I cried hoarsely, "now is the time for me to throw off the mask."

His keen gray eyes showed no emotion. He raised a finger for the waiter and pointed to his brandy glass. And when Martell was brought again, he pointed to the Otard, which was twice as expensive.

"You see before you a man who also has suffered from American civilization," I began. "An unhappy marriage"—

the Colonel lowered his eyes—"not the slightest of the difficulties, but also a temper wounded by just those qualities you noticed with such acumen. Well but uselessly educated at our oldest university. A soldier to whom the names of European rivers and forests are not mere geographical terms. Returning worn in spirit to my wife's home, a suburb of St. Louis, a friendly town of lawns and elm trees, I gazed at the October chrysanthemums and smelled the burning leaves and entered my father-in-law's thermostat business."

His eyes became glazed. He had eaten a phenomenal amount. It was a sign of the restaurant's mismanagement that the detritus was left on the next table to recall how much had been consumed, and the emptied wine bottles standing among the dirty plates like chimneys of burned-out factories reminded me of the German cities I had seen in 1945.

"I shoveled snow in winter and mowed the lawn in summer. At the surface my life was what you would see on the covers of a dozen mass-circulation magazines. But I was suffering from the limitations of our community. Nothing stirred it, not even money, except sex or violence. The youngsters from these nice homes who acted like hoodlums and harlots were achingly envied because no better antidote for boredom could be found. Yet where else could one go? This town of gardens and discussion groups was the ideal of American society. I lay awake each night twitching my feet until my wife's nerves wore away. Complications arose——"

"That is very interesting. Perhaps I have eaten so much that my mind no longer functions as sharply as it should," the Colonel interrupted. "But I find no place for myself in this discourse. You should have known the younger members of the business community of Kishinev. Gypsy orchestras, sleigh rides under a robe of marten furs." He sighed, "Une vie perdue."

"No. That is the past. Let me tell you of the future."

III

The Colonel and I arrived in Dallas two weeks later and went over to pay a call on General Hashbarger. Five years before, at a faraway business party I had met the General, a wiry little blue-eyed man with fading blond hair and the extreme nervous energy you find in certain officers as if they were always about to stride into a barracks and quell a mutiny, a tight surface sharpness covering a profound stupidity. The General was in food, or foods, pushing corn shreds, jackwheat flakes, and sorghum crisps around Texas the way he had once hurled his convoys into southern Germany. The vigor and logic he was employing at that first meeting in favor of immediate preventive war against Russia made me see him as our man.

We were ushered into his office: Mr. Dawson and Colonel Fewchuk to see him.

"Glad to see you, Colonel," he said to Porphyry Filipovich, one professional to another, a hunger to use titles and plan things, for desks of big corporations are full of old soldiers and there's not much for them to do.

"General, five years ago I heard you speak about the strengths and weaknesses of Soviet Russia," I began after he lit a cigar for Porphyry Filipovich. "No thirty-minute speech ever made a greater impression on me. Even today I bet you I could repeat it word for word."

The little blue eyes flashed.

"The Colonel and I arrived in New York from Paris Tuesday, and you, sir, are the first person in this country I've come to meet."

The eyes turned cold and eager. I nodded to the Colonel, who took from his pocket an envelope which General Hashbarger opened and read.

"Dear Tom," (the letter began. Porphyry Filipovich's publishing connections had let us print up a lot of stationery, and the signature he had traced from the guest book of the

Tour d'Argent, another capital investment, though I had had to beg Porphyry to eat more moderately): "Colonel Fewchuk and his friend Oliver Dawson have some mighty interesting things on their minds you might care to hear—and to forget too if anyone starts asking you about it." And the signature was General Gruenther's. He was head of SHAPE then. Fat chance for a has-been like Tom Hashbarger ever getting to check on matters with his old buddy. I saw the note enshrined in the family archives. The years were dropping away. He was already five thousand miles from Dallas.

"General Hashbarger," I began, "do you know where the Colonel was a week ago today?" I let him sit a moment. "Lemberg. Or if you prefer, Lvov."

You could hear the wheels spin but the gamble was worth taking. These old soldiers pride themselves on geography.

"That used to be southeastern Poland. It's Russia now!" he burst out.

"The Ukraine," Porphyry Filipovich intoned.

"By God, man——" He stared at the Colonel.

"Lemberg." Porphyry Filipovich stared moodily at the table, memories of his martyred people overwhelming his heart.

"How the hell did you get out?" the General demanded.

"An old German Storch. With a field in the Carpathians and one our Romanian friends manage to ignore, the Colonel got back to Istanbul," I filled in.

"By God!"

"I met the Colonel in Istanbul and we flew on to Paris together."

"But why do you want to see an old army mule like myself?" the General cried out in a forlorn attack of common sense. "I just hold down a desk. Those bright young gentlemen out there——"

"General, I'm not a bright young gentleman, and I'm not interested in one of them. I'm interested in a man!" Porphyry Filipovich's deep voice held a human understanding that the

General had not heard for a long time. His heavy Russian accent gave a universal quality to the appeal. Lincoln or Clemenceau would have spoken with the same pain-racked voice. "Mr. Dawson told me——"

"There it is," I broke in. "We'll lay our cards on the table, General. You know what the Ukrainians have suffered from the Russians. The destruction of a people, a language, a whole culture—there isn't much you can find in history to match it. Colonel Fewchuk's wife——" But his face grimaced. It was not right to go so close to the human heart. "What you may not be aware of, General, is that the sole partisan movement actively fighting Communist tyranny is the one in the Ukraine. In the Carpathians, in the forests, even in the little twisting streets of Kiev, you'll find men who are fighting for the freedom of their homeland."

"That sounds terrible!"

"There's organization, there's communication, of a sort, at a wicked price they have to pay, but what is necessary——"

"We need guns!" came like a groan from Porphyry Filipovich.

"That's the gist of it. You can't fight with sticks and stones."

Some of Porphyry Filipovich's agony had entered into the General.

"But what can I do? God, I'd like to strike back!"

"Well, you can guess it's got something to do with money," I said with a wry smile. "We've a real source of munitions— this'll amuse you—with an ex-Communist in Trieste who's selling us the guns the Reds were stockpiling back in '45. German and American machine guns all nicely coated with grease. And the Germans are manufacturing a beautiful little two-way radio: carries ninety miles, weighs ten pounds, as big as your two feet, but it's not cheap."

I sighed. It is sickening to tie freedom to finance.

"I'm not a rich man."

"General," Porphyry Filipovich interrupted again. "Mr. Dawson slants things too much one way. Money is needed. I know that. A lot of officials have to be persuaded to look the other way—though that's easier than you think. Money we can find, but it's what I said before: men."

He spoke slowly. Each word had to be dragged out. A veil rapidly rose between him and us, so that you had a vision of him disappearing into a forest, or up a rocky hillside wreathed in mist. The human being becomes a shadow and then it is gone. A man one rarely sees in Dallas now or walking along Madison Avenue. "We need to rely on someone, a few men of faith. Faith," he repeated the word to himself "Trying to keep faith."

"We had to start with someone we could trust," I finished. "I've lost touch with the States these last years. That's why I came here, to start with one man I could be sure of."

"Gentlemen, I'm deeply humble."

We rented a car and left Dallas for three days to go rabbit hunting around Corsicana while General Hashbarger arranged a dinner with his friends. Porphyry Filipovich hadn't hunted since he had left Kishinev, and my supplying him with that meant more, I think, than all the meals I paid for. We hiked all over those yellow hills, beating up through the draws and under the blackjack trees. The second day we must have covered twenty miles on foot. I've never seen a more tireless walker. He slipped through the scrub pine like a ghost, and I was always surprised to see a bunny as the result rather than a dead NKVD agent. We ate what we shot. He'd gut and skin the rabbit, ramming onions and peppers into all the open spots and dousing it with paprika, turn it over a low fire on a stick, and then we'd wash it down with straight bourbon. Sometimes he'd stew the little animals in a sort of horseradish sauce. You could feel the holes eat through your stomach. At night he wrapped himself in a blanket and lay down on the ground while I made out the best I could in the car. Those three days gave us both a brown, tough, and for me a worn appearance that I suppose is common for partisan leaders.

In theory, when we met at the General's house, we had flown to Mexico City and back. Porphyry Filipovich kissed Mrs. Hashbarger's hand, which stopped her conversation before it began, and we could sit and drink our highballs in silence. After a while our host showed us his souvenirs: the swastika autographed by an SS general, his Luger, his snapshots of Dachau and his German girl, himself as a brand-new lieutenant back in '17.

Then the guests started to arrive. It was perfect weather for such a gathering. The first autumn crispness sharpens the air and people are wondering what the winter's project will be. In Kirkwood that means which discussion group shall we join, but not in Texas. I met Mr. Pike, a pear-shaped mortician who had made himself big with a string of funeral parlors based on some revolutionary principle—self-service or drive-in, I forget which—and Mike Hamish, a big oil man from West Texas, though from the way he kept laughing at the others' jokes instead of telling his own, not as big as he'd like, and a lot of other new friends. Porphyry Filipovich let me handle all the preliminary socializing. He hardly spoke at all, which up to a point adds to a stranger's prestige. Mrs. Pike wanted to know about the little red ribbon in his buttonhole, and I told her it was a shred of the Ukrainian flag that he and his boys had divided up just before a Russian attack wiped out the battalion.

It was getting late before the really big man came, the man for whom General Hashbarger was merely the lure: big Seth Cassell, and his daughter Sarmina. Big Seth, who wore chocolate-and-blue cowboy boots and little silver steerhead buttons on his vest, owned enough cattle to clog the Chisholm Trail, but he rested fundamentally on oil and the twenty-five percent tax deduction for dry wells. Cassell was the wealthiest and most ruthless crackpot in Texas. He gave away money as casually as he went to the toilet. His charities made a fine splash, but when they sounded patriotic they were propaganda and police outfits if not outright blackmail, and when they sounded educational they were earmarked in such a way that even a college president couldn't smile at them— busbies for the band when a school didn't have the cash on hand for next month's payroll. Seth Cassell's love of destruction might be just what it took to slide him into our pockets.

Sarmina. What of her? A lot of ink has been wasted on the daughters of American millionaires: their beauty, vigor, cruelty, frustration. The only ones I have seen personally, besides Sarmina, were in Texas when I crept around the edges of the big world with my thermostats, and I don't care for them. Marvelous creatures, like young horses, brimming with health, not a day of constipation in their lives, they possess strange powers and fire their first servant when they are twelve and can drive a car a hundred miles an hour; infinitely talented when you first meet them because they have started everything, water skiing to harp playing, and never found it worthwhile to finish anything. Love included. They travel East to college with a trunkload of tweed skirts, cashmere sweaters, and Bermuda shorts. But people aren't friendly. They are Jews and girls with Italian and even Armenian names and the weather is bad and they come home again to look after Daddy and wait for a husband. When they marry, Daddy builds them a nice house in the corner of the lot where the young couple can go up to the big house for cocktails every evening, and when they are divorced, as Sarmina was, they move right back.

Golden blond, bare-shouldered, that glorious body untarnished by motherhood, Sarmina stood erect in General Hashbarger's living room and gazed about selecting whom to greet and whom to ignore, her smile flashing on and off like a neon blinker.

"A week ago when I met Colonel Fewchuk in Istanbul," I began after the General had introduced me, "I never expected we'd be in Dallas with you all tonight, but as I listened

to his story of that last raid into the foothills of the Carpathians——"

"Here, young man, let us listen to the Colonel," broke in
Mr. Cassell.

I was the first to look over at Porphyry Filipovich, almost
lost, big though he was, in a vast armchair. Like Garibaldi
or Tolstoy or any other great simple figure, he was able to
employ his weaknesses as a positive strength. A college president would have hummed out with his charts and human
interest stories, but Porphyry Filipovich became barely conscious that we existed. He raised his strange, haunted eyes
and fastened them on Seth Cassell's for a long, long look
and then on his cigar again and shook his head bitterly at
the insurmountable job of communication. A rumbling noise
came from that armchair and we knew he had begun to
speak.

"Hot summer, dry, streams dry, river beds just mud, sun-
flower fields withered, rye harvest bad. Hard winter. Spring
in my country is like young girl"—his sad eyes regarded
Sarmina—"but the springs wither, like our girls. Only in the
forests, deep, deep, with pheasants, deer, kuropatky, kuropatky——"

Like Laocoön with the serpents he struggled against the
word. His clenched fist trembled.

"Partridge," I said.

"Partridge. Partridge." It had a good sound. "Partridge,
wild buffalo, lost in cool moss and ferns. Forgotten in millet
patches and dusty wooden villages along Dnepr and Bug and
Dnestr and Prut . . ." He drifted off into geography and I
became alarmed, but the others sat there mesmerized. No
voice, no accent like his had ever come into their sheltered
lives. "And forgotten in cities. Freedom loves forest and
swamp, mountain. My boys——" His eyes flashed wildly at
them and his voice suddenly turned into fury. "Do you know
what it means to lead company of lads who love you and to

give them an order that will have nine out of ten lying dead next day?"

"Yes, son, I do," Seth Cassell replied gently. His eyes had filmed. In fact, all their eyes had filmed. Except for Sarmina. Her eyes burned.

"I am fool. I should control these attacks from Istanbul." He shook his head in guilt and doubt. "But I can't give order like that to lads and stay back in safety. Lenin could. I can't. I beg you to understand." They nodded. They understood the heart's weakness. "What we wanted were hostages. Strike at police themselves, strike at hideous heart and show our teeth and have their men in our hands to protect our boys in prison. We fell on that convoy. Like a thunderbolt!" He leaned over and struck the floor with his fist. "A hundred dead. Twenty-two prisoners."

"Did you save your boys?" asked the General.

He shook his head.

"They tied them down and poured gasoline over them." He couldn't finish.

"What did you do to the hostages?" Sarmina demanded.

"We made them remember. Their major was still alive. We lashed him to the back of wild bull and waved fire in its face. For captain, we tied down the tops of two young birch trees and fastened his feet to them, and girl came with knife and slashed rope." Our audience was pretty ashen except Sarmina, whose cheeks were flushed and whose bosom swelled until she looked unbelievably gorgeous. "And the men? We sharpened twenty stakes and put them up in middle of highway and sat each one of them on tops. Two were still living when patrol found them."

In the numbness that followed Mr. Pike still managed to lean over and whisper: "What do they do with the girls?"

"See me afterwards, "I hissed.

"But doesn't terror just mean counterterror?" came Mrs. Hashbarger's trembling voice.

"You are Christian woman. You are like our own women who keep ikon burning in corner and come to greet stranger with bread and salt, the moral depth of our women that thirty years of enslavement has not destroyed. I bow before you and your good heart." And he did just that. But again the falcon flew into the brazen heavens. "Terror tells our people that liberty is still alive! We strike back!"

"By God, that's right!" the General cried, grateful for the way the Colonel had treated his wife.

"And as our movement spreads into the cities——"

"But why can't you get support from the American army? What do we have to do with all them goings on?" whined Mr. Pike. I was proud to see Sarmina's look of contempt.

"General Gruenther——"indignantly began the General.

I stopped him. He had gone too far, even with this group.

"I think we all know the answer to that question," I said quietly. "The army doesn't drive down the middle of the street with the bugles blowing. But even with the most secret ways, we can't go too far. Our allies——"

"Damn cowards!" exploded Mr. Cassell.

"Exactly. The game is too big. Our partner—I'll just call him Fitzhugh now, though someday Americans will be proud of him and his own town, a Texas town, you'll be glad to know, will set up a monument. Fitzhugh was shot down last month in Istanbul. A man closer to me than a brother could have been. Not a word. Not even to the CIA men. They know but they look the other way. The Colonel was in Kharkov. I was alone. I hired a boat and rowed into the Bosphorus in the middle of the night and dropped his body into the water. It was a lonely hour."

"But how much are you looking for, Dawson?" This from Mr. Hamish in the back of the room.

"Right now, two million."

My face showed the strain of getting back to money again.

"You're not expecting us to put up everything, are you?"

"No, gentlemen. A check for fifty thousand is waiting for

me in New York, but I came to Dallas because five years
ago I heard General Hashbarger speak about Communism.
I knew I had met a man that night and I knew I could trust
any man he led me to. There's a lot of money in New York.
But there are a lot of other things going in and out of New
York. I don't want New York's support! I want something I
can trust, that's a solid rock. That's why I came here!"

A shudder of strong emotion shook the group.

"What do you want from me, Mr. Dawson?" Mr. Cassell
boomed.

"One hundred thousand dollars."

"You've got a nerve!"

"Mr. Dawson *has* a nerve," Porphyry Filipovich quietly
interrupted. "I am one to tell you that. He never would. That
night in Istanbul, when they murdered young Fitzhugh, Mr.
Dawson was man who followed NKVD agent to other side
of city and killed him with own hands and got papers back."

"I'm not like Seth Cassell. I'm a small man, though out in
Midland I'm big enough," Mike Hamish called out, "but I'll
be the first crackpot in on this and here's my check for ten
thousand dollars."

We hit the gospel trail after that night. Big Seth Cassell
hadn't tipped his hand yet though he invited us back to
Dallas in three weeks' time to stay at his home and meet
even bigger men. We worked the other towns—Houston,
San Antonio, Austin, the rim of the Permian oil basin at
Midland, where I felt less at ease because the boom had
brought in too many Easterners with dark gray suits and
small critical minds. I was as much of a foreigner as Porphyry
Filipovich and they treated me in much the same way we
Americans are apt to act toward Europeans. More of a foreigner really. Porphyry Filipovich found more and more that
reminded him of the Ukraine. His past changed, not only
from the Kishinev little-theater days but from freedom fighting as well. He became a landed proprietor. Servant girls
danced the czardas in their petticoats upon his table and he

killed bear with his father's old bear spear. This delighted the audience but we didn't pick up much money. Why should a bear hunter rate a check for ten thousand dollars? From Midland we were due in Amarillo, but my nerves were shredding away and I didn't want to see either Porphyry Filipovich or another Texan for a while. Up I flew to Chicago while he went back hunting.

I checked in with my secretary at the Drake. We had a suite overlooking the lake and took most of our meals in the Camellia Room, for I find those flickering blue flames around the shashlik and the crepes very restful. Evylyn was a good-natured girl who thought it cultured to talk about food and drink, so I'd tell her about the Tour d'Argent and other famous places. I bought her pretty clothes—she was a girl very easy to please if you spent enough money. We went to the aquarium and walked along Michigan Boulevard and got along great. At night I heard Texan in my dreams and Porphyry Filipovich's accent, like holding your nails to an emery wheel, and I'd wake up Evylyn and get her to talk in that beautiful flat Chicago voice of hers.

The closer the plane got to Dallas, the deeper my heart sank. Maybe the dream of becoming a great financial adventurer was like the old one of becoming a rhumba dancer, not for me.

Sarmina met me at the airport in her blond Cadillac with the "Texans Eat Beef Every Day" bumper sticker. The Colonel hadn't showed up yet, she informed me. My days with Evylyn had reminded me just how easy it is to get along with most women. As a bachelor in Philadelphia my father used to drop in at midnight on the restaurants where rich old men took vigorous young women, and at that hour the old men were ready to go home to bed and the young women had already been wined and dined, which allowed my father a pleasant evening for little money. But what pleased Sarmina, besides rolling through a red light at sixty miles an hour, I didn't know.

I was not happy to see her and have to start inventing new lies so soon, but she asked me about the Colonel. That story I knew perfectly and I could relax and watch her profile and the motions of her arms and legs as she drove us home.

One thing is reassuring about a real Texan house: everything costs a lot of money. No one is nervously trying taste or imagination to make up for a tight budget. We sank into the living room carpet up to our ankle bones, and a man's skull could have been cracked with any one of the crystal ashtrays. I was surprised, nevertheless, when a blue-haired woman waded across the carpet to greet me. Having Sarmina, Big Seth scarcely needed a wife and I'd been ready to believe that Sarmina herself had never possessed a mother. Despite her expert cordiality I kept on my guard. Big men's sons aren't much, though the discovery of penicillin has cut down the hazards of raising them, and the daughters are so close to the old man that they pick up the megalomania without the judgment; but the wives have been left behind, no matter how much they buy, and some of them acquire a dangerous rationality. We fenced carefully and I was relieved to hear Cassell's heavy feet.

"The Colonel with you, sir?"

"Nary a hair of him," he declared. "Have a drink?"

Maybe Hromulko—" I began to myself. Time was running out.

"Who?"

"No, that couldn't be. Not here."

"What you mumbling about?

Vassily Hromulko. NKVD. I thought we had given him the slip."

In Texas?"

I looked at him with a disdain that Big Seth Cassell doesn't often receive.

"Is it that hard to get into Texas?"

"Do you think he has gotten the Colonel?" gasped Sarmina.

"You don't get the Colonel," I replied coldly. "But if Hromulko was able——"

Where would he be?" she asked, strangely anxious.

I acted decisively.

"There's a chance. Can I borrow your car?"

"I'll drive it for you!"

"God, no! This is nothing for a girl to be mixed up in," I warned and looked over to Mr. Cassell for support, but he was proud at his daughter's spirit.

"Don't waste your time, Mr. Dawson," the girl said.

She pushed me out of the house—"Be careful, Sarmina," came her mother's voice—and into the Cadillac. She pulled open the glove compartment long enough for me to see the pistol inside. Then we roared down the driveway. "Where to?"

Laconically I gave her directions at each crossroad as we headed towards Corsicana, hitting eighty on the straight stretches. I said nothing more. My silence gave me a little mystery too. Actually I did have a hunch. At one cabin where we had stopped for a drink of water, the slatternly sixteen-year-old who served us had been so taken by Porphyry Filipovich's accent and his arrogant courtliness that she stretched herself around him like an alley cat in the sunshine. We had picked off three rabbits and seen deer sign. Perhaps the combination had brought him back. Sarmina was not such a fool, however, that she couldn't tell the difference between a man hunting rabbits and one lying tortured in the hands of the NKVD's Texas section. I looked at my watch nervously—it was difficult at that velocity not to do anything nervously. With her ready sympathy Sarmina increased our speed by fifteen percent.

At sundown we came in sight of the cabin on its hilltop. Sure enough a new orange car was parked outside. My hunch had paid off. I motioned to her to slow down.

"Oh, oh," I muttered somberly.

"That's Hromulko's car?"

"Maybe so. Turn around. Behind those blackjack trees there."

Excitedly she whisked the big car around. I grabbed the pistol before she could reach it.

"We're in this together," she snapped.

"You be ready for the getaway. That's the crucial part. Maybe I can surprise them. I'll do my best, Sarmina. If you hear shots and I don't come out, head on back."

"Shall I tell the police?"

"No, sir!"

She didn't demand any explanation. People like the Cassells aren't accustomed to rely upon the police. Leaving her in the shadow of the blackjack trees, I loped up toward the house, taking advantage of all cover to reassure Sarmina of the danger I was running. An NKVD agent in that cabin might actually be less dangerous than the Colonel if I burst in on him without warning, but I was riding a tiger. Gun in hand, I kicked open the door upon a scene of proletarian revelry.

This juvenile delinquent was seated upon the knees of an unshaven, greasy Porphyry Filipovich, one hand around his neck and the other holding a glass of bourbon. The leathery old mother, a whiskey grin on her face, was messing around with a stew pot. Porphyry Filipovich had just reached for a bone from a great platter of quail and rabbit scraps resting on the table and glared at me as if I'd been a serf from one of those hunting estates.

"Beat it! Let's go!" I shouted in French, shooting my pistol through the window to impress Sarmina. "We're due back in Dallas." *Bang.* The mother threw her spoon at me while the daughter leapt from his lap at my throat. *Bang,* through the ceiling. "Ladies, please, let me explain!" I said, trying to smile and firing out the window again. Porphyry Filipovich gave a shove that sent me crashing into the corner but at least freed my throat from his friend's clutch. "We got to get out of here!" I yelled feebly from the floor as she kicked at me with her bare feet. "You do good in Dallas tonight or it'll be the cops." His mind was beginning to work. He pulled the girl into his arms for a tremendous hug, and then her mother. I picked myself up and examined the rifle: deer cartridges, not buckshot. "Out the door, get going!" Then, thrusting the rifle into the hands of the mother, I said, "You're two sweet girls. My friend will never forget you." I was putting my trust in all the bourbon and doubtless the two of them would tussle a bit for possession of the gun, but that was a hair-raising run down the slope with those bullets whining past our heads. I turned at the bottom and fired my last two shots at the cabin, and then we were at the blackjack trees and falling into the Cadillac, which had reached sixty by the time I got the door closed.

"Get hold of yourself," I commanded Porphyry Filipovich in French again, trusting that Sarmina, who was driving with the lights off, had never bothered to learn any tongue but her own. "Tonight's the last chance."

"Were the tortures awful?" she asked. Just then we slipped between a trailer truck and a Greyhound bus and his moan was answer enough.

IV

The guests began showing and I limped around meeting the important new people along with General Hashbarger and the funeral parlor magnate, Mr. Pike, holdovers from the first group. Mrs. Cassell was present but the real hostess was Sarmina. She wore a blond gown that matched her hair and on that great exposed chest a necklace of oversized turquoise and topaz. "Evenin', Uncle Joe," she'd call out in a specially thick regional accent to some old man, "welcome to the li'l old water hole," and they'd kiss and he'd pat her bottom, which I suppose he'd been patting since she was nine. The noise became deafening, not the crackle you hear at a New York cocktail party but something out of the plains with these old bulls roaring at each other from opposite sides of the room.

Just before dinner was announced Porphyry Filipovich appeared, in a black silence and one of Mr. Cassell's suits, which gave him a sort of apelike quality because the sleeves barely came to his wrists, again all to the good when people have had too much of the perfectly tailored representatives of fine charities. And though I had interrupted him in the middle of that meal of slaughtered game, he cut slices off his steaks as big as a girl's fist and drained each wine glass at a swallow. This pleased the others, proud to see a stranger do justice to Texas beef, but I couldn't eat—among other things he'd left his passport behind at the cabin—and I couldn't even enjoy Sarmina's chest.

"What's the news from Istanbul tonight?" that wretched mortician asked me flippantly. I wasn't going to let him fool around and began a dead serious monologue about our intelligence reports. This flimflam was just what those thrill hunters had been waiting for, and they stopped rattling their forks and listened, though I was so full of seven hundred apprehensions I couldn't concentrate. But Porphyry Filipovich came through. He raised his hand to stop me and the heads swiveled toward him, for it was the first thing he had done all evening except eat.

"Mr. Cassell, can you guarantee security of everyone here?" he pronounced.

I felt ashamed of having doubted him.

"Why, they're all from fine Dallas families, Colonel Fewchuk," Mrs. Cassell exclaimed, but the others were modern and knew what he meant and looked around at each other with excited, insecure glances. A Mr. Vilmorin had been born in New York and the eyes ended upon him, but he was Cassell's guest and the old man put his fist out on the table and said: "You can trust these people, Fewchuk."

"The strikes at Kharkov——" I began again, more sure of myself. Again his grave face stopped me, the heavy eyebrows raised toward the service door. What a fool I'd been!

"The staff.'

"Martha's been with us twenty years!" cried Mrs. Cassell. "That new Leroy went to college," Mr. Cassell warned and we nodded our heads. Mrs. Cassell rang the bell. The older butler came.

"Tell Leroy to take the car and pick up another case of Chablis at Quaglino's."

"Yes, ma'am."

As easy as that.

"The Colonel don't look good," Mrs. Pike next to me whispered.

"He'll make his drop five days from now. He's been fighting a long time. It tells on a man. Even him."

General Hashbarger leaned towards me with a displeased face. "What do you mean, strikes?"

An error. Dark-eyed girl on horseback with submachine gun, fine. Strikes, even in Kharkov, no dice.

"Hundred and fifty killed," Porphyry Filipovich said.

The pressure shifted. The supper was going nicely but we weren't in this for a steak dinner.

"What's on your docket now, Fewchuk?" Mr. Cassell blared.

Again the Colonel looked at the service door; no more than an automatic gesture, but his life had depended on such care a hundred times.

"The money for the guns we have. Mr. Dawson cabled Giancarlo in Trieste. Giancarlo and Mr. Dawson will get them through to Vienna. I'll go back" (he couldn't help a sigh) "to Istanbul and we'll fit out the old DC3. But this time I'm off to Kiev. Kiev, that's the city now."

"Where's that? Where's that?" Mrs. Pike whispered.

"We're linking up with the Carpathian bands to the west. A murmur is spreading across the country like grass fire in

August." The old lyric croon had come back to his voice.
"Tired eyes are beginning to gleam again, jaws tighten, our
young men like falcons, our young girls gentle as gray willow
doves, proud and fleet as young mares of steppe." He looked
straight at Sarmina and her bosom swelled. "Hope that their
sons will not be born slaves. Old people dream of dying free,
for message is coming . . ." His fist jerked and knocked over
Mrs. Hashbarger's wine glass. For a moment he watched the
blood-red stain spread into the outline of his native land.
"Message is coming, out of Texas" (the air trembled, the
candle flames and the cigar smoke, with his voice) "world
like Ukraine, where horizon never ends, and over at edge of
sky cloud of dust rises and sweeps across plain and it is
young man on sweated horse galloping, riding with message,
and that is your land and mine. And the same fight for
freedom, the corpses washed in tears, the same punishment
we've endured from the North, lonely as man's fist raised in
defiance against sun——"

"Yowhee!" someone yelled. Mrs. Hashbarger was weeping. How bitter I felt, belonging to neither land. Then Porphyry Filipovich began to sing. His eyes closed, bass voice
barely master of his feeling, the Ukrainian anthem. We sat
there—I had a hunk of steak in my mouth I couldn't chew
and couldn't swallow—in that song, sad, too brave for sadness, the end of each hero's road only death, death itself
meaning nothing. His hand gripped his wine glass so tightly
that with a tiny click it broke, but he did not notice, nor at
the end, the little drops of blood that fell upon the cloth.

"He cut his hand," Mrs. Pike whispered.

He stared at the table, lost again in his homeland, then
slowly he raised his eyes until they rested on the proud,
beautiful face of Sarmina Cassell, and we all knew that only
a woman's beauty can equal a man's love for his country.

"By God, Colonel, if I was younger, you could call on
me!" General Hashbarger cried out hoarsely. "But you take
this thousand-dollar check, and you buy machine guns and

when they spit lead know that's one Texan's reply to the worst tyranny man has ever suffered."

"General, I rather have you beside me than a check ten times as large," the Colonel answered him, and we smiled proudly at these two old soldiers who had met across half a world.

"Maybe my money would buy you some of those guns too," said Mr. Pike. "Here's five thousand."

This raise of the General's ante was clear poor taste. Mr. Pike received no invitation to join in the parachute jump. But a noise came from the end of the table. Seth Cassell was pushing back his chair. This was it. A general watching his troops disembark on a hostile coast, a girl who awaits a beau in her first strapless gown—a host of cloudy metaphors surged through my mind.

"Colonel," he pronounced, "I make you an honorary Texan." We all cheered. So far so good. "We folks down here know what freedom means. Whether it's from Washington or Moscow, I reckon that tyranny is the same. You've sold me. Here's my check."

A hundred thousand dollars. There was a simplicity to the amount, even for those people, that left them silent. Porphyry Filipovich rose.

"What does this piece of paper mean? You write it out, you throw it on the table. You know what it means?" His voice rose to a shout. I was beginning to tremble. The evening was too much for me. "One thousand machine guns. Five hundred silken parachutes to bring our people hope from sky. Hundred radios so words of direction, and final clarion to battle. Freedom, that's what it means!"

That brought us to our feet, thrilled to have witnessed the meeting of two great men. But another movement, the raising of Sarmina's perfect golden arms over her head (a glorious gesture for a woman with such arms and such a bosom), and she lightly unclasped her necklace and threw it on the table before Porphyry Filipovich.

"To the bravest man I know," she said simply. "May it serve other women better than it serves me."

Topaz and turquoise isn't much. They'd have to be broken up and the settings melted down. He stretched his hand toward her—you've seen the gesture in a hundred statues: the meeting of the Mississippi and the Missouri, France reconciled with Britain, agriculture and industrial engineering—but it was fine.

"Sarmina." The pair were alone now. We had all vanished. "Sarmina." Someone started "The Eyes of Texas Are upon You," which they sing down here when they're wrought up, and we sang and whooped while those two stared into each other's eyes. I managed to pick up the checks and she rolled that necklace into a little bundle and dropped it into his pocket.

Seth Cassell was in high spirits. Mr. Pike's face twisted as if he'd been sucking lemons, but for a big man like Cassell, writing a check was an act of catharsis. His spirit was free. He challenged me to Indian wrestling and flattened me out on the rug. He challenged the Colonel and the two of them grunted and panted, and when the Colonel won we were all glad, Seth too, for it was the Colonel's night.

There wasn't much else to do. Who could play bridge, at any stakes? Who could chat, knowing what we did? The guests went home.

"You're a mighty big man, Seth," I said to him in the biggest way I could, as if silken oil gushed from the deepest recesses of the earth just to enrich me, as in a way it did. "You're the father of a great-spirited daughter, too."

None of his admiration for the Colonel lapped over on me, but I saw he liked my new simple way of speaking. As we were going to bed, Big Seth turning off the lights for economy, I glanced out on the terrace and there was the willowy golden back of Sarmina barred by two black wool sleeves and bent under the force of the Colonel's embrace.

V

At eight o'clock I came into Porphyry Filipovich's room and pounded the snoring terror of forest and steppe awake. That check of Cassell's had been made out to him. We had to go down to the bank and cash it—a check on the Dallas First National cuts no ice in Trieste—but I worried about an amount of money so large it might stir up a mean spirit of suspicion between my partner and myself. Cash the check, I explained, drive out to Corsicana in another rented car to pick his up—no one getting angry about car theft—and his passport and hop the first plane to Paris. A little mistake perhaps with the KNVD and we'd disappear.

I could have been speaking Choctaw.

"Get up. Let's get moving."

"Nyet."

"All right." No one could have been more reasonable. "I'll get the car and the passport myself. Then we'll go down to the bank. Okay?"

Not a sign.

Downstairs Leroy said that Miss Sarmina was apt to sleep until twelve. If I took her Cadillac and hurried—hiring someone near the cabin to return the other car—I'd be back by eleven and we could still reach the bank before noon. I set off and soon pushed the machine up to eighty. You could hardly drive it slower. I must say it was a fine car. And the excitement of barreling through some of those little towns at that speed kept me from worrying about my troubles. Well, I hit the cabin at a quarter to ten. The first thing I saw was the orange car piled into a ditch at the bottom of their drive, its fender all crumpled and the chromium twisted like macaroni. I opened the cabin door. The girl was sitting down, arm in a sling, while her mother was applying a wet compress to some nasty bruises on her face. They both looked at me suspiciously. I can't say I blame them. A cold fall wind was blowing through the window I had shot out, and the plaster from the ceiling still lay on the floor.

"Hi, ladies."

"You ain't fixing to shoot out nothing more, are you?" the mother wanted to know.

A kettle was heating on the stove and two fruit jars of hot bourbon and water stood on the table.

"You had a bit of trouble with the car, I see."

"Daing thing jumped out of my hand," the girl snapped.

"If I may be so bold," the mother asked again, "what was the meaning of coming in here tarryhooting around the way you did and then handing me Porf's rifle? I was so blame mad I might have hit you."

"That's all right. Let bygones be bygones. I just came for Porf's things."

"They're around," the girl said, waving her good arm.

They sure were. The old woman got apprehensive.

"If he left that there money behind there's no point in your grabbing hold of it. Maybe he wanted us to have it. By gum, we have a hard enough time getting along."

"I'm certain he wanted you ladies to have the money," I said. "But did you happen to see a little green book?"

"That's it. Right over there."

Under the bed. I jumped at it and then almost fell over. The photograph page had been torn in two.

"Good Lord!"

"What so dad-blamed important about a photygraph?" whined the girl. "I didn't think I'd never see him again the way you two stomped out of here so I tore it out and put it up in memory of a real nice fellow."

There it was pasted on the little mirror over the sink, Porphyry F. Fewchuk written across the forehead and Department of State stamped on the bottom. My eyes started to fog over, my heart was pounding all wrong—we have a weak heart strain in our family. I grabbed a vegetable knife—

the mother's hand reached for the catsup bottle, they didn't trust me in that little home—and began to scrape it loose. It came (poor paste), but a high-priced specialist would be needed before Porphyry Filipovich left the country on that passport.

"You don't leave a girl any memories, do you?"

"There was two thousand in that wallet," I snarled.

"Cheap!"

I staggered out of the cabin, back into the Cadillac and back to Dallas at the usual pace. Nothing was running right. A cop got on my tail, some ignoramus who couldn't read the license plate, but at 105 I shook him. He wanted to live. I was beginning not to care.

Well, back to the Cassells' house and what did I find but Porphyry Filipovich (wearing one of Big Seth's sport coats with a foulard carelessly knotted at the throat) and Sarmina having breakfast together in the patio. They were dawdling over their coffee and what had probably been a dozen pieces of toast and jam and—breath of Eastern Europe—a pair of little glasses and a bottle of peach brandy. No one was in a hurry to do anything. I was ready to choke.

"Hi, Ollie," she called airily. "Have a glass of peach brandy with us."

I sank down, still feeling the wheel under my hands and a blur of telegraph poles and cars whirring off at right angles.

"We should get down to the bank if we're going to make the one-twenty to New York. The Paris plane leaves at eight."

I was going to Paris. Porphyry could use all his ingenuity to get his own damn passport repaired.

"We can go tomorrow."

"I sent the cable to Smotryzki," I said sullenly.

He looked at me contemptuously, me and my playacting.

"He will wait."

"Medvenko will get the wind up." Silence. "Friday's the

last day with a dark moon. Sofronny can't be trusted too long."

I was shouting this gibberish in the hope of arousing something. Sarmina gave me a sympathetic smile.

"I am going with Porphyry Filipovich," she announced.

"You?"

"Women can fight beside men. We'll stand together, he and I."

"We can't wait till you get a passport," I replied weakly as I refilled my glass.

"I have a passport. And I know how to parachute jump. Porphyry and I will meet that plane at Istanbul."

That was their worry. He had studied the Marquis de Sade and he could hack up her torso and mail it home in a steamer trunk for all I cared, but the check was made out to him. The only check in my name was that thousand dollars from General Hashbarger. Above all I didn't want to meet Seth Cassell again. Getting his dough and then abducting his daughter filled me with such inner turmoil I just couldn't give him a simple look right into those fine frank eyes, and if you don't look at men like that all frank and simple they go right down and stop payment on their checks.

"Porphyry Filipovich, you're a tremendously lucky man to have won Miss Cassell," I said, putting my arm around his shoulder. "You and she together will create a legend not inferior to that of Guiseppe and Anita Garibaldi. Nevertheless, to be able to satisfy her craving for direct action, not shared to the same extent by her parents, get ready and come down to the bank so that we may all three climb on the one-twenty plane for New York."

Few acts in my life required the concentration of that calm little speech.

"I'll get my bag," I finished cheerfully. "Don't take much, Sarmina. You can buy the proper things in Istanbul. It has a surprising number of smart shops."

A suede jacket and mustard-colored pedal pushers for her travel wardrobe. I wove my way back into the house and there by the doorway stood a dour, middle-aged man with horn-rimmed spectacles and a briefcase.

"Mr. Dawson, I presume?" he asked.

The FBI, I confess, was the first thought that raced through my guilty mind, but he wore a blue suit, not gray.

"Yes, indeedy," I answered, clinging to the regional manners as long as I could.

"Ogden P. Slocum."

"Howdy."

"I'm in mental health."

Of all the damn fool self-descriptions that one took the cake, but I was finished being surprised by anything.

"That's just grand!"

"Stupid! he exploded, obviously under a bad strain too. "I raise funds for the Mental Health Foundation."

Now I caught the pitch, but I was too lightheaded to think seriously.

"Ha, ha, 'Quarters for Queers'?"

He was having trouble controlling himself. I was making a dangerous enemy.

"Mr. Cassell had promised me fifty thousand dollars last month."

"'Nickles for Nuts.' For feeble-mindedness, no less important, 'Dimes for Dopes'?"

"And he told me that you and your Lithuanian buddy had just rolled him for a cool hundred thou."

"Listen, young man," I told him, deadly serious, "all the mental health in the world won't do you any good if you don't have freedom. I'm"—proudly—"in freedom!"

"Are you on the Attorney General's List? Have you been investigated by the Ford Foundation's grant for foundation integrity?" he barked.

"Simple men fighting for their lives in the swamps and forests south of Tarnopol," I screamed at him. "Proud young women being tortured to death in the cellars of the NKVD, and you——"

I ran upstairs for my bag. A glance in the mirror: white and creased face, flecks of gray hair, pores large—Oliver Dawson was getting old, not distinguished, just old. A grind of gravel in the driveway and I glimpsed Ogden Slocum's car disappearing. I had handled that childishly and he'd be out to jam a spoke in our wheel. I tumbled downstairs. Porphyry Filipovich and Sarmina had left the table, but they had moved exactly five feet and stood there clasping each other's hands and staring into each other's eyes. And he old enough to be her father.

"All ready?" I laughed.

"I'll go get a few things," she said carelessly.

He still didn't like me.

"If you are in such hurry you take one-twenty plane and I cash checks and meet you in New York."

And have all the worry by himself of carrying a hundred thousand in cash?

"We've got to stick together."

"I'll need money to pay Giancarlo."

The walls were beginning to swim.

"And pick up the new parachutes, I suppose."

"Yes."

"What are you thinking of doing with this then?" I handed him the passport with the torn-out picture stuck in it. "She pasted it on the mirror as a souvenir."

"Geraldine did that?" He began to laugh. "Sweet girl!"

A clatter of heels on the stairs marked Sarmina's return, in a pale beige polo coat. She would have looked beautiful in burlap, but a polo coat for a woman of twenty-five is doubtful taste.

"I took the rest of my jewels." She pulled a tangle of metallic stuff out of one big pocket. "We can sell these when we need more money."

"Bags?"

She laughed and pulled some silk out of the other. "Undies."

"The bank closes in fourteen minutes," I said casually.

"Let's get a move on then," she cried and we strolled out to the Cadillac. It was foolish of me to have worried. We were outside the bank seven minutes later. The doorman smiled and waved her in. The vice-president knew her too and held the blotter and smiled while Porphyry Filipovich endorsed the checks. Then he counted out one hundred five thousand dollars. Porphyry shoved the bills into his pockets. One parcel of fives was too bulky.

"Hold these," he said to me.

"Sure. Shall we make our reservations now?"

"Let's have a drink," Sarmina suggested.

We went into a bar and ordered a round of martinis. "Here's to us," she said as she clinked glasses with him. And for the second round: "The freedom of the Ukraine."

"The plane leaves in twenty-five minutes," I whispered.

I paid, too, being the only one with small bills, and we spun off for the airport. Our luck hadn't held, though. The last passengers were climbing the ladder.

"We'll buy our tickets on the plane," Sarmina said. "Daddy knows the manager."

She walked between the two of us, holding our hands and swinging her arms so that her jewelry clinked a little. By the gateway to the plane, however, I saw a portly figure in a blue suit waiting beside a couple of men in gray.

"Good Lord, I left my passport back at the house! I'll run back and get it and take the next plane," I exclaimed. "Meet you at the Hotel McAlpin."

"Take the car if you want," Sarmina called. "Cheerio!"

I turned and joined a large group of folks moving from an incoming plane toward the control building. A bus was just leaving. I climbed on it and dropped off at the first stop and changed rapidly two more times at random. A cheap little store sold me a suit that didn't fit while I tore up General

Hashbarger's check. Then I went to the movies, three shows in a row at the same theater. Night had come by now. I didn't look at any of the newspapers. In a bar I heard a man say he was going to Fort Worth and for a five-dollar bill he gave me a ride. He'd just returned from Korea and we talked about the army. I spent a few days quietly in Fort Worth. Then I hopped a bus for Pittsburgh because Pennsylvania has always seemed an interesting old-fashioned state. I visited the museum and took in some picture shows, but I was feeling lonely and restless and walking through the steel part of town I passed a saloon that had a sign in the window: BARMAN WANTED. Mr. Woytka hired me for my dignified, reliable countenance. It's a good-natured neighborhood of Poles and Ukrainians and since I've made friends with the widow of Mr. Woytka's younger brother, he said that he'd let me into a third interest in the bar if I could raise two thousand dollars.

II

THE PURSUIT OF HAPPINESS

"ODELL, WE'VE BEEN HAD," Mrs. Gossett muttered resignedly to her husband.

Mr. Gossett had been married twenty-seven years, and though he refreshed himself with fantasies wherein he was irresistible to intense young brunettes because he enjoyed such a many-faceted intimation of life's meaning and to blatant blondes because he owned a lot of money, there still swept upon him waves of sudden warmth as he realized that no other woman but Esther would have stood up as well after twenty-seven years. He squeezed her hand.

The madwoman at the wheel skidded into the turn, tires screeching a sheet of gravel into the thickets bordering the road. Mrs. Lowenhaupt's blond head snapped against Mr. Gossett's shoulder. She moaned a little in self-pity.

"Both the children are happily married," he said to comfort his wife, "and at this speed everything would be over in a few seconds."

The lunch had been leisurely, because this was a civilized, leisurely trip; but France is a big country and you cannot get from Calvados to bouillabaisse to sauerkraut in three weeks without tearing like hell between meals.

"Some people are naturally stupider than others," Mr. Gossett went on. "We just happen to belong to that group."

He spoke guardedly, but Laverne Lowenhaupt was too numbed by food and speed to hear, and in the front seat

Arlington Lowenhaupt and Renée Montrose had had enough vin rosé and Armagnac to think that taking this track at this pace was terribly exciting. They had left the Bordeaux country (Médoc, St. Émilion, soup made from pork fat, onions, and egg yolks) and were racing through the narrow valleys of Gascony (lamprey matelote with leeks) to Languedoc and thrush pie, *estouffade de tripe,* and Châteauneuf-du-Pape. Mr. Gossett listened to the sullen rumbling of his intestines.

The first week had passed of this gastronomical wander through France, or Gluttons' Gallop, as Mr. Gossett called it. The whole idea had sounded promising in March when he had first seen the picture of Gerald and Renée Montrose smiling out of an advertisement, champagne glasses raised to toast the reader. "Venez avec nous!" the big type urged. The trip that truly civilized people have always dreamed of, a leisurely *tour gastronomique* in refined company of the finest inns and restaurants of France. The essence of French culture. No crowds, no tedious sightseeing—$2200—all expenses. Mrs. Gossett was still exhausted and heartsick after the slow death of her mother. They both delighted in good food. Hartford and the construction business would keep.

The little group that met at the Hôtel Alexandre had not been the Gossetts' exact concept of elegance. Arlington Lowenhaupt owned three funeral parlors in Kansas City, his wife Laverne owned a topaz big enough to be useful to a mason, about her only belonging that didn't have double Ls woven or stamped on it. "Wouldn't know tournedos from turnips," Mr. Gossett muttered. Mrs. Harvale from St. Louis was a lady in the sense that if you have money and dress well it is easier to be idle and self-indulgent than if you don't. Delphine, her eighteen-year-old, liked to eat and could profit from any measure of refinement that stuck to her. Then there were the young Farnsworths, Bunny and Margoulade, from Boston. They had inherited money and been everywhere. Outside of the excursion boat to Provincetown, this trip was almost the sole novelty left to them.

"At twenty-two hundred a head I suppose it's difficult not to be refined," said Mrs. Gossett.

At least the Montroses fitted the bill. In his dinner jacket, with his boyish figure (close up one saw the little orange wrinkles around his eyes), with his effortless urbanity that assumed that any companion of his was just as effortlessly a gentleman, that any lady he talked to merited the compliments he found so easy to bestow, Gerald Montrose lived up to the claims of his advertisement. He had fallen in love with France, as he said that first evening. And France had brought him Renée too. In repose Renée's face was a little sharp, but most of the time, it was alert and vivacious as she listened with the others to a story of Gerald's or explained to one of the guests how *soupe à l'oignon* was made.

"In St. Louis," Lucille Harvale remarked to Mrs. Gossett, "you always assume that a person named Montrose has some relative named Rosenberg," but she said it without conviction.

At Paris the explorers settled in to the discipline of their trip. The gilded chairs, the worn velvet hangings in the restaurants Gerald chose whispered of a vanished world of Rothchilds and their diamonded companions. Mr. Gossett looked up at his reflection in the tarnished mirrors and thought how well he would have fitted that world—his four matched chestnuts with their white fetlocks and the little scarlet ribbon in his buttonhole.

The two Peugeots headed first for Normandy. Gerald knew a little *auberge* where they found oysters, omelets—the same creamy dream that has made Mont St. Michel famous but a million miles away from its shop cases of imitation Quimper—*Sauté de veau aux petits pois*. A small glass of cider because this was Normandy and a couple of bottles of the weightless Muscadet. The eight pilgrims sat under an apple tree and understood Gerald's words that the right sort of food and wine formed a part of the defences civilization has erected against barbarism. The presence of young Delphine Harvale (stopped from requesting Coca-Cola) made them feel too that they all shared in molding the future. In St. Louis someday, when God would open her womb, she would raise up boys and girls to absorb certain shades of discontent, to yearn for proper gradations and assumptions unknown to their wienie-munching contemporaries, that would reflect a little bit on the whole band.

Into Brittany for a lunch of stuffed snails and roast eels and strawberry tarts at a little harbor restaurant—size and cost did not figure on Gerald Montrose's scales of quality—overlooking the sea. Then south to the Loire Valley, not for the châteaux common tourists plodded through, but for Vouvray and carefree Bourgueil, *coq au vin* and lark pie. And they all smiled excitedly when Gerald spoke of the hidden little chateau he would take them to right in the middle of the St. Emilion country. There they could frolic in matchless Bordeaux and taste the *caneton rôti* with ginger and a pinch of nutmeg.

Certain tensions, however, began. The breakneck driving between the leisurely meals left the pilgrims shaken and jumpy. Mr. Gossett, like a grizzled chief of police whose ear catches a different timbre in the usual bazaar noise, suspected that his stomach had never been trained for this style of eating. Mr. Lowenhaupt, developing an antipathy for Margoulade Farnsworth and her doctrinaire precepts on food, rebelled by ordering Sauterne with his entrecôte. Sauterne was good, steak was good. Neither Gerald nor Renée protested. More than one road leads to Rome. Margoulade, however, was driven to fury. She tried to explain the harmonies of taste and color, the responsibilities good eating posed along with its privileges. She might as well expound the cult of the Sacred Heart to a Vermont Unitarian. Only as she went into relative specific gravities did he show some interest. He himself had studied the action of liquids of different weights. He asked for the use of Mrs. Gossett's half-empty glass of Nuits-Saint-Georges and poured it into his Sauterne. The Farnsworths' faces froze.

"Rosé," Mr. Lowenhaupt said happily. The pilgrims could not help themselves as they stared at the glass. Slowly the top half became solid red while a slightly tinged yellow filled the lower.

"And that proves?" coldly asked Bunny Farnsworth.

Mr. Lowenhaupt picked up his spoon and stirred the two liquids together. Then he gulped down the glass.

"Great stuff!"

The basic folly of the trip, however, was the thinness of food as intellectual diet. There is a limit to how often one can discuss the difference between Bordeaux and Burgundy. Food stories just ended in snobbery—what Mr. Lowenhaupt had paid at the Pump Room, the time Mrs. Harvale ate frog's legs with the Von Gontards, the cliff-side restaurant outside of Beirut where the Farnsworths picked apart their fried locusts.

Mr. Gossett was the first one to collapse. A lunch of lamb tripe and fried mushrooms with one of Gerald's amusing little local wines at that hidden château on the Garonne and he was done for. Renée Montrose raced her Peugeot across Gascony. Mr. Gossett suddenly saw the little convoy as the symbol of modern civilization—speed without goal, the thinnest of covers over a pit of toiling, anguished, bottomless suffering.

"Do you mind stopping?" he asked in a strained voice.

"We'll be at the hotel soon," Renée called back cheerfully.

"Goddam it, stop!"

She slammed on the brakes. Mrs. Lowenhaupt was thrown on the floor. Only one bush was visible, in the middle of a field with four cows. Mr. Gossett loped across to it. He trudged back, avoiding the pity on his wife's face and the disgust on the others'.

At the inn everyone else exclaimed about the evening shadowed valley, the pink plastered walls, the great sweep of the grape arbor. He experienced the aged, rotting toilet. A pariah with his bottle of mineral water and his dish of boiled rice, a skull at the feast. The case sent Mr. Lowenhaupt's mind back to his own profession.

"It's hard to know where to draw the line," he reflected, picking at the nuts in his pistachio cake while Mr. Gossett listlessly read the label on his mineral water bottle: gravel, stone, gout, obesity, nephritic degeneration, but of what value to him now? "Two carloads of teenagers ran head on into each other. Five dead. Now I should have been reasonable and split the business with a couple of the boys, but I had two new ambulances to pay for and the only thing to do was to fill 'em up and handle the whole job myself. Laverne kept sending me up pitchers of hot tea and sirloins—"

"Rare?" Bunny broke in.

"Yes. Charcoal black on the outside. She's a swell cook." He paused to recatch the thread. "Those kids were sure going fast."

"Arlington worked twenty hours straight," Mrs. Lowenhaupt stated.

"We only had two display rooms, but because the families were friends I put them together and it turned out okay because they could all comfort each other. It was taking a gamble—there were times I was ready to fall on my face—but you just can't play things too safe. I don't think it's right to blame Mr. Gossett."

Mr. Gossett started at finding himself in the middle of this tale.

"I suppose you consider each corpse an individual problem," Renée Montrose said with a little smile.

"I still take care of the toughest jobs myself. And all the beautiful women," he added with an arch gallantry. "That would include you, you can be sure of that."

"Comme vouz me flattez!"

"What a thing to discuss at table!" snorted Mrs. Harvale. Mr. Gossett assumed that he, in his ugly reminder of the realities of metabolism, was responsible for this lowering of tone. Jokes were made about hamburgers and iceberg lettuce with Thousand Island dressing. Gerald offered to buy tickets back to Paris or at least stop to let Mr. Gossett see a doctor, but the contractor from Hartford did not trust foreigners.

He had the time now to try and put into some sort of shape the reflections from thirty years of hard work. A dozen times a day feeling the brush of the dark angel's wing as Renée passed on hills and roared blindly through crossings, humbling himself in the outhouses of picturesque inns, hunched with his dish of soda crackers while the rest tore into their crayfish pies, he knew how right he had always been that the aim of civilization was merely to keep man from seeing what stood right in front of his face. The more flesh the more worms. Each hour wounds, the last one kills. Gnomic wisdom of forgotten sundials. By every vehicle of communication it controls, society commands us to indulge ourselves. Duty, to ourselves, to our loved ones, to the man standing at our side: buy, spend, satisfy each desire—a car in three colors, a bottle opener fashioned from false false teeth, a whiskey so old, so honorable that to own a single bottle asserts one's breeding. He would walk barefoot from Hartford to New Haven.

Avignon. Mrs. Gossett was laughed out of a wish to visit the palace of the popes. "Sur le pont d'Avignon," sang the Farnsworths as they went off to dance. *Aubergines provençales,* a homely vin du midi, a dish of ripe figs that Mr. Gossett could not resist.

On the drive to Marseilles he could hardly move. He merely shut his eyes as the others played with the fish heads in the bouillabaisse. The next stop should have been further east on the Riviera—baby octopi in olive oil—for the Harvale girl and the Farnsworths wanted to swim. Mr. Lowenhaupt had been musing about beach girls in bikinis. But both the

Montroses were febrilely building up the unknown delights of Savoyard cooking. As a contractor Mr. Gossett guessed this was a symptom of the fixed-bid blues. He had suffered them often enough. Each twenty-two hundred dollars had been paid in advance, but Armagnac and petrol come high. What the Montroses saved on Mr. Gossett's crackers they lost on Mr. Lowenhaupt, who had dropped any fleeting interest in boiled lamprey and was sticking solely to steak.

The pilgrims grumbled at being cheated out of their flesh-pots. The guides' gay scorn of the tourists one found in St. Tropez got noplace. Grimly they climbed into the hated Peugeots and tried not to look down into the valleys as the Montroses—"those Rosenbergs," as Mrs. Harvale now called them—spun north toward Grenoble.

One lift for morale remained. This was France. Its inhabitants have learnt the meaning of pleasure in the decoration of human existence. No possible onlooker will reappear in Kansas City to recall what should be forgotten. Only the Gossetts were excluded, she too elderly and reserved, he loathed in his illness. It was easy, therefore, for Mr. Gossett, who sat well back so that his companions were not offended by his bone-white potatoes, to notice the little pattings and pinchings under the table. On his trips to the toilet he could hardly avoid the *tête-à-têtes*. Bunny should not be cross. Lowenhaupt was an overfed clown who had to be jollied along because he was a client, but Bunny himself was the sort of cultured gentleman—and a lot nicer than merely that—Renée had always hoped would join their little trip.

Renée's job, of course, was more complex than Gerald's. He needed tact and finesse and sheer brute speed to get from one woman to the next. Mr. Gossett admired his skill but did not envy him.

One hideous drive had brought them to a mountain hotel famed for its celery-stuffed goose and salad of thistle hearts. Gerald ordered hot baths and a carafe of rosé for each wayfarer. Mr. Gossett gradually came back to life. Seated on his balcony, he watched the evening sun shining on the snow and rocks of the mountains while along a heavily shadowed valley track a girl and collie were driving a herd of cows. France was beautiful. The people seemed straightforward and hard working. Even the damn food was good if he ever ate again. He clenched his fist in protest.

A door opened on a balcony below. Mr. Gossett turned his head to look through the fringe of geraniums down to where Gerald Montrose had appeared. He was wearing his maroon blazer and filled his pipe thoughtfully as he too looked out at the slowly moving herd of tinkling cows. Then the door opened again. Mrs. Lowenhaupt came out in a flowered gown. She was obviously worked up. Gerald stopped her by pointing to the cows with their busy collie, then up to some object on the mountain. She relaxed. He kissed her lightly on the cheek and slapped her lightly on the bottom. She laughed and disappeared. Mrs. Harvale appeared next, also in a bathrobe, also wrapped up in a complaint. Gerald had to listen, to talk for quite a while, but then she put her head on his shoulder and looked down the mountain valley he pointed to.

There was a pause after she left which gave Gerald time to relight his pipe. The next woman was Margoulade Farnsworth. She spoke intensely, patting her hands together in emphasis. This time Gerald made no effort at all to listen but set down his pipe at the corner of the balcony and pulled her roughly into his arms. She shoved him away and hit him, but the second time she put her arms around his neck. Before she left they embraced again. Almost immediately Delphine Harvale came out on the balcony and wound herself around the tour director. "My God!" gasped Mr. Gossett, awed by the pace. She must have been waiting in the bathroom. Delphine kissed and hugged in the same manner as she would have eaten a handful of chocolates. Finally Gerald was left alone. He picked up his pipe again but it was dead, and he knocked out the ashes against the edge of the balcony.

Mr. Gossett's son-in-law was a teacher of English who complained that every book report he read contained the sentence that Sinclair Lewis or Kenneth Roberts makes you know his characters like they were your next-door neighbors. Mr. Gossett felt one of life's blessings was that you really never knew your neighbor. Over the stuffed goose (he risked a veal cutlet) nothing seemed different. Only late at night, when the other noises of the hotel stilled, could he and his wife hear angry voices from the Montroses' room.

North the flagging eaters rolled, through the land of *truite au bleu*, into Burgundy, whipped on by promises of the feast awaiting them in Dijon: snails, parsley ham, truffles, cheesecake, and the glorious melody of the very names of its vineyards—Chambertin, Meursault Goutte d'Or, Pommard, Côtes de Nuits Saint-Georges. But the palliative the Montroses had offered turned into dragon's teeth. Laverne Lowenhaupt and Margoulade Farnsworth approached love from opposite paths—pinching in corners versus intense intellectual talk—and despised each other. All the women were shocked by the thrift of Delphine's method, to hold out her arms and her expressionless face in any slightly sheltered corridor where she met Gerald. Arlington Lowenhaupt, offended at having Bunny as competitor, took to addressing him as "Son." He had been promised his reward at Colmar—sauerkraut, sausage, pig's-foot jelly, gallons of good beer—and for the last week the others had generously looked forward to his big face grinning in greasy surfeit. Instead a savage argument broke out, on the improbable grounds of whether it was good taste to put whipped cream in a demitasse, and only Mr. Gossett's alertness stopped the undertaker from striking his rival with a beer stein.

Gerald silenced the row with a parade-ground burst of temper. The Peugeots would turn toward Paris. At Chalons-sur-Marne there would be a nice soufflé, kidneys fried in champagne, dandelion and bacon salad, and real Reims champagne. That was food for gentlefolk. Any boorishness and the whole mob could munch ham sandwiches and be dropped off at the first Metro station. But as the silent group straggled up with its luggage the next morning, Mrs. Gossett ventured to request:

"Couldn't we have just a snack and see the cathedral at Reims instead? It was the first cathedral I saw in France when I came here as a young woman, and it would mean a lot to me to see it again."

"I'm afraid not, Mrs. Gossett," Gerald answered with a forced smile. "It's north of our road and I want to get you into Paris not too late in the evening."

"Oh, come now," protested Mr. Gossett, but the director was adamant.

"Reims is not a first-rate cathedral. All the stained glass was destroyed in the war."

"After all——" began Mr. Lowenhaupt, but Renée cut him off with her rasping starter.

"Wait till you see that soufflé," Gerald snapped and the mutiny collapsed.

"I suppose we'll all become fat as butterballs," each woman had remarked to Gerald their first night in Paris. "No, ma'am," he smilingly replied, "the French don't let you do that with their cooking." Mr. Gossett glanced at the tight, lined face of his wife. No one could say she had put on weight. Through the Vosges now, past the iron mills of Lorraine, in Nancy a whirl around the Place Stanislas to silence the architecture buffs, then west on route 4 as fast as the machines would travel. Not a word had been spoken all the long morning in Renée's car, Mr. Lowenhaupt keeping his head buried in a road map, the others dully staring out the windows.

Then the signs announced their arrival at Chalons. Renée made a left turn.

"You're missing the town," Mr. Lowenhaupt warned her.

"We don't have to go through it," she explained. "The inn is out along the Paris road a bit."

"It's only forty-two kilometers more to Reims."

She laughed at the reappearance of this whim.

"If we went there after lunch it'd be eight o'clock before we got to Paris. You'd miss the first act at the Folies Bergères."

"Let's skip lunch."

Renée glanced at his rigid jaw and at the brow black as a Kansas thundercloud and shrugged her shoulders.

"You argue with Gerald."

She signaled to the other car. Both stopped. To her husband she spoke a few rapid words in French. Gerald was clearly in a poor temper, and with difficulty did he try to address Mr. Lowenhaupt as a human being.

"That's ridiculous, Lowenhaupt. Everyone is tired and hungry. I've made reservations, and no one wants to go out of their way just to see one battered old cathedral."

Arlington Lowenhaupt had a mission. Once he had worked twenty hours straight to neaten up five mangled teenagers and he could handle any problem.

"Mrs. Gossett said she wanted to visit Reims. It means a lot to her. We can pick up some cheese and bread here and whip right up. At the rate you two drive we'll be there in half an hour."

Mr. Gossett knew he should be the one defending his wife's privileges, but the conflict was already too engaged.

"The cathedral will be closed at midday," Gerald said through clenched teeth.

"We'll pay someone to open it," replied Mr. Lowenhaupt. He was magnificent now in the calm of his assurance.

"I've made reservations," Gerald snarled, trying to control himself. "You just can't break them like this no matter how much money you throw around. The soufflés will fall!"

"Let them fall!"

A spontaneous smile flashed on every face. Eyes sparked, shoulders snapped back. Gerald made a last futile appeal.

"Do the rest of you want to miss lunch and see this"—

with a terrible effort he swallowed the adjective—"cathedral?"

The heads nodded. Even Mrs. Harvale shared the same proud smile. Gerald glanced at his wife. She lifted her eyebrows in acceptance of the senseless.

"Okay," he snapped. "But first I'll ring up and cancel."

"I'll buy the grub," Mr. Lowenhaupt said.

The undertaker had divided the loaves and fishes by the time Gerald Montrose returned. The pilgrims had won but at the look upon his face their chatter ceased and they hurriedly took their seats. He slammed the door of his car and roared off at top speed. Renée followed as fast as she could. Chalons lay behind by the time she shifted into top gear. Gerald was making them pay. For a while Mr. Gossett leaned forward to watch the speedometer edge up to one hundred twenty kilometers, one hundred thirty. He leaned back and took his wife's hand.

One might find comedy at sight of the terrified grimaces they passed, at the futile contortions of a gendarme. Or calculate whether one had a ten percent or a one percent chance of survival when Gerald skidded his car around a blind corner. At a village he shot between two platoons of marching schoolchildren, swirled away like autumn leaves a second later as Renée passed. A flock of chickens exploded in front of the first car. Renée sent an old dog, which had stumbled back into the road to see what had missed it, whirling into a tree. Twenty-nine minutes after leaving Chalons both cars rolled into the cathedral square at Reims.

An ashen Gerald crawled out of his car. He held on to the door to keep from falling but he whispered defiantly: "See, shut tight."

Mr. Lowenhaupt kept silent. Weaving a bit, still grasping his untasted cheese sandwich, he did not bother to try the fastened portals but marched straight to the caretaker's house and banged on the door. They saw him gesture at the martyred edifice, they glimpsed the arrogance of the thousand franc note in his hand. The caretaker shook his head but took the bill. The little group tottered jubiliantly to the cathedral.

"Mr. Lowenhaupt, you are wonderful!" gasped Mrs. Gossett as she looked up at his radiant face.

He spread out his arms like some great bronze Christ summoning the tempest tossed, and in his wake they tiptoed into the empty building.

Gerald was not a good loser. He jerked his head toward the white windows.

"Well, here it is!"

"No, Mr. Montrose," Mr. Lowenhaupt replied calmly. "We are taking a tour."

The shriveled guide, with an ugly furrow across his skull showing that he had received his job as a *mutilé de la guerre,* spoke no English, but his French was so clear and direct that they could almost understand him as he gestured at the wounded statues and the naked windows.

"It all comes back to me now," Mrs. Gossett exclaimed. "We'd driven in from Germany and I was so excited seeing my first French cathedral."

The guide was painstaking and unhurried. The little group followed him without a murmur, even into the crypts and the treasure room, and Delphine ran up the staircase to the tower so that she could describe the view.

"By God, the French could really do things when they wanted to!" stated Mr. Lowenhaupt. Silently the others assented, silently they returned to the Peugeots where the Montroses waited. The last lap was tiring but bearable. Gerald's spirit was quenched and the kilometer readings never reached a hundred.

"Anybody be our guests at the Folies Bergères?" Mr. Lowenhaupt demanded, smiling at all his companions as they stood in the lobby of the Hôtel Alexandre.

"There is a horror show at the Grand Guignol. I think I shall see it alone," said Gerald Montrose to himself.

Each couple wanted only privacy. No one even made the gesture of offering to exchange addresses. A cup of bouillon and a ham sandwich in the bedroom was Mrs. Gossett's sole desire. But she kissed Mr. Lowenhaupt good-bye, and the pilgrims wore quiet smiles on their faces as they separated to follow the porters to their rooms.

III

A SIMPLE SOUL

IN A WELL-ORGANIZED COMMUNITY TODAY, some sort of committee exists to take care of every human problem. Open the phone book and ring up the proper institution. If the committees are sensibly indexed, it may never be necessary to use real sympathy or intelligence at all. Only a rare couple like the Hawthornes will belong to half a dozen committees and still refuse to accept the system. Or, on the other hand, a girl like Maureen Regler will not fit in because she is too simple to understand what committees are for, and because she is so pretty that some people will always make exceptions for her.

In face and personality Maureen would have felt at home in a German village of a hundred years ago: pale yellow hair, dreamy—or vague if you prefer—pale blue eyes, a pale, rather round face, a half-smile that showed a mind easily satisfied by its reflections upon the world around her. If she could have spent her evenings darning the socks of little brothers, if she could have looked after the cows on a sunny mountain meadow, above all if she had been placed in a part of the world where appearance and essence were the same, she would have been perfectly happy. From her retiring, ailing mother, from the hundreds of B movies the two had seen together in Kirkwood or St. Louis, she assumed that life should be taken at face value. The world was composed of good people, whom one helped or felt free to ask help from, and bad people whom one avoided. In actuality few people had ever helped either Mrs. Regler or Maureen. Still, neither mother nor daughter observed life broadly or very clearly, and what they didn't understand they ignored.

Mrs. Regler, a seamstress who altered dresses skillfully as daughters grew older or mothers larger, had come from one of the German towns along the Missouri, a timid woman prepared neither for marriage to a red-faced, loud-voiced carpenter twenty years her senior nor for his death on the rug before her eyes, from angina. When it is almost as cheap to buy new dresses as to let down old ones, a community no longer has much need for seamstresses. Mrs. Regler worked long hours and made little money. She listened to sad serial programs on the radio and found pleasure in the pale beauty and gentle kindness of her daughter. While Maureen (the name a pre-partum fancy of her mother's after a cinematic pirate's sweetheart) occupied herself with the housework, they talked about the radio programs or the movies they went to once a week. Evenings Maureen used to read aloud in her soft, pleasant voice from the library books she brought home.

Maureen was pretty enough to attract attention, especially when she turned about fourteen, but her shyness saw her continue to be ignored by both boys and girls in Kirkwood's high school, who valued vivacity above all else. She had her pleasures and duties at home. More of the latter now because her mother suffered from stomach disorder. Mrs. Regler had been trained to rely on strong sweet tea in time of trouble, that along with a vaguely optimistic point of view called Faith. By the time she was willing to see old Dr. Ogden about her pains, the cancer was too far along to be modified and Mrs. Regler did not live more than a few months in the hospital.

Maureen moved in with the family of her father's sister, who lived in the nearby suburb of Webster Groves. The new home fitted one of Robert Frost's definitions: a place where when you have to go there they have to take you in. There were four Wohlschlaeger children whose pleasure was quarreling. The parents scolded and slapped at this, but they identified selfishness as practicality and bad temper as alertness. Maureen was classified as stupid. Oddly enough, though, her training in movies and radio serials fitted her surprisingly well for this ordeal. Pain and death—cancer even—came into the world all the time. Orphan was an honorable title. Every heroine had to endure some set of vicissitudes like these cousins. If she had had some time for reflection she could have fitted all the events into a reasonable pattern from which time and accident would free her, but there was no chance. Even if she did the dishes by herself someone would drop in to the kitchen to point out how she was doing them wrong. Even in bed she had to listen to Clara talking or to Clara breathing through her clogged-up nose.

The Wohlschlaeger children went off to school each morning in a thick squabbling pack that Maureen must join, but in the afternoon, because she was older, her classes let out later and she could walk home by herself. Shifting to Webster Groves she lost the few loose acquaintances she had enjoyed in Kirkwood, and her sole pleasure became these solitary and increasingly roundabout walks home. Out of her twenty-five-cent weekly allowance she used to buy ice cream at a drugstore. And there it was that she met Corporal Booker Wallas.

Now the story becomes so stereotyped it could fit any Sunday newspaper: Problems of Our Youth. Booker had been in the army a year and discovered that he had lost contact with his old gang. Next to him sat this pretty blonde who listened to every word he said. Maureen was ill at ease with boys, certainly with a soldier, but this one was good looking and trying hard to be nice to her.

Here, however, training in cheap fiction did her no good. The kind stranger was always an important figure. You recognized right away, no matter how unobtrusively he might be introduced, who was going to be the hero. Booker had no desire to be a hero. He would have been satisfied with buying her a second ice-cream cone, but she seemed so impressed by him, so willing to laugh at his funny remarks, that it would be wrong to pass up such an opportunity. Was she free to go to the movies after supper?

The Wohlschlaegers raised no objection. Booker met her at the movie house. Then they had a soda. He said he would drive her home in his brother's car, but he took a longer road so they could park for a while and kiss. Maureen had no objection. It had nothing to do with her life at the Wohlschlaegers' house. It gave her a little pride to be able to offer something that another wanted so very much to enjoy. She was free again to go with him to the movies the next night and park again in his car. "You know what all this is about, don't you, kid?" he said hurriedly just before the end. They went out two more nights. Then his leave was up and she never saw him again.

This lovemaking brought her more direct pleasure than she had ever known before. At the same time she was disappointed at how little else was involved and how rapidly, as soon as Booker left—and she knew from the beginning how long his leave lasted, there was no deception here—her life returned to the way it had been. He answered a couple of letters, but by the time she realized she was pregnant it was perfectly clear that he didn't care a thing about her.

Unsanctified pregnancy has lost the literary drama it once enjoyed. If Maureen suffered no pain of guilt, she also possessed no pattern of conduct to follow and no counselor to go to. So she did nothing, noticing with apprehension and curiosity the changes that were taking place. As the books said, she did become nauseated in the morning, she did find it hard to stand by the sink in the evening. In sudden despair she confessed to her aunt. She was prepared for disapproval, not for the words that fell on her head. What a hypocrite!

What a little tramp! What wasteful expense! She could sit right down and send off that soldier an air mail letter, and if he didn't answer she could march right over to his parents' house and demand action. Maureen refused. She trusted her own judgment now, not her romances, for she could grasp how, in the long run, things would be worse if Booker did marry her than if, as was more likely, he did not. That she was sure about.

School finished for the summer. The oldest Wohlschlaeger boy got a job at a drive-in. The rest enjoyed that much more leisure to talk about Maureen's fix. Now, for the first time, she understood what misery meant. She had nothing to do. The house was impossible. Someone must help her. She had a right to ask for understanding and advice.

"You can get a room in St. Louis. You can get a job there. No one will know about you. There are organizations that look after girls like you," her aunt yelled.

"We'll send you money," added her uncle.

That settled it. Again she refused. Something instinctively told her that such a solution, so convenient to her aunt and uncle, would mean her destruction.

"All right then, what do you suggest?" her uncle demanded.

She didn't know. She would try to work out a solution.

"You'd better do it pretty quick."

The urgency distressed her. Essentially she was sure something would turn up. In the books, on the screen, someone always appeared to give a hand. Still, it was illogical to expect this savior to enter the brown shingle house on Kulm Avenue. She would have to find him. She took the bus to Kirkwood. There she might run across old classmates who would ask questions, but she hated everything about Webster Groves by now.

She got off the bus by the bank building and looked down the street. People had their morning shopping to do—groceries, children's shoes, new tubes for the television set. Who would be interested in her story? This struck her so clearly as she was crossing the street that she stopped in her tracks. A horn made her hurry for the sidewalk. The sudden strain recalled to her how much her body had already changed. The whole idea was utterly stupid. She was stupid. She was all the things her aunt and uncle said.

Then her old faith in what she believed came back. She left the shopping center and walked slowly over to Taylor Avenue. Here under the elm trees, passing by the nice big white houses, she felt better. In one of these must surely live a family of nice rich people whom she could serve and who would give her love and protection until her baby came. She knew how she would behave and talk. They would not regret their generosity. Each person Maureen passed she examined carefully. But to imagine the ideal family in one of these houses and to stop a man or woman on the sidewalk were two terribly different things. She had read a few old-fashioned books where pregnant girls committed suicide and then were mourned by the people who had treated them badly. She reflected about this for a while, her eyes on the sidewalk ahead of her slowly moving feet. The possible methods were all involved and painful, but the essential part was that the victim was bitterly mourned. Booker had probably forgotten her name. The Wohlschlaegers would go to her funeral with a sense of relief.

She felt very tired. Back she walked to a drugstore on the main street and ordered a small dish of ice cream. I will eat this ice cream slowly. Then I will decide what to do. She took tiny, tiny bites. Not many people sat there this time of morning besides a couple of housewives with their coffee at the other angle of the counter. They were discussing an unfortunate friend sorely tried by illness and poverty, and Maureen listened, eager for one more human story, anxious for anything that would slow down the disappearance of her ice cream.

"I don't know what she would have done if Mr. Hawthorne hadn't helped," the younger and plumper stated earnestly.

"I'll say," agreed the other. "Albert Hawthorne is one of the few Christian gentlemen Kirkwood still has."

Finishing their coffee, the two women left. Maureen sat motionless. The name of Albert Hawthorne—and what a dignified name—had come to her from heaven. A Christian gentleman—what else was she seeking! Her heart pounded. A part of her mind frantically warned her not to believe anything. Albert Hawthorne did not exist. He couldn't possibly be as good as those women had said. Maybe he was tired now of being good. But she put down fifteen cents for the ice cream and went over to the phone booths. Two Albert Hawthornes had Kirkwood numbers, one in the colored part of town, on Electric Street, but the other on Taylor Avenue. Just where he should! What should she say? What reason could he and his wife—Maureen took her existence for granted—have for sheltering her? The address, however, 532 North Taylor, gave her an objective. Back she walked, quickly this time until the last block, when fear slowed her. Yes, the house she wanted! White sides, black shutters, a black door with a big shiny brass eagle knocker. A lawn with a magnolia in the middle and an elm by the driveway. She stopped. If anyone came out that door she would speak to him.

The door remained closed. No face appeared at the curtained windows. Her heart sinking, she turned to go. Then a spasm of courage forced her down the brick path to the black door and she actually banged on the brass knocker. Nothing. So back, wearily, to the bus stop by the bank and the bus home to Kulm Avenue. She prepared a peanut butter sandwich and a glass of milk. When her aunt asked what she had been doing with herself, Maureen only answered "I don't feel well" and went and lay down. Later on in the afternoon she listlessly washed and ironed some of her clothes. The next morning she cleaned the house, dusting every last ledge and corner so that no one would catch her idle and look her in the eye to ask when she was going to leave.

A foolish dream. But at five o'clock she made up her mind that anything was better than sitting one more minute in that house. She would try again. Then she would kill herself or move into St. Louis. At the corner of Kulm and Maple she caught the Kirkwood bus, already almost full with people returning from work. She forced herself not to think. At Taylor Avenue she got off and walked straight to number 532. But at the driveway she had to stop and had to start thinking again. How cool and beautiful and dignified the house was. At the Wohlschlaegers' there were broken toys in the yard and the porch steps sagged. Again no one was visible and this time she lacked the courage to strike the knocker. She counted ten, and then counted again, clasping and unclasping her hands. There was no way out. She turned around to go. A tall middle-aged man in a gray suit was watching her from the sidewalk.

"Is there anyone you are looking for here, young lady?" he asked her.

Face and voice reserved but not unkind. A spare, intelligent face, not like the puffy ones of Mr. Wohlschlaeger and the storekeepers. He held himself erect, hands clasped about the handle of a briefcase.

He was the sort of man she had hoped to see. Maybe for that reason she couldn't say a thing and found herself able only to twist her handkerchief.

"Is there anything I can do for you?" he asked again with formal courtesy.

"Oh, yes!" she wanted to cry out, but she asked instead, "You are Mr. Albert Hawthorne?"

"Yes."

"I am—my name is Maureen Regler," she stammered. "How do you do?"

He made a slightly impatient gesture with one hand.

"I came here because I am in trouble and I heard someone say you are a good man," she forced out.

Mr. Hawthorne regarded her somewhat wryly, without surprise.

"You are expecting a baby?"

"Yes."

She answered him without any demanding display of emotion except a tightening of her face. It was a hard thing to say. He seemed a bit pleased by this forthrightness, but his guarded manner remained.

"My work doesn't bring me into much contact with babies."

"I know that," Maureen admitted. Then she drove herself to tell the rest of the story because she must either say everything or run away.

She ended her little speech at top speed. Mr. Hawthorne blinked his eyes a couple of times, but she had no idea what he might be thinking.

"And what made you choose me?"

"I heard two women in the drugstore yesterday mention that you saved a friend of theirs who was sick and poor, and I thought I would go to you because I had no one else." He made the slightest of grimaces with his mouth. Maureen tried to keep from stammering, tried to make her plea sound reasonable and not desperate. "I'm a good housekeeper. I learned from my mother. I can cook. I'm very neat. I can iron and sew. I can do the ordering and take care of things."

The two of them remained silent. She straightened her shoulders because for a moment her proposition did seem a fair and respectable one.

"I'll be damned!" he exclaimed softly to himself. "And therefore we are to keep you in our house and look after you when you are not well and pay for the baby when it comes? I assume that your aunt and uncle won't give you any help?"

"I never want to see them again!" Maureen said. "The

whole story is a stupid one, but"—she sighed with the ex-
haustion of her strain—"all I can say is that I will not be a
load upon you and I promise that I'll carry out my end of
the bargain. I'll leave when I can take the baby with me.
Then I'll be strong again and I'll be older and know better
what to do."

"How old are you now, Maureen?" Mr. Hawthorne asked
in a more kindly voice.

"Seventeen. In March. I've finished junior year of high
school."

He nodded.

"Come along and tell your story to my wife."

He motioned her to precede him down the path. The
hallway was what she had dreamed. She saw herself reflected
in the large gilt mirror at the end. Her feet pressed into the
thick green carpet. There was a crystal vase of nasturtiums
upon a table so smooth and gleaming that she had to touch
it with her fingertips. They would not be sorry if they did
this thing for her! A woman's steps sounded from a side
room. "Hello, Albert," called a friendly voice. Mrs. Hawthorne was not pretty, spare as her husband in her features
and with a long jaw, but kind it seemed in her eyes, and
again, Maureen felt, here was the face of someone who
accomplished things and did not merely complain.

"Dear," Mr. Hawthorne explained, "This is Maureen Regler. She has a rather curious story and I'll ask her to tell it
to you."

Mrs. Hawthorne led the way into a sitting room and had
Maureen sit down. She took a chair opposite. Mr. Hawthorne stood by the window and watched Maureen while
she told her story again. The girl brought out more details,
to Mrs. Hawthorne's questions, about her mother and their
life together and her aunt and uncle, and she spoke frankly
about Booker Wallas and her complete lack of resistance to
him. Her words came wearily, but if Maureen was unable to
handle deceit in others she was also unable to give any other

impression than what she was, an appealing and gentle girl in trouble.

"The hard part of what you ask, Maureen," Mr. Hawthorne said when she had concluded, "is the unlimited amount of responsibility you expect us to assume. You are a minor. I would have to get matters quite clear with your uncle before you could live here. You are going to need a good deal of money for clothes, not to say doctors' bills. And you know yourself that sometimes people don't get along. It's not a matter of our calling it quits in a couple of weeks if things don't work out. You'd be in an even worse shape then than you are today. Don't you see?"

He spoke with genuine kindness to try and make the hard sentences acceptable. Maureen sat straight in her chair, looking at her hands together tightly. Her usually pale face was as white as paper, but she looked at him firmly until he was done. She reflected a moment. Then she stood up.

"I can't think of anything to say. You've been very kind to listen to me like this, but I can see I've wanted to ask too much. I'll go back to my uncle's house."

Her intense unhappiness, her determination to keep it from showing, to not add weight to her appeal with a burst of tears, made it impossible to let her go.

"Wait a minute, Maureen," Mrs. Hawthorne said impulsively. "We can still give you some help. You were looking for a job and I need someone to help me with this house. It wouldn't be too hard work."

Maureen stared at the older woman with her wide pale blue eyes and shook her head. Her voice was barely audible.

"No. If it was just a matter of working for you by the day, you could find someone a lot more efficient than me."

Mr. Hawthorne thought he understood.

"What you are trying to say, Maureen, is that you want us to give you everything or nothing."

She made no sign of disagreement.

As Mrs. Hawthorne said later, what the girl wanted above

all was love, but she couldn't come out and say that when the two of us were pressing her as hard as we could. Mr. Hawthorne suddenly realized what the girl was begging for. After that it was impossible to refuse it.

"We'll help you, Maureen."

She shut her eyes and shivered a bit so that the older people were afraid she would faint. All she did, however, was sigh and manage to whisper, "Thank you."

Mr. Hawthorne tried to lighten the tension.

"We've never seen you smile, Maureen. Will you?"

She lowered her eyes a moment and when she raised them she was able to smile shyly at them both. That effort broke her defenses. Her face twisted up and she burst into tears.

Maureen was to come the next morning. Mr. Hawthorne said he must speak with the Wohlschlaegers, but she begged him to wait until she had left the house. She would tell them she had found a job as a maid. They would ask no questions. And Mrs. Hawthorne didn't need to pick her up with her bag. Maureen wanted to see no contact between these two worlds.

At nine-thirty, accordingly, from an upper window Mrs. Hawthorne saw the girl coming down the sidewalk, carrying or almost dragging a heavy old suitcase for twenty steps, then carefully going around to pick it up with her other arm. She hastened down to help.

"That's much too heavy for you, Maureen."

"Here I am," was all the girl said, but she smiled again and made Mrs. Hawthorne's practical morning thoughts vanish.

The Hawthornes had a son who was a lieutenant in an engineering company in Korea. Their older son had been killed at a Texas air field just before the other war ended. A still older daughter was married a thousand miles away. The house was large and empty. In all she asked for Maureen might give the two of them exactly what they needed. For this reason Maureen was put in the daughter's room instead of the small, equally empty maid's room over the kitchen. Maureen wasn't surprised at this and only exclaimed at how pretty the curtains were.

In fact nothing seemed to surprise her. She had lived so richly in her world of fiction that any arrangement, good or bad, fitted into one pattern or another. Mrs. Hawthorne was a director of the local hospital and headed the library board, not merely to keep busy at anything, like too many other women, but to make up for the early years when three children kept her shut in her house and because she and her husband felt that people who understood responsibility should hold responsibility. She had a lot on her mind. Therefore to have Maureen look after the house—too loved to leave, too large for the older woman to handle now—was a blessed relief.

Maureen was perfectly content. The stairway was no fun to run up and down, but she planned her work so that everything was done in one room before she moved on to the next. She polished the silver and the brass without being told. She neatly mended the old linen napkins. In this beautiful house of refuge nothing should be less than perfect. She made a reasonable cook. And each time that Mr. or Mrs. Hawthorne entered the house she greeted them with a smile. Mr. Hawthorne compared her gratefully to the flowers because she was pretty and didn't say much.

Both the older people had had a good deal of experience with human beings. They served their community and many separate individuals in it because that fitted their concept of a Christian life, not because they had any optimistic notion of human nature's likability. Maureen's good temper and diligence, her transparent devotion to them both, her unwillingness to intrude her own personality other than in a desire to serve and to please, were all more than they had really expected. Tacitly they each set up a week, a month, two months for the bloom to wear off and one more ordinary human being to appear. But Maureen had drawn up a rigid personal contract with some unseen authority and never abated on what she owed.

She rarely left the limits of the house and garden, where she weeded in the morning when the Hawthornes had left and the day was still cool. In fact, almost her only outside contact was to play with the cocker spaniel from next door if it wandered into the yard. She liked working with the radio on, humming along with the hit tunes and reflecting to herself why some became popular and others were forgotten, but her soap operas she ignored. She had sensed that her guardians thought poorly of them, and in a way she was a sort of heroine herself now and didn't need them. Mrs. Hawthorne made unobtrusive attempts to improve her reading. Books, like everything else, possessed a different value in this house. Maureen blamed only herself if a story confused or upset her, but Dickens, with his color and crotchets, the heartbreaking misadventures of his young heroes and heroines, made an exciting discovery; and sometimes in the evenings, when Mr. Hawthorne was away at a committee meeting, she used to read aloud, stumbling a bit over hard words or dialect and then at some comic episode bursting into a peal of laughter that for Mrs. Hawthorne filled the whole house with youth and happiness.

The first trouble occurred when Louise, the oldest child, came to visit in late August with her two boys. Maureen was attentive, almost deferential in her desire to be of help, but the week was a misery for her. Louise's gay sharp wit reduced her to speechlessness. One of the boys asked loudly, "If Maureen is going to have a baby, where is her husband?" That issue had never existed for the Hawthornes. Louise's visit brought it clearly to Maureen's attention and she was made to feel ashamed. Louise held a far greater right to be accepted and loved than she. Louise obviously had the right, when Maureen was out of the room, to raise the practical questions that the parents had set aside.

Even after Louise's departure Mrs. Hawthorne could hear her weeping at night. It took some weeks of long conversations with Mrs. Hawthorne about the details of birth—hardly mentioned by poor Mrs. Regler—and the care of a tiny baby, of the growing excitement of making and buying things, for Maureen to recover confidence.

A few days after Christmas Dr. Rutledge delivered a baby girl. Maureen wanted to call it Edith after Mrs. Hawthorne, a happy, busy grandmother again, but Mr. Hawthorne, still fearing too much responsibility, suggested that a nice gesture would be to use Anna, for Maureen's mother. He was the only one to see the cold words "father unknown."

With the baby and with Maureen rapidly strong and slender again, the atmosphere of the house changed. Noise and confusion, lines of diapers hung in the basement, the anguished whisper, "Please, please, little sweetheart, please don't cry!" that came through the wall to Mrs. Hawthorne's ears as she lay in bed and sent her mind back twenty and thirty years where youth was not all the time of joy and eagerness we like to think. Mr. Hawthorne recalled his old comparison of Maureen to a flower: not only because she moved gracefully and lightly again, but because of the mindless way she gave her entire self to the task that Nature had set. To rise from her bed in the middle of a January night, to rock back and forth with the baby at her breast, to kneel beside the crib and gaze dreamily at the red face and tiny fists—she had as much conscious awareness of what she did, of the world around her, as a lily in the field. It was hard to realize that she was only seventeen; it was impossible to think that she had grown up in Kirkwood and gone to that noisy brick high school. The forgotten soldier who had fathered Anna did not exist. The child had come untouched from within Maureen alone.

Even at table her eyes were remote as she listened for a possible cry. Only when her hands were occupied in mechanical chores like sterilizing bottles or handling the laundry could she talk and laugh with one of her guardians as before. The baby having arrived, the exciting event for them now was the return of Roland from Korea. His term of duty ended in spring. He would have four months to get himself adjusted and to earn some money before he went off to Yale Law School. Maureen listened gladly to his mother's stories. She liked the bright and generous face in his pictures. The house would be full of life.

"He might even be back in time for my birthday!" she exclaimed.

"If you have some gasoline and a lighted match, what do you get?" Mr. Hawthorne asked his wife one evening.

"An explosion, silly," she replied.

"Both are useful, good things in themselves, but put them together and you get something else."

"That's very profound."

He reflected a moment. "How do you feel about Maureen as a daughter-in-law?"

"Oh. That's it?" She was rarely surprised by anything her husband said. "The issue hasn't seemed a terrifically urgent one to me." She knit another row of the little pink sock. "I think I'd rather have her as a daughter than as a daughter-in-law."

"I'll make you a bet," he said, "and you can set the odds. If Maureen stays in this house one month while Roland is here, we'll have her as our daughter-in-law. Maybe that's perfectly satisfactory, but I guarantee that that will be the end product."

"Albert, you're going too fast. She's completely wrapped up in her baby. Roland has law school ahead of him, and I'd think he'd want a better-educated girl."

He shook his head. "All of which adds up to nothing. Roland will have been overseas fourteen months. He comes home to find a pretty girl of eighteen living in the room next to his who, so far as I can see, is constitutionally incapable of saying No. If there were any way to prove it, I'd also bet you she already sees herself as his wife."

Mrs. Hawthorne replied thoughtfully: "He could find a lot worse one."

"No." He wouldn't give in. "That isn't the issue. For Larry, we couldn't have been luckier. Maureen has every quality he wanted in a wife. And she'd give him a baby every year so he'd never be able to stop working. Roland is different. He has the finest mind of any young man I know. He'd make a brilliant lawyer. He clamps hold on the main argument like a bulldog. He'll take in a dozen contradictory and modifying issues and he can still make up his mind and stick to his decision. But he doesn't have a Chinaman's chance if Maureen smiles at him. He'll be her prince the moment he opens the door."

Mrs. Hawthorne didn't speak, but she was worried by the look on her husband's face as he pushed himself out of his chair. "The world's so damn full of second-raters——"

He couldn't finish.

"Listen, Albert. The girl's never had an education, but she could learn. I didn't know so very much when I married you. And I wasn't as pretty, either."

The irrelevancy irritated him. "Some people can keep on learning. Some people can't. I'd rather talk to Maureen than half the women on the Community Council, but let's keep seeing her as Roland's wife. Now and ten years from now. Love and good food and babies, and he'll be clutching at any job he can lay his hands on."

It was difficult from then on to bring anything new into the argument. Mrs. Hawthorne disliked her husband's assertion that Roland would be in Maureen's bed within a week after his return, but she was surprised at her own failure to disagree with the inevitability and the quality of the marriage he described. Two points, however, were firm in her mind when she got out of bed the next morning.

"Albert, do you regret our decision to take in Maureen?"

"No."

"Do you see our sending her away from here before Roland returns?"

"No."

"Let's try to keep that in mind, then."

As Maureen had suspected, on her visit Louise had brought up all the practical objections to Maureen's presence in the house and managed thoroughly to irritate her father. Certainly, it's nice to be nice to a pretty girl. But to have rejected that plea would have been to admit that everything he believed in all his life was just words. They had been richly rewarded, every day, with Maureen's voice singing in the kitchen. They had sheltered her and helped her to bring forth new life.

What is life? Mr. Hawthorne thought about that going to work, coming home, in bed, at his desk. A little more than half a year and how completely Maureen's personality lay upon their house—her step, the movement of an arm to push back her pale yellow hair, her smile when she was pleased that always brought her head a little to one side. Yet this was almost nothing. Her smile was only a little weapon—she would be the last to know it—at the service of the whole silent mechanics of fertility deep inside her. Three times with a stranger—it had taken him and his wife five years of heartbreak and humiliation before their first child was conceived—and the machine is set on its tracks and nine months later she is a mother.

He was the father of three children. One had been broken and burnt because he had been sent to fly a machine too fast for him. One had married a man whose sole pleasure in life seemed to be the money he earned and the things he bought with it. Louise had been a fine student at college. Now as a suburban housewife she thought it fitting to put all that behind her, and she wrote to her parents about the new furniture and the new car and the boys' successes. Mr. Hawthorne's stake in the future by way of these grandchildren was purely mechanical. One child was actually left to him. If it had taken nine months for Maureen to produce a child, it had taken him twenty-four years.

Roland had survived scarlet fever and Chinese bayonet charges and friends at school who had called, "Don't bother about that, come on out and have a good time." A letter last month had read: "Law has come to mean a lot more to me than I thought it would. Despite all the slowness and trickiness I used to resent so much, it means using reason instead of force and trying to find rules that will bind men equally instead of saying, 'I'll do what I want when I damn well please!'" And another letter: "How I am longing to get home again and start real work and learn something." Mr. Hawthorne's own field of law dealt with corporations, the way by which you could shift words about in order to save on tax money or concentrate power in the hands of one faction or another. Sometimes it was interesting. It had paid for this house and his children's upbringing and gave him freedom to do things like sheltering Maureen. But Roland was interested in the question of freedom and responsibility, the new relationships between the individual man and the community in which he lived. In law that will fit itself to new problems and still retain its old respect for objective justice, so that men do not live at the mercy of the sly and the strong.

"All our righteousness is as filthy rags." St. Paul's iron warning to easy goodness. And this act of righteousness could well cost the father his dearest possession. For the first time in his life, he was locked in an agony of silence, for who could shame Maureen away from their home when she was even more defenseless than before? Graceful as a flower, pure, good, offering with her smile her love and her fertility. Child after child, borne and reared and loved, with no regrets when she became old and shapeless, with not much fear, he was sure, when she had to die. Who would ask a man to be cold to that strange richness? Yet her gifts had to be paid for. Intellectual devotion that might allow one man to become something special, to do a little more than thrash around with the rest of the pack, how abstract and bare that would seem to her.

In Mr. Hawthorne's dreams and even when he was awake, her smile began to acquire a new meaning. He beat his fist helplessly upon his desk.

Maureen sensed that Mrs. Hawthorne was upset and this worried her, but she could not understand the reason for Mr. Hawthorne's sudden coldness. She had thought too much about the baby. She had not carried out her full responsibilities. It was time, by the original agreement, for her to go; yet she knew the Hawthornes were not people who insisted on formal bonds. They had always shown such kindness to her, and now, trying to do better, trying to look after little Anna more efficiently so that she would have more time to cook again and keep the house dusted, trying to smile and be gay, she exhausted herself and what did she accomplish?

One morning early in March she brought Mrs. Hawthorne a letter from Roland. He had been shipped from Pusan to a transit camp near Yokohama. Perhaps by the time they received the letter he'd be on his ship. "Tell Maureen how much I'm looking forward to meeting her."

She smiled, almost in relief, at this reassurance that she was one of the family, but there was pain on Mrs. Hawthorne's face and, it seemed, anger on her husband's as he kept his eyes on his coffee cup.

Mrs. Hawthorne felt utterly miserable, able to see what both Maureen and her husband were suffering. The girl might threaten their son's long-range future—in her mind she could understand—but how impossible to look at that honest, troubled face and really feel that threat in her heart. She kept trying to show Maureen that she was still loved, but these attempts were clumsy and embarrassed.

Maureen's confusion turned into fear. As Roland's arrival drew nearer, when everyone should be overjoyed, waiting for the phone call from San Francisco, the atmosphere became worse. For some reason she was the cause of it. Neither of her guardians wanted to meet her eyes. It was hard for Mr. Hawthorne even to say good morning. She suffered now to hear the baby cry in the day or the night because that reminded everyone that the self-invited guests were still around. Her birthday came in a week. That day would be unbearable if things kept on the way they did. Saturday afternoon, with Mrs. Hawthorne gone off shopping, she went into his study and stood before him.

"Mr. Hawthorne, what have I done? Why don't you like me any more?"

He turned around to face her. A girl of seventeen had more courage than he.

"Do you want me to take the baby and go away?" she went on, seeing that he was unable to speak. "I know I've stayed longer than we agreed to."

"Sit down, Maureen," he said, and pointed to the armchair. She sat straight, her hands folded in her lap, her pale blue eyes fixed on his face.

"Will you believe me when I say two things?" he began. "There's never been a moment when Edith or I regretted bringing you into our house. And"—he had to wait a moment again—"our own daughter isn't any more dear to us than you are."

She hadn't expected this answer. She blinked her eyes and shook her head with a little gesture of pain.

"Why, then?" her lips formed.

But it was impossible for him to say his brutal things. He couldn't even look at her. She had to force herself to do the questioning.

"Have I done anything wrong?"

He shook his head.

"Has the baby—have we been a bother to you?"

"Lord no, Maureen!"

The expected reasons weren't the right ones. She had to go further, where she did not want to.

"Does it have anything to do with Roland's return?"

He did not shake his head. She lowered her eyes to her lap. First she had to straighten out her thoughts and then she had to find the correct words.

"If Roland comes home when I am in this house," she said slowly to the floor, "you are afraid that he will fall in love with me and want to marry me—or have to marry me," she went on with her mouth tightened. "And that will hurt all his plans of going to law school and becoming a fine lawyer."

"That's it, Maureen. That's exactly what I have feared."

They were both able to face each other now.

"And I've never even met him," she said sadly, almost to herself.

"It would be very hard for Roland not to fall in love with you. You are a beautiful girl and he has a warm heart, and so do you."

She needed a little time to work out the contradictions that his statements seemed to contain. The conclusion made her blush.

"And I'm not good enough to be his wife. Oh, Mr. Hawthorne, you shouldn't have taken me then!"

"Maureen," he insisted, seeing her wrong path. "I don't mean that. If I thought my soul was as pure as yours, I would be proud."

She shook her head in confusion.

"What do you mean, then?"

This was almost the hardest to answer.

"The work he wants to do means a lot of preparation. It means, in many ways—it demands a sort of partnership between a husband and a wife to work out a career, to face the problems not only of their family but what he is interested in, so that the two people grow together in every way."

He could go no further. Maureen needed time again to figure out what he meant. Suddenly, for the first time, he saw her almost angry.

"I think I understand. I am a nice girl but I am stupid and I will hold him back. Is that it?"

He shoved his chair back and stood up to stride over to the window and back again. She saw things too clearly for any words to make them nicer.

"I can't disagree with you. You and Mrs. Hawthorne know what sort of a girl I am."

Tears stood in her eyes. He clenched his fists together.

"There is so much he might be able to accomplish——" he began and left the sentence in the air.

"And I would keep him from it," she said in a bitter sort of resignation. Then her spirit broke and she burst into sobs. "And I haven't even met him!"

Maybe I have hurt her worse today, Mr. Hawthorne said to himself as he looked out the window, than if she had gone to St. Louis and had her baby in a hotel. Her sobbing stopped. He heard her stand up.

"I think I had better go," she said, trying to speak calmly. "I have a little money from what you gave me each month. I think I could find someone to look after Anna while I got a job someplace. I am very grateful for what you have done for me."

Her eyes were red. A tear still rested at the side of her nose, but her face was composed as they regarded each other. He had to blink his eyes to hold back his own tears. What sort of a man have I turned into? She was forcing a smile.

"I didn't realize what trouble I would cause." Then she attempted to think practically. "Anna's asleep but I could pack all my things. Or maybe if I stayed until Monday because everything will be closed tomorrow. No," she reflected again, "Perhaps it would be better now. I could certainly find some sort of hotel."

It was strange to suddenly realize that she was the stronger of the two. He reached out his hand. The slightest of smiles came and left her face. She put her hand in his.

"Maureen. It's been hard for me to explain myself because I was ashamed of what I thought I had to say and I couldn't speak clearly. Roland is the only child I really have now. What happens to him means more to me than my own life."

"I understand that, Mr. Hawthorne," she managed to say.

"It's hard for me to speak, but whatever I've said to you has been the truth as I saw it. Do you believe me, Maureen?"

"Yes, sir."

Give me a little time, he prayed.

"Will you believe me once more if I tell you that I have been stupid and blind and cruel, and that it has taken this horrible hour to realize what sort of young woman you really are, and that I want to beg your pardon?"

She pulled away her hand in surprise and stared up at him with her mouth and her eyes open. She tried to speak but couldn't.

"There are some things it is hard for an old man to learn. I had to wait until now."

"But that doesn't change what you said. I agree with you, Roland is a brilliant person. I'm certainly not. If he and I live right next to each other, we'll probably fall in love. If he marries me, that will harm his career. I wouldn't make a good wife for a lawyer. It makes sense." She began to stammer. "It just hurts."

"Maybe it's taken me this time to learn I can trust you."

"I can't promise you that I won't fall in love with him if he lives in the same house with me and if he's kind to me."

"That's not what I mean. That's impossible to ask."

And as he tried to finish his statement, another flash crossed her face.

"And I can't live here if I know that that's what you really think of me! You know I can't disagree with you, but you— you've humiliated me!"

"I've humiliated myself." He struggled to keep explaining. "You see a lot more clearly than I thought. You feel deeply and you feel honorably——"

"You thought I didn't?" she demanded. "What do you actually think I am?"

He raised his hand, about to say something, then let it fall. They had reached just about the limit of whatever words could accomplish. It was unbearable to appear in this bankrupt position before her, but she was a good and beautiful young creature and she was absolutely right that he had humiliated her. He turned back to the window.

"Mr. Hawthorne, I am sorry that I got angry. I have no right to lose my temper," she apologized.

"Maureen, I don't seem to know who has a right to do what."

"But what do you want me to do?" she cried in anguish. "I don't know where I stand now."

"Can you try to——" but he suddenly checked himself. He could not lose her or hurt her. He was seeking to spare her pride by punishing his own. But was he doing her any real good? At great effort was he merely teaching the girl that, if she insisted, people would go very far to please her? Maureen was clearly puzzled by his indecision.

"You said you trusted me. What did you mean then?"

"I can trust you to be decent and honorable. That's all I have the right to ask," he replied almost absently, trying to see her as if she had appeared for the first time, erect beside the desk in the dark plaid dress his wife had bought. He remembered that she was a mother. It was easy to forget when one looked at her face and its soft, still unformed contours. Maureen never bothered to curl her hair, brushing it straight back with a thin dark ribbon to hold it in place. That fairness of her hair had held his glance the first afternoon as they stood in the front yard. That and the simplicity and honesty of her blue eyes, and their firmness. He had misjudged her pride.

"What is the matter, Mr. Hawthorne?" she demanded. "You acted as you thought best."

"You buy knowledge at a high price."

"I don't understand you."

If he had taught her what power she possessed in her honesty and simplicity, he would have given her a dangerous tool.

"I try to look into the future. I try to foresee the way people will act and then I and my partners and our customers make up our minds how we want people to act and then what sort of legal restrictions we can design so that they will act the way we want. Because the things I see and plan are apt to come true, I earn a good deal of money. But when I plan what cannot be planned, then maybe I end up in blindness or cruelty or pride."

"I think I see what you mean."

Not completely. The words were convincing. And pride is evil. But if it was brutal to dwell on matters of knowledge and power in her presence, it was not false. She was made for love. She was worthy to be loved. Rolnd would not be able to help himself.

He smiled sadly at her. Since he had to say something, he said: "What you and I think we know suddenly becomes a lot more complicated, and that is hard to take."

She gave a rueful smile at this. "Yes. It is."

"So all I can do, Maureen, is to ask you to live in this more complicated world with us. In our house. And to believe that I've learned a few things. And"—he paused, for even if he was right he still had no regrets—"I have to ask you to trust me."

She looked at him for quite a long time before she held out her hand.

"I can trust you."

IV

A GLASS OF MANDARIN

"THE MANDARIN, MONSIEUR."

The Arab waiter presented him the drink on a tray. One look and Christofek regretted the spirit of curiosity that would clutter his life to the grave—have you ever spent a weekend at Atlantic City? A viscous film crept up the surface of his glass. The melancholy liquid tasted like old hospital dressings. It was obviously made to be drunk—you saw the label in every bar, with Negro dwarfs prancing about a great maroon orange—and it was not in the French character to drink in a spirit of penance.

"What's it like? I've always wondered whether to try a glass," said the young woman with the pile of magazines at the other side of the table. She was Mrs. Judy Williams. She had arrived from London and was waiting to take the plane for Meknes. Her husband Roy was a captain at the airbase there. He came from New Rochelle. She, however, had grown up in Scarsdale.

"It's not worth the effort."

Perhaps the memory of a childhood sip from Father's glass, when the franc was worth a lot more than it is today, gave the Mandarin a nostalgic appeal.

"It looks sort of horrible."

"It's a very sincere drink," he replied more cordially. It was two hours until the plane back to Oran would be ready and he could free himself from the loudspeaker's cacophony and this wasteland of red leatherette armchairs. "It looks and smells and tastes horrible. Now then, why do the French drink it?"

"The French do lots of funny things," she laughed.

She had white teeth, blond hair, neatly painted toenails. Her face a little too bony, but her print dress was bright and fresh, her legs smooth and long. It was a pity to lose all this in one more chat about national characteristics.

"André Gide," Christofek began because the story had occurred to him this past week, "wrote about a time when he was traveling through the Congo, and the absolute proof of native inferiority to the Frenchmen he met was that when you finished your meal and ordered a drink the bearer would be just as apt to bring you the vermouth as the brandy. Gide thought this was an important point."

"You certainly meet a fascinating cross-section of people when you travel," she observed brightly.

That was not true. He had met her.

John Christofek sold electrical calculating machines from Casablanca to Cairo. He lived with his wife in a pink villa in the suburbs of Oran. The machines were complicated and very expensive. Once each month Christofek tried to call on his customers and hold the operator's hand so that she wouldn't scream that they could whip her or fine her but if this contraption was not thrown down the elevator shaft. . . .

This morning Monsieur Cosnard had returned from a trip to Oued Zem where his sister-in-law had been one of those murdered.

"You know, monsieur," he said reflectively, "with some of the bodies you would not be able to tell whether it was a man or a woman."

Christofek had worked this North African concession for three years. At Monsieur Cosnard's words his memory went down the opposite path. A French sergeant was disciplining a queue of Arabs who stood against a wall with their hands clasped behind their heads. One by one the sergeant grabbed each man, spat in his face, slapped him on both cheeks, kneed him in the groin, spun him around, and kicked him off down the street. He was a rocklike man. Some Arabs fell to the ground when he hit them. Still he had a great deal of work to do and his gasping breath sounded as clearly as the blows and the harsh groans of the Arabs. Then one of the Senegalese guards saw the silent witness standing back up the street, and the sergeant yelled at Christofek to get the hell out if he didn't want to enjoy the same treatment.

The tired voice of Monsieur Cosnard had continued: "You might understand about cutting the throats of the women and children, but if you looked into the gardens they had disemboweled the rabbits and torn the wings off the doves. And I know they were laughing when they did it."

"My sister was pretty worried about my returning to Morocco, but after all we're Americans and there hasn't been any trouble yet up Meknes way."

"I envy you being able to get away."

"It was nice, I can tell you, to hear English again everywhere I went."

The different postage stamps he put on his letters home to Oran or home to St. Louis reminded him how far away he was. He could still see the little boy with his album and feel his anguish that he might never find any of those countries where the magical bits of paper came from. Now airport buses, the same garish flowers blooming upon each newsstand—"Marlon Brando's Forgotten Love"—the droning to and fro of these airborne subway trains, and the great world shrinks and cheapens.

One of Christofek's machines, if properly used, would do the work of a dozen clerks. That meant he was as much the enemy of these girls in their nylon blouses as the café seducer with his waxed moustache and celluloid collar. That meant he was loathed by every genuine Frenchman as the symbol of American commercial imperialism-cocacolonization. But it was exactly the speed and rationalization of these machines that might give this middle part of the world a chance to stand up to the menacing twin giants. Christofek had a sincere affection for the warm, feminine flavor of perspiration and cologne these offices exuded. The heat made the sallow faces glow, brought tiny drops of moisture to the downy upper lips and stained the armpits of the blouses. It made the girls' laughter shriller and their tempers sharper. Their tight skirts clung damply so that when they bent over the outlines of their pants and their sanitary belts were visible. He took Marie-Françoise Belbassa to a café and bought her a glass of Mandarin and listened about her mother's diabetes and remembered that she liked snails. And Marie-Françoise would remember his careful kindness and be patient with his electrical calculating machine.

Marie-Françoise got more money and an interesting job. Josette and Claudine and old Madame Moirot hated him. Christofek's arrival meant severance pay and an embarrassed expression of sympathy in the classic capitalist tradition. You could point out the womanly qualities of these machines with their housewifely humming and clicking, their slight tremble when you touched the keys. Hot and overused, they gave out a sweet oily fragrance. This, of course, was nonsense. If Claudine hid little of herself in her nylon blouse and tight skirt, she also let Christofek imagine too clearly her return home. Did she help her mother with the dusting and listen to the radio and file her nails? Did she give herself to her lover in the evening because the day had been empty? Madame Moirot had traded youth and beauty for magenta hair and power: "Yes, Madame Moirot knows everything!" Was she going to live with her daughter? Where would her cat sleep now? Would her son-in-law complain that she ate too much meat? They all would have time to think. Are my hips fatter? If it was Oued Zem last week, will it come again to Casablanca? The weary, uninflected voice: You know, monsieur, with some of the bodies you would not be able to tell whether it was a man or a woman.

"North Africa is so funny the way you get the contrast between the most modern things and then other things go all the way back to Bible times."

He nodded. If she wore a robe, and a veil up to her eyes, she might be beautiful. One could imagine a beauty of wild flowers or young foxes. The veil repeated that woman's strength was mystery. Does her husband no longer care? Has he forgotten what he was given when in her arms, her soft body that is all the richness of the world?

"Isn't it terrible what those Arabs have done? Some of the newspaper stories have just been sickening. Still, you've got to admit that the French have been awfully greedy."

Long slim fingers and fullness of breast and then this journalistic bathwater that she poured over his head. Interesting facts, neat conclusions, gleaned in the waiting room, at the beauty parlor, around the swimming pool, read, digested, forgotten in the rhythm of chewing gum. I am happy and therefore I deserve to be happy. At Meknes there were enough atomic bombs to turn a score of Russian cities into ashes. These bombs and Judy's husband made Russians smile and tell heavy jokes when they traveled in foreign countries— not the acuteness of French intellectuals nor the iron discipline of their sergeants.

"They're awfully cruel to their animals."

Perhaps Christofek hated Arabs because nothing that protected him—his calculating machines, his money, his green passport—had any force for them. They were so many, so poor. They desired his death, to remove one more intruder, but also to enjoy his fear and pain and to mutilate his corpse. They mirror our worst: the sadism of schoolboys, the greed of old café proprietors. They blackmail the world.

He knew a Jewish family in St. Louis who had adopted a Polish war orphan raised in Maidanek and Dachau. One day, returning from high school, he demanded a Buick convertible. It was not a request. He had to have one. And to the reasonable arguments of his foster parents he used one

unvarying clincher: You bastards were having it easy while
I—I saw my sister burned alive in front of my eyes.

The atrocity has shifted, to these words that justify and
demand everything. Yet Christofek had never imagined how
loud could be the blows of one man's hand upon another
man's face. The street had trembled. The French pay me ten
cents a day. Trachoma eats the eyes of my children. If I kill
you, you have no right to complain.

"Did you read that a British plane flew to New York by
lunchtime and was back in England for supper? Distance
doesn't mean a thing nowadays."

Did he sound like that? He also had done some reflecting
on this question of distance. Christofek used to live in a
suburb of St. Louis called Kirkwood. His parents' home was
on Taylor Avenue, not in the nicest block, only a stucco
bungalow with a heavy, airless porch, but near the dignified
elm-shaded houses with dark green shutters and polished
brass doorknobs. The colored maids and yardmen and gar-
bagemen who worked at these houses lived a mile down the
road in Meacham Park. In Meacham Park sewer ditches
separated the shacks from the unpaved roads littered with
the broken glass of old bottles. Sometimes babies were bitten
by rats. Christofek had bicycled down there on some errands
for his mother and that had begun his education.

"It must be wonderful to have a job like yours that lets
you travel so much."

"Yes, indeedy!" he replied. "I was in the bar at the airport
at Khartoum last month and I was drinking Gordon's gin
and an English flier and another American were drinking
Haig and Haig and some one brought up the same issue. If
you get in an airplane and flew five thousand miles, I thought
then, the bar boy would be a different color, but the same
men would be drinking Gordon's and Haig and Haig and it
would be easier to fly those five thousand miles than to walk
five hundred yards to the first native house like that one."

He nodded to the Arab hut just beyond the wire fence

protecting the airport. It was made of wattle, burlap, and strips of corrugated iron, the one three-dimensional object in the sun-quivering world outside their window. Judy Williams stared at it curiously. She frowned.

"That's interesting. I never thought of that before." Thought took away her eyes' sparkle and made her face less pretty. "But suppose you did make that walk from here to there, what could you ever say? What would you do?"

"Go up to the door and give the first person you met a fifty-franc piece. He'd be so stunned you could walk right in and make yourself at home."

"That seems sort of insulting."

It was to her credit to think of that, but he had decided to tempt her.

"You can't insult an Arab. If you've got a thousand francs you can buy a baby if you want one."

"That's not even three dollars!"

"They'll beat up the price if they think you mean business, but I bet you won't have to pay two thousand."

"That's horrible!"

If she offered them five they would run out of the house in fear of the police. Or they would kill her to get the rest. She put on her dark glasses to get a better look at the house.

"The plane for Meknes doesn't leave for over an hour," she said reflectively.

"I'll do all the negotiating. I'll put up the fifty francs, too." He added, "If you wanted a grandmother, you could get one for seven hundred francs."

"Don't say things like that!"

She made no motion to get up, but she couldn't let go of the idea and return to her magazines. Christofek sipped his Mandarin and watched Mrs. Williams play with her bracelet.

"How long would it take to get there?" she asked at last.

"Five minutes each way."

"It's a silly idea."

Christofek ordered the waiter to keep an eye on Madame's

bags. The four o'clock sun was brutal, the wind blew dust into their faces, but she walked briskly, holding on to the brim of her hat.

We are going to inspect this Arab family and see what baggage they carry through life. Mrs. Williams is wearing a new print dress and in her suitcases are underwear and toothbrushes and letters from her mother and souvenirs from London. Yellow goes best with my hair but my husband prefers blue.

And if this Arab family and Captain Williams and his wife were all cast upon a desert island, who would be the most naked? Her tools are mostly ones worked by electric switches. His no longer have the slightest contact with human utility. They would be hungry and sunburned and she would have one child after another because they lacked the materials to prevent pregnancy. But what would they give these children? What beliefs and skills, what patterns of beauty, what songs?

Just before the entrance gate she stopped.

"Let's go back."

"Anything you say."

Christofek had lost interest in going to buy an Arab baby, but she started on again, past the incurious guard at the gate. Across the road and they were in the yard of the hut. A dog snarled silently at them. He cringed away when Christofek stamped his foot, and the noise brought out a little girl in a torn cotton shift and a scrawny boy with one blue blind eye. Then through the burlap door appeared a woman of thirty or forty with a sunken chest, thin scaly arms, and a stomach protruding in pregnancy. She stared at the strangers in fear.

"Bismillah."

"Bismillah," replied the woman doubtfully.

Christofek held out the copper coin. "Madame wishes to enter your house," he said in French.

Her eyes flickered from one face to the other before she grabbed the money. Christofek pulled aside the burlap so that Judy Williams could enter. A baby sat on the floor, flies on its face. In one corner crouched an old woman. A piece of iron upon two concrete blocks made the stove, and behind this stood a box holding two oranges, a bottle partly filled with a brown liquid, a half-loaf of dust-colored bread. The back wall was the side of a wooden packing crate with U.S. AIR FORCE stenciled on it.

One glance and the hut was theirs. The adventure had been completed. But the Arab mother twisted in front of them to peer up at this woman. She had noted the bracelet and shoes and handbag clutched like a shield, but she strained to peer behind the sunglasses and Christofek saw her two wild green faces, hands up to the half-opened mouth, reflected in the lenses. The eyes behind the green glass were no less wild and the face so chalky the lipstick looked like metal. Judy Williams gave a little jerk of her head as if to shake away the cloud of panic—flies swirled off the ceiling where her hat brim scraped it—and Christofek felt ashamed he had brought her to be turned into this caricature: If you touch me I shall scream.

Then she darted for the doorway. She hadn't time to pull aside the rotting burlap. It knocked off her hat and tore. "God be with you," Christofek repeated to the Arabs, and picked up her hat. She almost ran across the road, turning her head away from the smile of the airport guard, but the heat suddenly slowed her pace. Christofek held out the hat.

"I don't want it! It's dirty!"

"And what did you expect?"

She fixed him with a look of hatred. His own miniature faces stared back at him. Then they went on in silence to the door of the airport.

V

FREEDOM

AT THE CREST OF THE HILL the soldier turned to look back at the town. The rooftops, the church spires alone were visible, none of the people in the square or any of the army traffic he had put behind. Once again he set himself to hiking steadily between the fields of potatoes and turnips, marking his pace with the stick he held like a pilgrim's staff. The time was a little after noon. His shadow flowed over the ground at the right of his feet, which meant he was walking west, toward the sea, as accurate a direction as he wanted.

The last real decision Ethan Toller had made had been in Normandy almost a year ago. When the mortar fire lifted, the rest of the patrol picked itself off the ground, but not the sergeant. Corporal Toller decided it was safer to run than to walk, no more hopeless to attack than to run away. They reached the crossing of the two hedgerows, and a moment faster than the German on the other side of the ditch, Toller pulled the trigger of his submachine gun. The German fell back dead. At hysterical speed the two handfuls of men fired their guns through the hedge, hurled their grenades over it, and in eight seconds Toller's gun was empty and every other American was dead. The noise of breaking branches made him turn. A German had crashed into the ditch behind, two insane eyes and a black machine pistol. Toller had infinite leisure to look into those two eyes. Then the German jerked his head, jerked his thumb toward the gap in the hedgerow, and Toller's life as a prisoner began. Eleven months of this had been spent at the Moosberg Kriegsgefangenerlager on the border between Saxony and Silesia, where he occupied a bunk next to Jerry Sangallo's. Now he was free again. He took his directions from the sun, the low chain of pine-covered hills to the north, and the distant blue mountains way off to the southeast. The weedy potato furrows and the dead branches in the fruit trees showed him—and he was no country man—that no one was looking after these fields and orchards. When he finished his beans and chocolate, he would go up to a farmhouse and tell the woman he would hoe weeds in exchange for food. He went through the gestures to use, holding out a weed in his hand so that she would understand.

The path swung into a shallow valley, and all view was cut off by the bramble borders and the wandering, unkempt apple orchard on both sides, except straight upward, to the sun and a drifting of small cumulus clouds. That was all— not a face, not a voice, only a woman's footprints in the dust. Suddenly he stopped and knelt down, pulled off his boots, his socks, and set his feet upon the warm dust and the cool earth. The pebbles underfoot made him limp for a few minutes, but he didn't mind.

At Moosberg Ethan had become an expert on skies and learned the constellations and the types of clouds. Underfoot, however, were the cinders and the mud. Outside the wire was Oberfeldwebel Treitzschke. Inside were the ninety-five men of his compound. He had nothing to do with the leader of the patrol who forgot all about the fragile personality he had to protect and turned into a fighter ant scrabbling mur- derously toward the enemy. He had also lost contact with the reasonable life of a young businessman and his wife, a life of slow building—care of two little boys until they should be men, paying off a mortgage until the house was theirs.

Feldwebel Treitzschke was the sun and moon, a figure of phlegm, choler, melancholy. Each morning roll call they must listen for what his mood might be and to the threat, almost the plea, that each prisoner had the personal responsibility to see that his anger did not break forth that day and destroy all the decency that should exist between man and man even in wartime. Joe Springarn, the Lagerführer, held a more contradictory authority. To enforce obedience to Treitzschke and above him Hauptmann Kleinschmidt, to enforce a rigid and uniform resistence against the Germans—he handled both jobs at the same time. He didn't see any contradiction. Order was will, the iron will of this ex-hardware clerk from Corsicana, Texas, and behind his will the mountains of discipline and patriotic duty.

Ethan could accept these men and the barbed wire, but Sangallo's brutal North Boston monotone grating day and night eighteen inches away from his ear became a sound out of hell.

"She said she didn't want to and that was okay by me if she just let me stick my hand in a little but she said that'd tear the blouse so why didn't she unbutton it but the buttons were those real little tiny ones and she got all tied up with them so I shoved my hand under her skirt and she got sore and I said if she didn't want to tear her damn blouse——"

Always the same ending—the woman sobbing and cursing, whether she was a proper, foolish little girl or a two dollar whore,—and Sangallo going his way with a "That's just too bad, sister." His life moved in a series of jerks, like an old-time movie, but with absolutely no connection between the episodes, with an absolute denial of cause and effect. Sangallo was the only man in a world of ghosts. You killed him or you accepted him the way he was. Once Ethan did try to kill him. He hurled himself upon Sangallo, overturned him in his fury, trying to bang his head into marmalade against the floor until Joe Springarn dragged him off.

There was very little to do. Each man builds up a capital of body and soul. Ethan's was draining away from lack of food, toothache, monotony, and hatred. Sangallo lay on his back, humming tunelessly, beating time against the bunk, jiggling his head from side to side. Snow turned into mud. The war was coming to an end, but would they live to see the end? Germany was Feldwebel Treitzschke written large, and its fury would burst out and destroy all the helpless beings in its power. But when blue cornflowers bloomed in the wheat field outside the barbed wire, the Russian guns could be heard. Every day red-starred Stormoviks roared over the camp. Peasant women and old men whipped their carts along the road, a cow with swinging udder dragged behind each one. Treitzschke fawned and grew vicious, both at the same time.

One morning the machine gunners on the guard towers fired burst after burst through the roofs of the tar-paper barracks. The Americans flattened themselves to the floor. They tried to crawl under the bunks while the ricocheting bullets tore off splinters and smashed the window glass. Silence. Noises of haste. The Germans dismantled the machine guns and threw the kitchen equipment and Hauptmann Kleinschmidt's furniture into the camp trucks. Like a madman Feldwebel Treitzschke ran from compound to compound. "We're only going on a reconnaissance! We'll be back! And if we find any of you have forgotten your discipline——" He stamped his foot and could not finish his sentence. The three trucks raced away. An hour later two Russian jeeps with an officer wearing shoulder boards and half a dozen towheaded, round-faced boys drove up from the opposite direction.

The first flowers of freedom had already bloomed and died. Even before the trucks disappeared all the locks had been smashed. The men ran out into the wheat field, yelling, wrestling joyfully in the sunshine. The cornflowers in Ethan's hand were the first living things, living or beautiful, he had held for a year's time. He could almost see his wife's face.

"Hey, look at the camp!" A cloud of black smoke was pouring out of one of the barracks. "Sangallo's trying to burn the camp down," someone yelled, and the men ran back. Joe Springarn summoned a meeting of the Lagerführers. When the Russian jeeps pulled up, therefore, it was he who saluted the officer with the maroon shoulder boards and the strange false teeth made out of stainless steel.

The Russians left. Springarn appointed a pair of sentries for each gate.

"Just who's going to be trying to break in, Joe?" Ethan called out to him. "And who are you keeping from breaking out?"

"The Russians are running a war. They don't want a lot of sightseers goofing around," Springarn replied.

"If I want to take a nice little walk, Joe, are you going to stop me?" questioned Sangallo.

"We're free now. We've got to keep up discipline," Springarn answered him, which was sidestepping the question, not Springarn's usual way of handling things. He ordered the construction of baseball bats and announced a baseball round robin between all the compounds. That evening another Russian jeep drove up with a job lot of German rifles and machine pistols to arm the sentries, which was the delayed answer to Sangallo's question.

There were some weird bats carved out of scrap lumber, but nothing so weird as the baseball games played on that field of young wheat. The gaunt, sunken-eyed Americans yelled and batted and ran slowly around the bases. Sometimes the Russian tanks stopped a moment. The infantrymen riding on top grinned in bewilderment. German prisoners straggled past on their first march of the endless journey eastward. The peasants were drifting back too, most of them without their cows. And on the same road trudged other civilians in ragged black clothes, Russian and Polish laborers starting home at last.

"Baseball?" one of these men stopped and said to Ethan. "Ten years in Pittsburgh"—the explanation for his English. "That's wheat"—he pointed at the young blades being trampled down. And angrily—"What the hell you play baseball for now?"

The Russians and Americans had met on the Elbe. All day there were men sitting around the little radios they had built secretly, waiting for news of the war's end. Ethan had almost forgotten what he had expected it to be like. Three American ambulances did come with food, cigarettes and medicines, and took back the sickest prisoners and those wounded by the machine gunners. One evening a convoy of a dozen trucks arrived to evacuate the whole camp.

The convoy loaded up at four-thirty, when the last stars were still shining. The ugly taste of the past ten days began to fade. Moosberg would vanish like Feldwebel Treitzschke. A terrible joy just to stamp one's feet on the steel floor of an American six-by-six again. Nothing else in the world sounds exactly like that. But why did the convoy have to travel with tarpaulins pulled over the top of every truck? All the towns and summer fields outside while they rocked back and forth and stared at each other's faces.

"Get those tarps back again!" Springarn yelled. "That's the way the Russians want it."

They reached the Elbe by nine. The men almost fell out of the trucks, waving good-bye to the Russians, stretching for a look at the sign: "You are crossing this bridge courtesy of the 488th Combat Engineers." An MP with a white helmet meant home.

At eleven-thirty the convoy halted for lunch in the square of a small railway town. Once again, like the morning they ran into the wheat field with the cornflowers, every detail of the world was golden new for the ex-prisoners who clambered out of the trucks and settled themselves on the hoods or upon the benches of the little park opposite the railway station. And while they opened the cans of beans or unpeeled the oranges of their picnic lunch, they could gaze at the church, the red sign of Jo. Knottig Kolonialwaren, or the vicious riot that had just started around a freight train. From

the top of the truck where he was eating, Ethan watched the
argument between the two American MPs guarding the train
and the shabby, weary crowd of men and women pressing
against the picket fence that protected the station. The MPs
must have spoken rudely, for the civilians yelled and began
to climb over the iron stakes. Shoving the MPs aside, they
tore the benches off the platform and battered at the car
doors. The two soldiers ran down the platform toward their
jeep. One of them had an idea. The jeep swung alongside
the parked convoy. "Hey, you fellows, give us a hand, will
you?" The picnickers laughed derisively and the angry policemen pretended they hadn't said anything and drove away
at top speed.

The doors of the freight cars had been smashed open. Some
boys climbed in and began throwing off boxes and sacks to
the mob on the platform. Now the Germans of the town,
who had been watching from the edges of the square, were
seized with fear that they would miss the profit. Two women
carrying a basket between them ran toward the station, then
boys with knapsacks and an old man with a bucket. The
rioters were clearly not German, however, and they turned
on the newcomers with such a dangerous fury that the towns-
people fell back irresolutely into the street by the convoy.

A clamorous honking heralded the return of the MP jeep,
followed by two truckloads of infantry. "Here come the U.S.
Marines," observed the man next to Ethan. The Germans
scattered, ducking between the convoy trucks and then peering to see what would happen, but the non-Germans kept
on with their sack of the train. The trucks halted at either
end of the station. Two wedges of soldiers cut toward the
wounded freight cars, compressing the riot into an irregular
black triangle. The base disintegrated into scraps of men and
women running toward the street, clambering over the picket
fence with their loot, but at one car the apex held firm. It
was harder to run. The rifles were pushing from both sides,
and the people were angry and ready to push back. The

spectators on the trucks, however, could already see the round olive helmets lined in front of the train. A soldier jumped up onto the car to clear out the two boys in it. One of the boys kicked him in the chest before he caught his balance and toppled him backward. Three other soldiers pulled themselves into the car, grabbed the boys and flung them out, over the olive helmets, right into the middle of the mob. The fight became crueler. Rifle barrels jerked into the air; the soldiers were using the butts. The rioters had only their fists. They began to run for the railing. But the soldiers were right behind them, using the rifle butts to knock the parcels out of their hands, shoving them along so that no one would change his mind. This brought panic at the picket fence. The fugitives were pressed too tightly to climb over, or they lost their footing and tore themselves against the spikes.

One slightly built girl in shorts, shoved so violently that she made a sort of somersault over the fence, landed heavily on her back and lay without moving. A man and a boy ran up and dragged her to the middle of the street. Still she did not move. The boy stood and shouted at the trucks with their watching soldiers. The front of his face was bleeding terribly from a rifle blow, but he spat out the blood in his mouth and wiped his sleeve across his face and, throwing out his arms, shouted again. There was no answer from the soldiers to his despairing words. Nor when he came closer and stared up wildly at the men in each truck could he find on any face the answer he wanted. A third time he shouted in his unknown language.

"Wipe your nose, sonny!" Jerry Sangallo yelled back.

Some fool laughed, though most seemed embarrassed and angered, and one soldier jumped down and rather shame-facedly held out a pack of cigarettes to the boy. He shook his head and he and his companion picked up the girl and carried her off.

Ethan climbed down from the cab roof. He went around

to the back of the truck, pulled out his blanket roll and his bag of personal gear, and walked away. If someone had asked him what he was doing, he would have found it hard to answer. Disgust, disgust with himself mainly, who accepted everything. Turning out of the square, he found himself in a narrow street with trees and brick houses, a few stores, a long, straight street that turned into a road without a person in it. Perhaps if he had seen anyone he would have turned around and gone back, but there was no one. He heard the noise of the truck motors starting up. The trucks groaned into motion, rumbling off in the rhythmic pound a convoy makes. Ethan started down the street.

He picked up a heavy stick that would protect him against dogs. Other matters he would worry about when they had to be faced. On that last patrol in Normandy, when the mortar fire killed the sergeant, Ethan hid himself in a cart track. The bombs no longer whined or screamed, they were falling so close, just a flutter of the air and then they hit. With his fingernails he was slowly digging the track deeper. A lizard darted in front of his face. It jerked its head curiously at him and stared with one beady eye, then jerked around to peer with the other. A snap of its tail and it ran off, anxieties on its little mind no doubt, but not the war that had flattened out these men.

He was going to be a lizard.

Walking now with bare feet he went more slowly, eyes sharp for what he passed—he had been too long in Moosberg to waste the smallest phenomenon, even the bluebottles on a cowpat. The unpruned branches of the apple trees sheltered a drowsy bird world, and twice Ethan halted to peer up at a nest for any signs of the young; another time he was amused by a little brown-and-yellow bird that hopped aimlessly between two branches without being able to decide what it should do. Patches of raspberry bushes formed part of the bramble border along the path. Most of the berries were still a hard whitish green, but some were ripe and he

greedily tasted the sweet sour dusty fruit. A dozen yards off
the path the bushes grew more densely. Painstakingly he
made his way through the brambles; closer to the bushes he
heard the rustle of a stream and saw the glittering of water
through the leaves. Then he heard a woman's voice singing.

An opening in the bushes let him slide down to the water's
edge. The little stream sparkled and trembled in the sunlight,
and when he noticed the naked woman standing in the water,
he saw her, where the sun struck against her body, as a white
column of light. She stood sideways to him, supported by
one hand upon a branch overhead, her eyes closed, her head
flung back so that the sun fell full upon her face, and as she
sang she let herself gently sway back and forth. Ethan stared
breathlessly at the wonder of her bare shoulders and the
curve of stomach below her waist. It wasn't desire that over-
whelmed him but a sudden flowing sympathy with her longing for sunlight and air, water, solitude. She shook her head
to let the breeze catch her hair. Then she opened her eyes
and saw Ethan.

Her body jerked in angry surprise.

"Geh weg!" she called out.

"Don't be afraid," he said in English without thinking,
then repeated it in German. Her shock made him sorry he
had spoiled her pleasure.

"Geh weg!" she called again and tossed her head angrily.
Her arms were thin. Her shoulder blades and the tops of her
hipbones stuck out. The young body looked tired and worn.
She had a pretty face, angry now but straightforward and
proud. She was not afraid of him but he did not have the
right to watch her bathe. Turning to go, he thought of something.

"Would you like some soap?"

She didn't understand. He took out of his pocket the cake
brought by the trucks to Moosberg.

"Soap? Seife?"

He held it out and then tossed it to her. The cake fell on

the sandbar by her feet. Holding her breasts, watching him carefully, she bent to pick it up.

He clambered up the bank. Ten minutes earlier he had felt blessed in his solitude. Now he was lonely. He lined his cap with leaves and followed along the raspberry bushes, looking carefully for the berries the birds had left. When he came back to the spot where he had turned off the path, the girl was still hidden. He didn't believe she would run away out of fear or leave with his soap. Lighting a cigarette, he sat down and put on his boots.

Still she didn't appear. He could hardly go back to the stream to look for her there. He became impatient. It was getting on to the middle of the afternoon and he had far to go. Then he heard a rustling of the bushes. She emerged in a black woolen jacket and a brown skirt, barefoot, her hair wet. From the way her body moved he guessed that she was wearing nothing except those two garments. She carried the soap on a leaf, smaller than when he had tossed it to her.

"Danke." With a slight smile she shrugged her shoulders. "I washed my clothes. I used a lot."

She spoke in German but her accent was not German. He offered her the cap full of raspberries. She took a small handful.

"No. Take all. I am sorry. I——" He tried to think of the right words. Feldwebel Treitzschke hadn't taught him much German. The girl waited for him to finish. "I did not have politeness."

She accepted the cap. Close up to him, barefoot, she seemed very small but self-reliant and sturdy in the whole way she held herself. If her narrow, bony, sunburned face was hardened by too much work and the habit of always being on her guard, it hadn't always been hard and it was still an open one with honest and intelligent eyes. The rather short nose was a bit comical, the firm mouth wasn't.

"I'm an American soldier. I was a prisoner in Silesia," he explained.

"I'm a Belgian. I worked in a munitions factory in Chemnitz."

He couldn't catch what she did but she made the outline of a shell with her hands and then a screwing motion.

"You mean fuses?" That might be it.

"I live in Antwerp."

"St. Louis. That's near Chicago."

"Well." She accepted and dismissed this exchange of information. "Thanks for the soap."

"Do you have food? Are you hungry?" he asked, trying to detain her.

"I have bread and wurst."

He lit a cigarette for her.

"If you are going west, so am I. It's dangerous to travel alone."

Drawing on her cigarette thoughtfully, she raised her eyes to try and judge his face. A small diet and sunshine—a prisoner has a lot of time for sunbathing—had given it a leathery texture. It was drawn a bit to one side from his way of smiling, because he hadn't been accustomed to smile just out of amusement. She nodded.

"I'll get my things."

When she reappeared from behind the bushes in her heavy worn shoes and bent beneath her knapsack, she looked even less like a person who needed his help, and he could not see any connection with the young woman singing dreamily in the sunlight. They marched along the path, the soldier with his staff, the girl, head forward, thumbs stuck in the straps of her pack, a little bit behind. They didn't speak. It was hard to communicate in a language foreign to them both, and they didn't have anything yet to say to each other.

The orchard fell away. The path turned into a road in open country with the same landmarks of the hills to their right and the blue mountains way off to their left and a dark rise of forest some miles straight ahead. The sun shone in their faces. The wind blew against them and blew the high cottony clouds across the sky and the shadows across the fields. They plodded along steadily and they could measure the ground they put behind them by these pastures and potato fields they passed. The position of a farmhouse in the valley shifted and the folds of the hills opposite them changed. They were crossing Germany. They were taking themselves out of this land of captivity. He looked back at the girl behind him and when her eyes met his the two of them smiled at each other.

Twice they passed small groups of men hiking in the opposite direction, toward Poland or Czechoslovakia, who looked with some curiosity at Ethan's uniform and his shoulder patch and with less curiosity at the girl and exchanged a nod of greeting. Then they came to a large hay field which a slender, barelegged boy was trying to reap by himself. It was a job his father should have done. The scythe was too big for him. He tugged and strained at it. When he jerked the blade back he lost balance. He was fighting the hay field, tossing his head again and again to throw the hair out of his eyes. For a moment he set his scythe down to watch the two walk by. The boy stared at them defiantly—Look what I can do—but as they looked back at him from the edge of the field, they saw another expression mixed with the first: "This is a terrible job, won't anyone help me?"

"Poor boy," said the girl.

At the top of the next hill a huge yellow dog ran out at them from a farmyard, hideous in its slathering, motiveless fury. It ran at Ethan and then cut behind the girl. She gave a cry. Ethan pushed in front of her, struck out with his staff. The dog recoiled, circled, lunged again to slash at the girl's legs, but the staff kept it at bay. It was convulsed with its own rage, with growls so deep they sounded like vomiting. Maybe it ran out like this a dozen times a day—its mistress was already shrieking from the steps of her house—but Ethan had had enough. He struck again at the dog. It grabbed the end of his staff. He jerked it free enough to jab the end down the dog's throat. The dog screamed. Ethan jerked the staff completely free and brought its other end with all his might upon the beast's head. Two more blows and the groans stopped.

The woman ran to the edge of the road and was shrieking at him now. The dog had been her only defense. He shrugged his shoulders and the two of them started on again.

"I'm glad I wasn't alone," the girl said. "I am very afraid of dogs."

Now they began to talk and Ethan found out that she had a gentle voice. Her name was Maxine Heermansch. She traveled alone because her companions at the factory in Chemnitz had not waited for her when she fell ill. In Antwerp she was a textile worker, had been one since she was seventeen, but after a strike in 1944 the Germans arrested both men and women, sending them as forced laborers into the Reich, and she hadn't been lucky. Could he tell her anything about Antwerp? She hadn't received any news from home since the liberation, and the German papers said that the city had been wiped out by their guided missiles.

"Why are you traveling alone?" she asked him.

Her German was simple enough for him to understand, and if he used English pronounced with a German accent, the language of Feldwebel Treitzschke, that seemed near her own Flemish. But this was hard to answer. He didn't know how to fit in the baseball games and the soldiers on top of the trucks eating their lunch and watching the riot.

"I was a year in the prison camp like this"—he pressed his hands together and interlaced the fingers. "I wanted to be by myself."

"You're not a deserter, are you?"

"No."

She was satisfied by his answer, but he hadn't thought of that word before.

When they sat down to rest and to eat his chocolate, she remarked on his wedding ring, and he told her about his

wife and his two little boys. Out of her wallet she showed
him some snapshots of her family. In one they were all
drinking beer at an outdoor restaurant, her shapeless mother,
head thrown back in the middle of a laugh, her father (a
foreman at Maxine's plant), very clearly the boss of the
family despite his Sunday afternoon good humor, sitting with
his arms folded across his chest, a tight little moustache in
the middle of his upper lip, her scrubbed and handsome
younger brothers. One of her heavier older sister holding a
small baby. One of Maxine with lipstick and a marcel beside
her fiancé grinning in a Sunday suit, his hair curled a bit by
a wet comb. They went to the movies together on Saturday
nights and on Sundays, if it was nice, they'd bicycle out
along one of the canals and picnic or go to an inn to drink
a bottle of beer and dance. Their families had been strong
against marrying when Dirk might be conscripted by the
Germans and nothing was certain. Instead she was the one
taken away, and it seemed a shame now that they hadn't
married.

They got to their feet. He took up her heavy sack.

"Let me carry it," she protested, but he acted as if it were
his right. For a year he had been idle and of no use to anyone.

Maybe she was as tired as he, for they both plodded along
in silence again. The weight of her pack bent his neck. He
looked at the road ahead, his feet as they took step after
step, and Maxine's. The direct and simple nature of the
young woman held his mind. Those pictures of her mother
and her older sister showed how quickly her good looks
would go, but they would find her a husband.

"If we find a town you can get us a ride on one of your
trucks and maybe some hot coffee," she said.

That was the practical way he could serve her. His rejection
of the army had no significance for her. He was either a
deserter or he wasn't.

They came to a crossroad. The traveled road led around

the low roll of wooded hills now in front of them. The other, more nearly a path, disappeared into the pine woods.

"I'd think this one would bring us to a town more easily," Maxine said, nodding toward the bigger road.

"I don't know what we'd find in a town," he answered doubtfully.

"There'd be American soldiers in it, wouldn't there? They're in all the towns."

"I don't think so in this section. That path through the woods looks more direct."

He knew he was trying to deceive her.

"I'm tired," she sighed, stretching and rubbing her back. "It ought to be possible to get a ride. Any army driver would give us one if you asked him, wouldn't he?"

"In the morning perhaps. It'd be harder at this time of day."

He avoided looking at her. He was angry at himself. For her to spend the night in the forest with him didn't necessarily serve her best interests. Or his own loyalties. But he had been a man for so short a time he couldn't bring himself to give this up.

Maxine looked at him doubtfully, but until then everything he had said to her had been truthful and she was ready to believe him. She allowed him to lead the way and another half-hour's slow hike brought them to the woods. No sun reached the path, the air fell cooler about them. Though German thrift means that everything is picked off the forest floor and the dead branches lopped away, creating a perspective as distant as in a forest of telegraph poles, all they could see, save the path ahead, were these pine trunks and the low ceiling of dark green boughs. They were shut in upon themselves. This privacy, added to Ethan's bad conscience and the girl's doubt, constrained them. The only sound was that of the wind sighing through the tree tops. Again Maxine stopped to rest. To their surprise a thin and mournful black hen limped across the path in front of them. She halted, and cocking her head at the man and woman, uttered a self-pitying *klerp*—sad and old, a city chicken that had lived on half rations.

"Poor old woman," Maxine said.

Ethan carefully took his stick and got to his feet. The hen limped away with the same complaining *klerp,* stopping to eye him like a careworn housewife. He almost reached her when she became alarmed and cackled off at a right angle. His stick hit her on the side. The animal exploded in panic. Maxine jumped up to drive her back. A kick checked her and he sprang and grabbed the wings and wrung the brittle neck before he could think. He was not proud of what he handed to Maxine, but she accepted it and began to pluck the feathers.

Ethan found wood for a fire and set two forked sticks at either end and with Maxine's knife peeled a long green stick to serve as a spit. Then he took the naked bird, cut off the feet and neck, and cleaned it. He worked quickly, surprised by his own skill as he had been in killing the dog. He shoved the spit through the chicken and squatted down to begin turning it over the fire. Maxine, meanwhile, having put on a coarse gray sweater under her jacket that made her look bulkier and even shorter, had unpacked her sack and was hanging up the damp laundry on the pine branches.

"You turn the forest into a washhouse," he teased.

She laughed at this. Then she came to the fire, and kneeling down opposite him, toasted the liver and heart on a long twig.

"You're a good cook," she told him.

Her praise made him happy. Her face was reddened by the heat and as she smiled at him, holding out the wretched little scrap of liver, she became girlish and pretty.

"You'll burn the chicken," she warned. He had forgotten to keep turning the bird, but she seemed pleased to have him look at her so warmly. He felt light at heart to be cooking for her this animal he had killed, and after they had eaten it would soon be night and he could lie beside her and hold her in his arms. Perhaps his face expressed this too plainly. She lowered her eyes. But when she raised them again all the life in her face instantly froze. Toller turned his head to where she was looking. A man had walked to within a dozen paces of the fire without their hearing a sound.

He was big, a head taller than Ethan—the knife stuck into the ground out of reach and the stick lying off by a tree. The Wermacht jacket covered only half his chest and ended above his wrists and his bony hands. He had been nearly starved too. The skin was stretched tight across his skull and the eyes were sunk into shadow.

"Guten Abend," Ethan said.

The man nodded. A smell of singeing reminded Ethan of his chicken. He turned it again. The man approached nearer and Ethan saw the torn pants and broken shoes.

"Huhne."

The German word came out hoarsely. The three of them stared at the turning bird.

It was his duty to offer the stranger a share of their small wealth. Yet Ethan was afraid and wondered if it showed. He glanced up again at the black gaunt face. The man was looking at Maxine now, not the chicken.

"I am an American. I was a war prisoner. The girl is a Belgian. She was a forced laborer."

Ethan tried to break the silence with a little human information. Every man in Europe knew those German words.

"American?" The stranger reflected upon this. Then he stretched his arm a little further out of his sleeve and showed the tattooed numbers. "Sachsenhausen." And he pointed in the direction from which they had come: "Ukrain."

The wizened bird was as roasted as would do it any good. Ethan nodded toward the knife and Maxine reached over to get it for him. Lifting off the spit, Ethan disengaged a leg and thigh for Maxine. He gave her a faint smile as she looked at him to learn his mind and began to cut at the second thigh.

"Please. Eat with us," he invited the Ukrainian and pointed at the ground by the fire. Painfully the man sat down. He sighed. Ethan was digging off the thin breast of the chicken. The other half would go to Maxine. One wing for the stranger, the other for himself. Then he'd give him a cigarette—nothing else to be eaten on that carcass—and they'd go. Out of his jacket the Ukrainian pulled a small bottle and offered it to Maxine.

"Schnapps?"

She wiped the top and drank, burst into a fit of coughing and tried to smile her thanks. She handed it back and he passed it to Ethan. Ethan took a gulp of the oily gin, and then the Ukrainian drank. The next round Maxine only pretended. Ethan divided the remaining parts of the chicken. Again the man's eyes were fixed on Maxine.

"Ethan." He pointed to himself. At the girl: "Maxine."

"Vasilo."

The sky above the pines had turned to a steel blue. In the dusk the scattered pieces of Maxine's underclothing floated among the trees like little ghosts, and the ruddy fire glistened upon the smoothness of her cheeks and forehead and deepened the hollow of the Ukrainian's ravaged face. Ethan reached for his cigarettes. They were almost gone. It had been a dreary way to eat their supper and finish their supplies. A third time the stranger passed his schnapps and then tossed the empty bottle over his shoulder.

"Cigarette?"

He pulled out a charred stick for them to light up with. More fire was needed against the chill and he rose to fetch wood. A small sound from Maxine made him turn. She was leaning forward, with an unfrightened but curious expression of waiting on her face. The Ukrainian, eyes screwed up against the cigarette smoke, was bent over stiffly to one side. Ethan saw his hand fastened around Maxine's wrist.

He had shot and killed two German soldiers in Normandy, but he had never killed a man he had spoken to.

"No. Lass allein." The man did not move. "Chicken. Schnapps. Cigarette." He listed the things they had shared. "You go. We go." He pointed in the two directions. "Leave her alone."

Maxine raised her eyes to his, that same look of waiting on her face, cut in two with the fire red on one half and the other dark. He had never seen her before this afternoon. Now he had to kill a man for her sake. How strangely delicate her light brown hair seemed. He winked to catch her attention. Then he threw his wood on the fire. It burst out flames and coals. Maxine wrenched herself free. Now they all stood, with the fire between them.

"Listen," Ethan said. "We go. You go. Auf wiedersehen." The Ukrainian took the cigarette from his mouth and stubbed it out against his leg and put it away in his jacket.

"American soldier, you go."

Ethan motioned Maxine to go back. With a quick heavy step the Ukrainian ran at her. This time she looked frightened. She whirled away but her foot caught on a root and she fell. Ethan hurled a burning log against his enemy's back. The man grunted. When he turned a knife blade shone. Nobody moved. A bird began to sing. Ethan felt he could blink his eyes and the man would be gone, blink them again and he would be back in Moosberg.

The Ukrainian started to whistle, a mournful tune with a long pause between each phrase. He whistles and still he wants to kill me, Ethan wondered, but he kept moving away, slowly revolving around the fire to keep out of reach, Maxine on her feet now, limping. The little fires lit by the exploding brands flickered and cast new reflections upon the shirts and underpants hung about the trees. Ethan noticed his staff lying in the pine needles and grabbed it up. The gesture alarmed the Ukrainian, who leapt at him through the fire. Ethan struck him on the shoulder, but a terrible blow against his

ribs knocked him to the ground. He saw the black outline
of the foot lifted to stamp on his stomach. A hideous scream
from the girl made the foot pause. Ethan rolled over and
hoisted himself upright.

For a moment again the three of them stood still and silent.
The two men panted, bent over like cavemen, but this time
the Ukrainian stood between Ethan and the girl and suddenly
he wheeled round and started after her. Again Ethan grabbed
his stick, ran and struck at the man's wrist, knocking the
knife from his hand, and as the other turned back, he
punched him in the stomach with its end. The man tore it
out of his hands and grabbed his elbow, but the blows had
slowed him and his knife hand twisted to one side useless.
With the side of his palm Ethan struck out at the Adam's
apple. A grunt, a stagger, Ethan hurled himself at his throat
and the man fell. Under his hand he felt a rock. He smashed
it against the head below him. The skull cracked and the
hand dropped away from his arm.

Slowly he got to his feet. The firelight showed the great
dent in the forehead even if the skin hadn't been broken. It
glistened on the blood that began to flow from the nose and
the little trickle out of the corner of an eye. Unexpectedly a
hollow rattle sounded in the throat and after that nothing
else.

"Are you hurt?"

He shook his head though his side ached and he trembled.
She stood by him now, looking down at the body and then
at him. "He hurt you," she repeated. Absently he touched
his side, sighing in a misery he couldn't explain. He gazed
at her sturdy plain face. How far away he seemed from it.

"Let's go," she said and they turned back to the fire and
their gear, hunting for her knife, Maxine picking her laundry
off the trees. Once the fire leapt up as a log collapsed and it
flickered upon the streaks of blood congealed over the dead
man's face. Rapidly the girl kicked the dying fire apart and
stamped out the embers. As they stepped past the trees to-

wards the trail she reached out her hand to him. He squeezed it—it was the first time they had actually touched each other—and she lay her other hand upon his for a second.

They moved slowly. Only a loathing of the dead body behind them pushed him on. At last they reached the end of the trail's ascent. The forest stood a little more open and through the tree tops he saw the stars he had learned about at Moosberg.

"We can stop here," she whispered.

"Yes. Off the road."

They pushed their way cautiously through the branches until they came to a little clearing with ferns growing thickly in it. Ethan was afraid to make a fire which might lead the way for other wanderers, but with the last of the day's new skills, he plucked the ferns to pile up a mattress and folded his two blankets into each other and tucked under their edges. They laid their jackets on top to keep off the dew. Maxine took off her skirt and placed it underneath the blanket roll. Her thighs shone a dim white as she stooped to work her way in. If they lay still and close there would be enough room and by each other's bodies they would keep warm. But he stood beside their bed in his stocking feet and couldn't go in to lie beside her. His hands were soiled from hitting at the man.

"What is wrong?"

Her voice sounded quietly. He wiped his hands against the damp ferns and then eased himself into the blanket roll. The sudden touch of her bare legs made him tremble. She was touching against almost every part of him in this narrow, narrow bed. Her breath warmed him, the smell of her hair was around him, but he couldn't feel any desire for her body now, after all his longing for it, and all he could do was lay his hand upon her hip.

"You feel bad because you killed him?"

"Yes."

They lay still. Gradually her gentle breathing strengthened

him, and the feel of her legs alongside his. Her hand lay
against his palm and he unfolded it and began to explore
this miniature body with his thumb and his fingertips. Com-
pact and solid it was, with sturdy bones and the skin of her
fingers and her palm hardened by too much work, but as he
caressed it in a tenderness he hadn't been able to show for
a long time, touching the network of bones and tendons and
veins at the pulse and cradling it in his hand, it slowly came
to life. Her fingers pressed against his and caught them lightly
and made prisoners out of them. They passed over his face,
trying to discover who he was, stroking his cheek and pressing his lips and his eyes until he began to understand that
this resolute woman who had hiked beside him through the
afternoon was also the white body with eyes shut and head
thrown back singing naked in the sunlight. He put his arms
about her. The ferns beneath them rustled and they must
move carefully because the blankets bound them so tight.
They lay in absolute darkness but as they embraced roughly
instead of gently, they pushed the blankets back and held
each other under a sky of clouds and stars.

Later a confused dream crowded upon him, row on row
of brown shapes with white blank faces that flopped back
and forth, back and forth to some monotonous grating or
droning he knew he had heard before. The drone became
Sangallo's voice in the next bunk and then Sangallo rose
black upright as the stranger, panting and grunting as they
fought together, and Ethan had to wake himself up before
that rattle burst out of the dead throat again. He knew he
was awake but still he was pinioned, in some strange, soft,
warm way. The pressure upon him slowly turned into a girl's
arm and her soft chest underneath the sweater and her warm
bare legs. But still in the dream he had lost her and he turned
so as to hold her in his arms and kiss her until she shook
her head in sleepy protest.

When he woke again a clamor of bird calls, pipings, chirps,

and trills came from the pine woods and all the bushes about them. The sky was gray and he could distinguish the drops of moisture stringing along the pine needles above his head. From far away the grind of a truck changing its gears. He pressed closer to the woman sleeping beside him.

The next time he awoke the sense of sadness was already weighing upon him before he knew why. The torrent of bird song had subsided to a few scattered calls and chirps. Ethan pulled himself up to look at the wet woods and then turned to Maxine. His movement awakened her and her eyes opened to stare back at him. He had never seen her face so close. It was a stranger's face, dulled and lined from sleep, the skin coarsened by bad food, and its courage turned into the suspiciousness of early morning, and no warmth in those brown eyes. He smiled sadly for he knew his own gaunt, unshaven face offered nothing to bring her either pleasure or encouragement.

"I'll make a fire," he said, and kissed her on the forehead. The morning air was raw but he stripped and cleaned himself with a handful of wet ferns. By means of the ferns and bracken that had kept dry as their mattress he started a fire. Maxine climbed out of the bed but she clearly did not want him to look at her as she stood up in her sweater brushing the leaves off her wrinkled skirt.

Observing the can of beans he was heating, she remarked, "That won't be enough."

"It's all I have."

"You know where my food is," she replied, unimpressed by his fastidiousness. He toasted a sausage while she was combing her snarled hair and with her knife cut the bread. They ate in silence. When she did say something he didn't catch it. Cross at having to repeat herself, she kept her eyes on the fire and took a bite out of her bread and sausage right afterward to show she didn't want to speak again: "I said I don't want you to think I make a habit of this."

At first he didn't understand. Then he clamped his teeth shut to keep from replying.

They broke camp. If they turned back to the left they would come to the dead body and the bones of the other fire and the chicken. They turned right and started downhill. Once they had begun the day in silence it was hard to speak again.

"If we find some Americans you'll be able to get us some coffee, won't you?" was the longest remark she made.

Still, the rapid hike downhill could not help but raise their spirits. There were many things to rejoice in: the spotted mushrooms growing among the roots of the pine trees, a rabbit that darted across their path. When her foot slipped once he steadied her with a hand on her elbow. She smiled her thanks but something began to trouble her and a little further on she stopped.

"I'm sorry for what I said, Ethan. You're a good friend," she told him, her eyes lowered unhappily. He took her hand and when she did raise her face she let him kiss her. Now he became the unhappy one for he knew what he was going to lose.

They came to scattered farmhouses, first of woodcutters and then of peasants again as the forest ended and the fields of turnips and cabbages reappeared. A town lay in front of them, a German town of 1945 with a large school building on its outskirts split by a bomb. This beaten town still offered to Ethan a multicolored variety that a person who had not spent the year in Moosberg would hardly have noticed, but his appreciation was not as disinterested as on the day before. A few bakery windows had loaves of bread, for this was a country town, but who would give anything to them?

"Look," Maxine said, taking his arm and pointing down a side street. "There are some Americans."

He stared at the weapons carrier and jeep and the big square olive drab tent that closed off the small street. He saw the MP markings on the rear of the vehicles. There was no chance of passing them by now. Nevertheless, as the American army was represented by a boy in Wehrmacht gray scouring a griddle, his spirits rose.

"A little coffee perhaps?" Ethan asked him. "Amerikanische Kriegsgefangener. Some coffee for me and the girl."

The prisoner looked up at Ethan and sensed that he did not have any real authority.

"You ask the sergeant," he grumbled.

"There's always coffee." Ethan knew that much about the American army. "If it's there you can give it to us. And some bread too."

The German boy didn't dare simply to tell him to go to hell. His face clouded with indecision. Then it cleared, for the mess sergeant emerged out of the house beside the tent, turning to listen to some last words from one of even higher authority still inside. He was a heavy man with the shrewd, worldly face acquired by mess sergeants in a conquered country, and he cast a sharp glance at Ethan's worn figure and at the girl standing back by the jeep.

"Where the hell have you come from, soldier?" he demanded, in a not unkindly way.

"I was a prisoner in the Russian zone. I got out of the camp yesterday and I'd be obliged if you could let me have a cup of coffee."

"That's easy enough. Klaus, get them some coffee," he ordered the German, who disappeared into the tent. "You're just drifting around now? You headed anywhere in particular?" the sergeant asked with a certain good-humored suspiciousness.

"I'm going on west. The girl lives in Antwerp. She was a forced laborer in Chemnitz."

The German came back with a pot of coffee and two mugs and a sugar jar. He filled one and offered it to Maxine. The sergeant let them drink before he asked any more questions. Maxine closed her eyes to sniff the fragrance and then raised the enamel mug to her lips. This silent intense pleasure made all three men watch her. Seeing their look, she smiled in embarrassment and thanked the sergeant. "Dass schmeckt mir gut," she said, and forced out in English: "That tastes good. Thank you very much."

"Would you like some more?" he asked her, and the German refilled her mug.

"That's very decent of you. We're much obliged," Ethan said, lifting his blanket roll. Disappointed, Maxine nodded her head toward the jeep.

The sergeant picked up the thread of his questioning. "You still haven't said where you're going."

"It's simple enough," Ethan said with an exasperated smile. "I'm going home. I'm no longer a prisoner of the Wehrmacht."

"That's a bit too simple. You'll have to see our captain," the sergeant stated.

A young captain who carried a helmet and a pistol belt in his hand appeared on the steps outside his quarters and inspected the newcomers. Ethan was not reassured by the hard blank stare and the unnecessary neatness, a man preoccupied with orthodoxies who would register the two facts that Ethan wore an uncommon shoulder patch and needed a shave.

"That division of yours is a hell of a long way from here," was his opening remark.

"He got out of a PW camp yesterday and he's walking home," the sergeant explained.

It seemed ridiculous to explain that he had left the army out of disgust with the moralities of group life and that he was escorting this girl to Antwerp. He told the captain the factual details.

"Let's see your dog tags."

Tangible proof he existed. And a humiliating gesture, as he bent his head to remove the little necklace, that showed who was master. The captain examined them minutely.

"You say a convoy evacuated your camp? Why did you leave it?"

Ethan had had no practice in deception, except for the half-truths he had told Maxine.

"I shared the same damn lager for a year with those fellows, and I suddenly felt I had all I could stand."

"Well, you stay here then. If the convoy was going to the collection point at Coburg, we have a vehicle going there tomorrow and we'll send you along. Until then you stay right here."

Ethan held out his hand for the dog tags. Maxine looked in dismay at this impotence.

"What is the matter? What are they doing?"

"I can't leave. I have to stay here."

"But why? You said you weren't a deserter. How can they keep you?"

"I have to join the other prisoners. These are military police."

"I am sorry." She asked no question nor made any complaint about what would happen to her. "I didn't think we would be separated so soon."

The captain had buckled on his belt and climbed into the jeep.

"Sir," Ethan said to him. "Are you going westward at all? Could you give this girl a ride? The Germans conscripted her and she has a long way to go to Antwerp."

"Good grief, soldier, Germany is filled with people in the same fix she is. I'm not running a taxi service."

"I know that's true. But if you're going westward could you take her? She shouldn't travel by herself."

The demand was too simple to refuse. The captain looked at Maxine. "Okay. I'm going to Griesdorf. That's twelve kilometers."

Ethan lifted her pack into the jeep and motioned for her to get in. Then he turned to the mess sergeant.

"Could you give her some food to take along? She doesn't have much to keep her going."

"We don't have supplies to feed every refugee that comes by."

"Well, can you give me anything?" Ethan demanded. "By God, I haven't been overeating!"

A glance at his face showed that that statement was true. Without a word the sergeant went into the tent and returned with an opened can of hash and a large slice of bread. Ethan held them out for the sergeant and the captain to see. "This is my lunch. Thank you for giving it to me."

He walked over to the jeep and set the food in Maxine's lap.

'You'll need this. The captain will give you a ride for a little way. Maybe you can get another one at the next town."

"Is he leaving now?"

"Yes." He took the small cake of soap and the matches out of his pocket and put them in her hands. "Take these. What can I give you, Maxine?" Absolutely nothing belonged to him, except his wedding ring. Then he thought of his scarf and he took it off and wrapped it about her neck. "You'll need this at night. It will keep you warm." He tried to smile. She pulled a cheap silver ring from her finger and put it in his hand. For a moment they held each other's hands. A tear began to roll down her cheek. Ethan stepped back. The captain started the jeep. At an order from the sergeant the German boy ducked into the cook tent and came out with two more cans, which he handed to Maxine. The jeep backed around. Silently the two raised their hands to each other. Ethan watched the small shoulders in the black jacket and her light brown hair and for a second, as the jeep turned a corner, the profile of her face.

VI

THE GARDEN

THE CHECKBOOK COVERS were dark blue, the checks inside, his name—GODWIN HATCHARD—on each, paler in tint, each check separated from the others by perforations that rasped smartly when torn. The book was not exactly his. It stood for his father's life—oil wells and cattle, office buildings, a ranch of mohair goats—and his death. A room with doctors and nurses and Godwin on a chair outside, sitting, waiting. But the book belonged to him now. It would summon jovial college presidents as his visitors, wise and kindly doctors to talk about his health, long-legged young women to try and please him. Godwin, however, reflected that he did not have much time. If he was ever to find his own life, whatever that might be, he would have to act pretty briskly.

On his way up the ladder Jim Hatchard swore that his son would have the opportunities he himself had missed. This old oath differed from other men's because Big Jim understood that these opportunities would have to be demanded by the boy himself, not dreams of the father. Godwin liked books. His father sent him away from Dallas to the best school in Massachusetts. Godwin entered Harvard and majored in French history and literature. He bought an oboe. He took up fencing and to his surprise became very good at it.

When the war came he enlisted, but along with her love of music he had inherited his mother's poor eyes and her self-distrust. His superiors saw him unable to fire a rifle or give orders. He reflected too long on the ultimate purposes of action—why turn a squad left instead of right? Accordingly he spent three years in a limbo of futility, issuing maps, typing news releases. His last months of service, as headquarters clerk of an infantry battalion on Okinawa, reassured his father. It gave Godwin a sort of union card in the scar of his shoulder, but it did not convince him that either his life or anyone else's amounted to much.

He returned to Dallas for a few weeks. No one knew or cared how frightened or useless he had been under fire. He was welcomed and, except for his father, forgotten. "Daddy has been more ill than he would like you to know," his stepmother had written. Even so, Godwin was shocked by the gentle, vague hesitancy of the old man, the almost apologetic way he asked about his oldest son's future plans. Godwin now was the stronger. He should stay at home, with his stepmother and her massive topazes, with his stepbrother who, now that gas rationing had ended, would kill himself before seventeen, with his hard, shiny stepsister. She embarrassed him. His buddies' tales had taught him a lot about such young women and he knew secrets about her a brother shouldn't know. He had to get back to Harvard, the place where he had driven himself the hardest, and cleanse his fouled and idle spirit with hard work.

Godwin took his master's degree and was ending a first year of teaching when Jim Hatchard's last quick illness brought him back to Dallas. Now his only real family bond was expressed by this checkbook. His study of Racine and Watteau, that hard-won intimation of the elegance and concision of classic France, had unfitted him either to direct or to enjoy his station as a Hatchard in Dallas. On the other hand, no one else would ever be enriched by any shining individual light he could shed on his own subject. To write essays, to bring culture to a new America by correcting irregular verbs, to intrigue for a college post at thirty-six hundred a year when with a few hours' preparation he could write a check of six figures: that was make-believe. Better a red Jaguar like his sister's and pawing the girls.

So Godwin went to France.

If he could really find France, the opposite pole, in his mind, to Dallas, he might find some place somewhere. He told himself to take plenty of time. He had a right to demand six months to look around carefully before he considered suicide.

It was a pity that he started with Mont St. Michel. The shrill omelet hucksters reminded him of the whores in a border town like Ciudad Juarez. The culture on display was like the cowboy boots of a Dallas realtor. He tried again at Chartres and from there he turned his little Renault south to the valley of the Loire. Through his study each white château was almost a part of him before he ever saw the towers or smelled the stagnant moat. Shuffling through the rooms with his fellow tourists, he could recall the actors and flavor of the life—lute soft, rapier sharp—that here had been led. The diet was a rich one, but Godwin could not escape the conclusion, as he gazed down upon the roofs of Chinon from the vast white ruin where Joan of Arc recognized the poor doubting Dauphin hiding among the courtiers, that it had nothing to do with him.

He was unsure where to turn, but examining each subsequent château put off the next decision. From Chinon he drove to Ronçay, a château he knew little about but which his guidebook stated possessed the finest formal garden of France.

The wall of pollarded chestnuts along the road obscured any overall picture of Ronçay, but one could see it was built like a giant squared horseshoe opening on to the road, with one rear corner buttressed by a donjon in medieval style and the wings constructed after the fashion of the sixteenth century. Twisting gable ends, balconies and chimneys added fantasy to the limestone walls and the high roof. The gates being closed for midday, Godwin walked to the village for a lunch of crayfish tails and Vouvray and then lay down on the grass and watched the clouds drift overhead.

The gatekeeper's lodge, the stairway to the upper level of the garden, were so shabby that Godwin was astounded, when he reached a high terrace at right angles to the château, by the dreamlike geometry of boxwood displayed below him. In diamonds and squares of greens as varied as the mosses on a stone, the fragrant hedges enclosed a series of rose gardens and, the other side of a grape arbor and a narrow canal, an elaborately embellished checkerboard of vegetables. On a gravel court next to the château stood a double row of orange trees in tubs. To the far left of the terrace, beyond another row of chestnuts, shimmered a pond.

The short guide with a cast in one eye was no mere employee turning in a thirty-minute stint. He loved his garden and its elegant Renaissance symbols. Each of the four great diamonds had its boxwood clipped, with the roses a color to match, into a different aspect of love: daggers and tears for the sorrows of love, hearts, with white roses, for its purity, fleurs-de-lis and crowns for its nobility, yellow and masks for its falsity. The garden dated from the time of François I, but an eighteenth-century owner, led astray by the vapid informalities of the English fashion, had uprooted the original to set out willow trees and rocky grottoes. Not until the garden was purchased by Dr. Mostrenco, a wealthy Spanish physician and father of the present owner, was it restored to its authentic design. German soldiers shot swans with machine guns—what a metaphor for war! They had done no other harm, but the Mostrencos were now impoverished. As a memorial to France, a couple of gardeners clipped at the hedges all day and tried to keep the roses weeded, but——.

The group strolled slowly in the warm sunshine, enjoying the quiet crunch of gravel and the sweet muted smell of boxwood everywhere. Godwin tried to clarify what quality of France the garden expressed. It was not artificiality, for however oddly the box might be manicured, the pear and apple trees espaliered along the terrace walls, the limes and chestnuts pollarded, the true nature of each plant was never distorted. Nature was to serve man—no romantic pretense that savagery fostered anything pleasant—but man in turn served the purposes of nature. With pruning, weeding, fertilizing, each flower and fruit bore to its fullest, in beauty and harmony, a witness to the generosity of God and the skill and patience of man.

"And all her husbandry doth lie on heaps, corrupting in its own fertility"—the lines clarified themselves in Godwin's mind, of a France after another punishing war. It was true even here, all that needed to be done, as any careful passerby might see, even to this nobly disciplined garden. All those weeds, broken branches, were only details.

The guide finished the tour by returning to the château to inspect the gallery, also mentioned in Michelin. On the way they passed what looked like a chapel, in Baroque style, built out upon the upper terrace. A little theater, the guide explained, where every so often Mademoiselle Mostrenco presented plays written by herself and acted out by her friends.

"What sort of plays?" Godwin asked, suddenly curious.

The guide did not know.

The gallery possessed good names—Zurbarán, Velázquez, Goya—and mediocre, muddy canvases. One picture, a skull placed upon a book, was entitled *Truth and Vanity*.

"Which one is Truth?" asked Godwin.

"The skull," answered the guide, who had not been asked that question before. He shrugged his shoulders with a smile. "Or that's what the Spaniards would think."

"That girl of the proprietor who writes plays," interrupted one of the group, a stocky little wag in a beret who had forced out a comic remark on everything, "how old is she?"

"About twenty-five, I believe."

"Is she a good-looker?"

"She is quite dark," the guide answered, but the wag's companion jabbed his side and said: "Don't worry about that. You saw all those vegetable gardens, didn't you? You'd get your three squares a day."

The party came out once again upon the upper terrace. Godwin walked to the balustrade for one last look. This was what he had dreamed of finding. And he, if he was unable to create beauty himself, could recognize it and preserve it. In this ravaged time that was an honorable mission. He would marry Dr. Mostrenco's daughter.

Outside the iron gates again Godwin left his car where it was and took a long walk along a winding cart track. The unbelievable richness of the French countryside filled and sweetened his spirit. Avarice and odors composed most of peasant life perhaps, but this simple complexity of poplar rows, dung heaps, cabbage rows, vineyards, kept fruitful by toil, fitted God's will. The alternatives were an office in his father's building and those women with harsh voices and bright-colored cars. If Mademoiselle Mastrenco lived with such a garden, she might well accept the older concept that a man and a woman married to strengthen a property and to raise children. In balance and completion, love came later.

That evening he put on a new silk tie and rang the bell of the château. He was an American writing a book on the masques of François I. After almost half an hour the aged porter returned. Godwin was reassured by the shabbiness of even the private parts of the château, and when he was finally ushered into the salon, his eyes picked up the threadbare velvet as quickly as they did the old man and his daughter. The young woman's face was long and sallow—his first glance was for reassurance—but not misshapen or stupid or petty. Determined, handsome perhaps, a bit severe in its lack of warmth, and joined to it a body of womanly proportions.

"We owe your visit to a mutual interest in the times of François I?" inquired Dr. Mostrenco with courtesy shaded by reserve, or perhaps suspicion.

"I have studied the garden ceremonials up through the time of Louis XV, but of course they were perhaps most imaginatively developed under François."

"Louis XV was a monarch of decay," was the sour reply. "It is all too easy to find decay wherever we look."

"In America too?" asked the old man with a naïve surprise.

"The shine and polished metal disguise what has happened to the spirit."

The yeasty phrases caused the daughter's face to brighten and Godwin thought he could discern spirit in her smile.

They discussed François I and Louis XIV and the ills of romanticism. Yet the eighteenth century had seen French opera at its height, which allowed Godwin to mention his own study of the oboe. Ysabel, it seemed, played the harp. Was she acquainted with the harp and oboe duets of Lully? When a request for the more exact whereabouts of Dallas allowed Godwin to reveal somewhat elliptically his own share of the city's wealth, he felt that the goals of the evening had been achieved.

"Rush Lully oboe harp duets," he cabled that night to his friend Oliver Urquhart in Cambridge.

Godwin returned from Ronçay's inn the next morning to inspect with Dr. Mostrenco the archives that his father had compiled. They shared lunch together and in the afternoon Ysabel led him along the paths closed to the ordinary upon the terrace above. She pointed out the purity of the vegetable gardens, where no anachronistic potato or asparagus was permitted to mix with the species one would have found four hundred years earlier. She showed him how one hedgerow was actually composed of thirteen different varieties of box-wood. Her dry voice was clear, her words gracefully enunciated, her gestures expressive, her step light.

Godwin came each day. He talked about Racine and Watteau and also about Texas and the sterility of wealth without culture or responsibility. Early one morning Ronçay's post-man knocked at his bedroom door with the parcel of duets.

Oboe case under his arm, Godwin brought them to the château. Ysabel smiled politely. They might try an easy one. Godwin placed his chair where he would see her profile through the golden chords, her strong and graceful hands, and not her stubborn mouth. It was the first task they had shared, making music together in the liquid twanging of the harp and the dry nasal tones of his own throbbing reed.

That evening Godwin asked Dr. Mostrenco for the hand of his daughter. The old man inquired how much he was worth, and paused a moment, translating the answer into francs. Of course the decision must rest with Ysabel herself.

The next morning, under the eyes of a small group of tourists to whom Monsieur Perrin the guide was lecturing, Ysabel and Godwin walked silently through the garden. She stopped and faced him.

"Why do you want to marry me?"

Dr. Mostrenco had divined perhaps some of his reasons, or perhaps did not care too much what they were. But it was, without doubt, Ysabel's right to ask this question.

"I have always dreamed of finding a woman of intelligence and spirit and grace. I think you are that woman. I will love you and look after you."

He had nothing more to say. Without speaking they returned to the chäteau.

"I will give you my decision in a week," she told him and he left Ronçay for Paris.

In his hotel room he practised upon his oboe until his head throbbed and the neighbors banged on the walls. Perhaps he had been dishonest to express admiration for Francis I, a king whom he had always disliked as unprincipled, but he would live up to any agreement he made with Ysabel and her father.

When Ysabel greeted him back at Ronçay, uncertainty and perhaps even fear flavored her smile, but she did seem pleased to see him and his gifts. Dr. Mostrenco was the most excited of the three. Godwin must have his own room at the château.

The banns must be posted. The floors must be waxed. The Protestant must take instruction.

This latter task was no real bother, for the old curé was easily sidetracked into talking about the Mostrenco family. The first proprietor fascinated him. "Forte riche, forte riche," he repeated over and over, and in the hot, fly-buzzing study Godwin was sleepily pleased by "powerful rich." It sounded very Texan.

"He got that wealthy just as a doctor?"

"Yes, yes indeed, a doctor in Barcelona."

What golden hysterectomies, what lavishly coddled colitis. Godwin and the priest sat silently thinking of the wonder of science.

Toward the end of these lessons old father Hourliban revealed his more private hopes.

"When you marry Mademoiselle Ysabel and become a French citizen you can run for mayor and beat that Communist Jacquart."

Dr. Mostrenco saw no reason for a long engagement. Godwin sent Oliver Urquhart passage money to come and be his best man. Oliver arrived, with limited French but with a Gascon enthusiasm and high spirits that made the last few days bearable. He couldn't have been more charmed by the garden, by his host, by Ysabel. As the friend of such a sprightly, courtly young man, Godwin's own status rose.

Only once did Oliver reveal the effort this gaiety cost him.

"Making love isn't too hard, but Godwin"—and his voice grew anguished—"what in God's name are you going to talk about in the evenings?"

The wedding day came. Once Godwin's battalion had had the task of shoving the Japanese off a heavily fortified ridge. The attack was to start at nine, as dreaded by the colonel as it was by Godwin. "We've got six hundred pieces of artillery behind us," the colonel said more or less to himself, "and if we keep pushing along the damn thing ought to be over by noon. It's just a matter of living through those three hours."

The church service was followed by a reception and a dinner and then a ball. But at last Godwin could free himself and drive his silent bride to a hotel in Tours. In the bed they could not see each other's faces. They did not have to speak or even consider who the other person was.

The initiative was now his. As an unknown he had been accepted on the tacit assumption that he would do a lot. Dr. Mostrenco really cared about his garden and his château. What Ysabel cared for Godwin did not yet know. In his own mind the process was clear, the blood transfusion of American dollars that would renew the life of Ronçay, but it must not come so suddenly that the bargain appeared obvious, or so lavishly that he merely inflamed cupidity.

In the weeks before the wedding Godwin had made the acquaintance of the gardeners and the house staff, had seen their worn tools and noted down their almost nonexistent wages. In a little black notebook he made lists of what was to be purchased, what was to be repaired. Each morning now he discussed the day's plans with Dr. Mostrenco and asked him for permission to hire a glazier or raise the wages of the scullery maid. He listened to the complaints of Yves, the head gardener, and bought him clippers, copper sulphate, harness, twine, fertilizer. With Jacquart, the mayor and plumber, he crawled over the roof to inspect the gutters and under the arches of the cellar to inspect the drains.

Perhaps Godwin was never happier than during that fall and winter. He rose before sunup in the black cold château to win a couple of private hours for Racine or Montaigne. After breakfast he checked bills and supervised the gardeners and workmen. An hour of practice on his oboe after lunch and often a drive with Ysabel into Tours to purchase supplies. What will you talk about in the evenings? He listened to Dr. Mostrenco and played duets with his wife. In bed there was no need for words.

It was the time when the Marshall Plan was beginning in

France, and behind his back the workmen used to refer to
Godwin as Monsieur Marshall. Godwin did not mind. He
was almost drunk with his vision of fertility. What had been
once his mere waste had caused his wife's body to distend
with life. A pair of swans floated once more on the pond,
and the money that had procured them had an origin about
as mysterious. Who could touch its source? In the beginning
was the word, soundless electrical words above the water
whereby the bank in Dallas told the bank in Tours that it
might assume Godwin was richer again by ten thousand
dollars, a distant faithfulness like the gift of rain and sunshine. New strength and dignity came to all of poor tired
France in these dollars from Texas, and with the fat rolls of
francs Godwin was handed he had given useful work and
good tools to honest workmen.

He was proud of Ysabel's pregnancy, of the swans, of the
new plaster on the plumber's house and the new shoes on
the man's daughter. Out of party loyalty Jacquart presented
ferocious cost estimates for each new job, but he shrugged
without ill humor when his American cut them in half. The
new floor Godwin commissioned for the church Jacquart
dismissed as intellectual weakness, but the next project re-
modeling a building at the edge of the village as a clinic, he
treated with respect. As the man who always paid the bills
Godwin might appear slightly foolish, but he did not ask for
gratitude, and the workmen and gardeners and household
staff congratulated him sincerely when little Claude was
born.

Before the second Christmas Ysabel was pregnant again,
but Dr. Mostrenco did not live to see the birth of his grand-
daughter. The old man had shared Godwin's enthusiasm for
Ronçay. He had admired his son-in-law's ability to get along
with every type of Frenchman. Now the only witness to the
original agreement was gone. The silence with Ysabel fell
heavier.

"You really don't have anything to do now, do you?" she

observed. He had carried out his end of the unspoken agreement so thoroughly that a day came when he had nothing more to write down in his little black notebook. "I'd like to visit my cousins in Barcelona."

The babies were well taken care of, and the parents next went to Paris and let an apartment in order to enjoy the music and exhibitions. When February rain fell without ceasing Ysabel suggested a trip to Marrakech. There was no money, however, in the account in Tours. Walking about the streets of Paris and looking into the shop windows, Godwin had forgotten about checking its level. No answer came to his air mail letter. A new truck had been delivered at Rançay and must be paid for. He cabled Dallas. Silence again.

"You can't even get your own money?" Ysabel inquired.

The answer to his next cable was simple enough: the accountant who usually handled Godwin's payments had fallen ill and a careless assistant neglected messages. Once again everything could be paid for, and they flew to Marrakech to note the dramatic contrast between sun and shadow. But someone in Dallas neglects a little chore, and all life at Rançay suddenly gasps for breath.

Godwin walked slowly along the gravel paths with Claude holding on to his finger. If he narrowed his focus to Claude's world the other one might safely blur. They zigzagged to peer at a snail or touch a forbidden faucet handle. If geese hissed that was frightening, but then you could go over to the rabbit cages and tickle your hands with their whiskers and laugh at the way their noses twitched. There is magic in a bicycle pedal. The rubber pads of the foot rest are so rough and bumpy, the steel bar between them is so cold and smooth. With one finger you can make it twirl, or you can shove the whole pedal up and down and make the chain move too. The chain made hands terribly greasy but you could try and touch all the wheel spokes or stare into the dragon's eye of the reflector.

No one could ever measure how soft were the little boy's cheeks or how silken his hair. When he was tired he lifted up his arms and Godwin carried him. What other trouble could be made right so easily?

Jim Hatchard could do anything, but he had never made friends with any of his children. Godwin had surpassed his father. But even this he could not share with Ysabel. Of course she loved her babies, but a little boy grows up into French life by acquiring certain disciplines. If he tears his clothes on a bicycle or dirties his pants, he has failed his first responsibilities. Godwin rejected this. Claude's tears were too costly for a hundred suits of clothing. An accomplice would do away secretly with the soiled underpants and carry an extra pair in his pocket to make the crises less serious.

"What a thing for a man to carry around!" exclaimed Ysabel when he pulled out his handkerchief and the little pants fell on the carpet. It was shameful.

One day, however, Godwin read a newspaper story about the government's plans to make fuller use of France's architectural heritage. Light and music at its finest châteaux would attract tourists and remind the French themselves of what a civilization they had inherited.

This fitted Godwin's own concept of life. Ysabel could stay in Paris. He brought two young engineers back with him to Rançay, and the three of them tramped about the wet springy garden arguing where to set the floodlights and the loudspeakers. On a summer night would hover the scent of boxwood and roses. The lights would offer the weathered limestone and the infinite variety within the single color of green. And above it the music of Lully and Couperin and Rameau. And there would be more jobs, as Jacquart the mayor agreed, in the village.

Culture, however, is more than the effective utilization of loudspeakers. It is creation by human beings to make possible the creation of human beings, and one function of wealth in an imperfect world is to insist that sometimes beauty be given the highest priority. Godwin set about to recruit in Tours a dozen members of the symphony orchestra. This would become the Orchestre de Ronçay. He would be its director.

Both Dallas and Ronçay agreed that if you paid the piper you called the tune. Godwin was swearing allegiance to another set of laws, just as brutal, which said that nothing in the world took the place of perfection. He was no genius, but if he rose before dawn and played out each instrument's part on his oboe, his knowledge of these composers told him what to expect from a score. Ysabel had reluctantly agreed to be the harpist. Now they would share a task together and she might see how well he handled the orchestra.

For the last rehearsal the musicians drove out from Tours. The young engineer from Paris was dragging around his wires and microphones, angry because they got snagged in the orange trees, worried about echoes and the vitality of this eighteenth-century music. The ballet from Gluck's *Iphigenia* must be robust and delicate. This afternoon it was dull and lumpy, like a roughhouse of teddy bears. A fitful wind led away the sound and made the musicians nervous, but that wasn't the trouble. Godwin rapped for silence.

"I don't believe the bassoon and the cello have a strong control of the tempo."

The two men looked at him resentfully. The orchestra began again, the bassoon louder but nothing really improved. A second time Godwin stopped them. Something fluttered in one of the château windows. It was little Claude waving to attract his father's eye.

"That's not it at all."

He wasn't sure what to do. The first violinist spoke up: "If you allow me to say so, sir, you're not calling for the right rhythm. The beat is sharper than that."

Godwin offered him the baton. Politely but with alacrity the violinist stepped onto the podium. There was no question of the difference. Maybe they tried harder for him, Ysabel too, Godwin thought ruefully, but this was music as Gluck wrote it—firm, sharp, light. No instrument was forgotten, no details slid over. Monsieur Voinchet stopped and held out the baton to Godwin.

"That is what I mean, sir."

They watched him with a sort of laboratory curiosity, but Godwin, from his earliest years with his father, had trained his face not to reveal his heart.

"There is too clear a difference between your direction and mine, Monsieur Voinchet. I will play beside Monsieur Délignières."

The violinist's chair was hastily set beside the oboe player's, while Godwin took his instrument from its case and blew a few scales. The Gluck was finished, well. But in the Couperin which followed, the brightness and haunting grace of the whole piece was expressed by the oboe. Godwin knew that he slurred the grace notes and retarded when the fingering became difficult. Voinchet could not halt the orchestra to reprimand its patron. When the piece came to an end, Godwin bowed to his partner and withdrew.

The concert went off well and all the other ones of the summer. Godwin greeted the guests and reporters, set up a gas station and a second restaurant to accommodate the visitors, located another harpist to replace Ysabel, who said practicing took up too much time. Sometimes a few American soldiers came from the engineer depot that had been newly activated thirty kilometers away. There always seemed to be callers from Dallas who parked their Cadillacs in the courtyard. "We'd sure love to spend a couple of days and really get to know la belle France. You must be dying to hear all the news from home," their cards read. "You've got a nice little place here," they told him and in painstakingly enunciated phrases they shouted their appreciation at Ysabel.

The summer ended. Only a few tourists still showed up

every day for Monsieur Perrin to lead about the terraces. Ysabel had driven to Barcelona. Godwin walked silently up and down the gravel paths with Claude. With the money in his pocket, the gas in his car, how far could the two of them go? They walked further, along the windless yellow paths, where the peasants they met said "bonjour, monsieur" and expected no other answer. He liked passing the plumber's daughter, Oralie, because she always smiled at Claude and sometimes gave him a piece of candy. Once Claude was home with a cold when Godwin met Oralie. She inquired about the little boy and then they didn't have anything else to say although she continued to smile somewhat uncertainly. She let him kiss and hold her.

"Not so fast," she complained but she was not really cross. Perhaps her smells held him the most strongly—skin, hair, mouth of sausage and wine, dried grass, ferns. Sometimes he gave her money. When it rained they met at a bramble thicket so dense and twisted a little pocket at the bottom always remained dry.

Ysabel spent December at Ronçay. She talked spiritedly about a very artistic young dancer she had met in Barcelona, a Frenchman named Pascal Tassain who had been most interested when she had told him about Godwin's musical programs. Imagine what Ronçay might be if one went further and tried to recreate the masques of François I and Henri II for which the gardens had originally been designed.

"That was what you were writing your book on when you first called here."

"Yes, so it was."

From first sight he disliked the slender, faintly mocking dancer. The relationship of the three of them, or four if you counted Oralie, was so traditional, stale, rigid, French, that it sickened him, but he listened to Tassain's projects and admitted that he knew and loved his art.

"It will run very high," was the only protest he could make, at which Tassain made a polite grimace. "There's not a château in the whole Loire that will compare next summer with Ronçay."

"You could set the music and costumes," Ysabel said flatteringly. "I told Pascal that there wasn't a man in France better equipped to handle that side." The three of them squabbled all winter. Godwin could pay the bills and he could arrange the music and design the costumes so long as they were just what Tassain wanted. This was so obvious that Godwin despised the dancer for underrating him too far.

"Godwin, you are impossible when you act so stubborn!"

"If you don't like what I am planning, monsieur, it is always your privilege not to pay for it."

Godwin did not let them make him feel ashamed.

"You are an American. You have learned a great deal about France," Ysabel began, her voice trembling a little, "but you can't expect to have Pascal's grasp of what our music and style have been. Pascal is a great artist."

"Pascal could put on Offenbach in the garden and the garden is beautiful enough to carry it, but the music I have arranged fits the style of the garden and fits the style of the dances of that time. And, on the whole, I think the same can be said for the costumes. With all due respect to Monsieur Tassain, what he has suggested does not."

He looked at the fountain pen his hands were playing with. It was not courteous to watch the dancer's face while he was being defeated. And it was not the money alone this time that gave Godwin the right to win.

"In certain ways it is hard to argue with Mr. Hatchard," said Tassain quietly.

"Godwin, you are not fair!"

He looked up at her angry eyes. His face tightened. She could not hurt him. Oralie's thighs were as muscled as her shoulders and her hair smelt like dried grass. He was the seigneur. But perhaps it hadn't been any good for Ysabel to marry him. There was no longer any purpose for her to boil preserves or practice on the harp. She ate candy and that gave her cavities. She drove very fast and she was not really a good driver.

They went to Paris for Ysabel had many purchases to make, but the city bored Godwin now, and he returned to Ronçay to finish the music. It was good. He would fight for it with anyone. It was cold outside and sometimes he brought Oralie at night to the château. He possessed another interest too: he had accepted responsibility for his homesick countrymen at the engineer depot. It was a hideous place, a sprawling slash in the forest, absolutely un-French in the brutal waste of trees and land; but the men ought to see something of France, and Godwin held open house every Sunday with Oralie and other local girls to serve wine and food to the truckload or two who came. Because he had worn a uniform himself for almost four years, he knew what were the only things soldiers wanted. At the same time, if he showed them more of the hospitality of France, he might persuade a few that the world was really round. And if he could make the Negro soldiers, who made up almost half the unit, feel at home in a château they might refuse to feel at home in the ghettos to which they would return.

The summer came, so busy that Godwin was happy most of the time at first, with the château filled with slender nervous dancers, the parking lots crowded, people asking his decision on publicity and the installation of new toilets. He was proud of the number of American soldiers who came. He accepted Tassain's arrogance because the dancers were well trained and they danced to the music he had arranged. But it was just too obvious the way Tassain tossed the bills to be paid on to Godwin's desk, or the way Ysabel let it be assumed that she and Pascal Tassain had created the whole project while Monsieur was merely the director of finance.

Ysabel wanted a new car. Tassain wanted five hundred meters of gold brocade. Oralie wanted an abortion. A harshness came to his face. It was easy for them to ask and to sneer because he gave—by God, they could accept him in other ways! The plump little brunette in charge of the linen was afraid of what would happen if Madame found out, but she let him take her. So did the wife of the carpenter's assistant on duty in Algeria.

Godwin's birthday occurred the day after the last performance. Tables went up in the gravel court among the orange trees and there was a party for the dancers and musicians, the village notables, strangers like his stepsister and her second husband, some of the American soldiers he had come to know. Roses and asters, a dwarf forest of bottles, chicken, duck, lamb, laughter and music to shine up the surface. He had slipped away from his seat at the head table between Ysabel and his sister, and moved about the guests, a bottle of red wine in his right hand, white in his left, a half-smile on his lips. He had picked out the music, elegantly gay pieces by Scarlatti and Gluck, and he smiled a little more sideways at his sister, who had angered Ysabel by flirting with Tassain.

But people were rapping on the table for silence. Of course it must be Pascal Tassain to make the speech of honor, his glass slightly waving in the air.

The lark hovers in the western sky, the thrush warbles in the willow. How facile it is to imagine that day draws toward eventide. Yet how false. The day has but newly begun. A sun still rises over the plains of Touraine, warming its gentle rivers and stirring the roots beneath its soil until it becomes merely fitting that the poplar leaves glimmer silver and the wheat dark gold—Godwin, a wine bottle still in each hand, stood at the end of the table, the same half-smile upon his thin lips. What elegance and how absolutely plain to all except his stepsister and the soldiers eating fruit and refilling their glasses. Listen to Orpheus' lyre, good as new now. Gaze upon Terpsichore and Calliope in tasteful nylon gowns and rubber-soled sandals. How rosily glow their cheeks from rational meals of milk and orange juice. And poor stumbling France, upheld by golden arms—every protective fume of wine had drained from his head. He could feel his heart dry up. Words, all by themselves, to end every last hope. Perfect.

"Our Mycaenas, upon this day of triumph, crowned—antlered even"—some of the dancers snickered and the curé put on an expression of shock and some pretended they hadn't heard and the soldiers kept on with their drinking. Godwin set the bottles down and walked slowly toward the grinning orator. How far could he flee? Could he find his son in time?

"And thus we see, in dignity and honor——" but the expression on Godwin's face across the table halted the peroration. Godwin picked up a glass of wine and threw its contents in Tassain's face.

"Get out!"

A sudden burst of interrupted sound, but the silence so intense that the gasps, the slap of a hand upon the table, were lost in it. Tassain's face quivered once. Then he pulled out his handkerchief and wiped it. Godwin stood motionless. For a moment he had absolutely nothing to do. The dancer clicked his heels—"Monsieur"—and turned about. Poor Lady Macbeth's cry: 'Stand not upon the order of your going, but go at once!' Maybe they would all go. But Tassain marched only up to the château and on his tiptoes grabbed two rapiers that had been hung upon the wall as decoration. Then he swung upon his heel, the swords cradled in his arm, and marched back to the table.

"Monsieur, will you choose your weapon?"

Godwin stared at him sadly. The wretched fool. And yet who had first created this fancy-dress atmosphere, so authentic, so convincing, that no one leaped up to cry halt?

Godwin grabbed the proffered hilt. Tassain lightly vaulted over the table and threw his coat aside. The soldiers and dancers stood up excitedly. Jacquart the plumber, with his mayor's sash across his chest, indignantly stepped forward—I am sorry about Oralie—but when a soldier put a hand upon his shoulder he did not go further.

Tassain lunged twice. Godwin easily parried. The dancer was fast but not skilled. Godwin had kept up his fencing during the winters at a club in Tours. He had also drunk less. He would parry the blows until Tassain's wrist weakened. Than he would disarm him.

Godwin deflected another lunge and did not riposte to the obvious opening. The bad footing of the gravel disturbed the dancer. He was already breathing heavily, but the sad reserve of Godwin's face, his readiness only to defend himself, infuriated him, and he attacked Godwin's blade, trying to whirl it out of the way before he lunged again. Again Godwin parried and then slapped the side of his foil against Tassain's jaw. The head snapped from the heavy blade. One saw the whiteness and the line of red. Now was the time to summon the servants and throw the troublemaker off the property.

But there was no mistaking what Tassain wanted, the narrowed eyes, the narrowed mouth, the frozen crouch and outstretched arm. Godwin lowered his blade to rest his arm. He had a second to glance at the audience, Ysabel's white mask, fear on some faces, simple excitement on others. A couple of soldiers were grinning. So much to write home about.

Tassain attacked furiously. Godwin barely held off his blade. He must attack, finish this game, puncture the leg or thigh, bring the man to the ground and have him dragged off. He feinted at the face. Tassain was sensitive there. Godwin's wrist was in agony but so was the other's, from the pain in his face and the jerky way he thrust with his shoulder. Godwin kept striking his blade. One more minute and it would fall from his hand. He would endure.

Then he heard a little cry, running feet upon the gravel, a cry of anguish to match his own heart.

"Oh, Papa, you mustn't!"

A glimpse of the anguished little face, a figure running toward him because this was a dangerous game, what Father himself prohibited. For Godwin, a prayer of thanks, someone still cried for his safety. One thing he loved, and how could love be saved in all this stupid make-believe? He jerked his head to shout "Stay away!" The triumph on Tassain's face told him what he had done.

He wasn't surprised by the blow against his chest. The jerk of Tassain's arm to free the blade brought a sucking horrible pain and it twisted him over and caused him to fall on his face. He was surprised a bit because the blurred grey stones were so big and some were splashed brightly with red. A shrill voice kept screaming. There were a lot of feet near his face. The pain wasn't bad or the blood in his mouth, but oh, what sadness that this was all he had ever amounted to, and what would happen to the boy?

VII

O CANADA

SHE ENTERED with her husband and a leopard-skin coat. One glance and decor, food, and every lackluster individual in Rudy's Eats was taken in, judged, and cast out. Rudy presented himself sullenly, in his dirty apron. Hamburger? Trichinosis. Chicken salad? Ptomaine. Just toast and tea, please—can you boil water, can you brown bread without burning it? The rejection of his meager skills made Rudy nervous as well as angry, and when he served the toast, sure enough, black on both sides. But she had gone to the toilet. That was a mistake. The door of the unpleasant little room banged open, out she stepped, face white and set as cold lard, contaminated, and not merely in body; insulted, along with every decent woman and every step toward civilization since life in the caves.

She scrubbed at her table with a paper napkin, laid down a little white carpet on which to set the plate of charred toast, wiped her cup rim, and picked up her spoon in another napkin. But the dirt of Rudy's Eats seeped out of the table to stain her prophylactic carpet. It was imbedded in the glasses and plates; the murk would have stayed under the surface even if Rudy had scalded them. A touch of any piece of silverware left a fingerprint that would have delighted the FBI. What could a lady do? She stared wide-eyed before her like an elderly doe cornered by wolves, and monosyllables to her husband slipped through her tightened lips like dimes.

Above her hangs a stalactite of flypaper, Rudy's longpast concession to hygiene, encrusted with moldering clumps of flies, an agglutination of bodies so thick that a fly driven by some Teutonic wish hunts carefully for one precious dot of stickiness before she can stretch out a leg and abandon herself to voluptuously buzzing and writhing. The lady herself begins to buzz and writhe. An expensive psychiatrist might persuade her that she really loves dirt, because filth alone stirs up such a boil of emotion. She is rocking in her cramped booth, oblivious to her frightened husband, not merely indignant but ashamed, self-loathing, because she too is soiled now.

But what is this that goes through my own brain? An asphalt square, proud and brittle brown lines on parade, packs and beltings slaved over with pipeclay, remnant of empire. The world has changed, though we know it not. Little brown men riding over the jungle paths on cheap bicycles will slip behind and cut us off, leave us like blinded elephants, and our teeth will fall out from scurvy in the prison camps but how well the webbing was pipeclayed, how afraid we were of the sergeant major. Aten—the lines quiver—aten—aten—a world gives birth, the leaping up of jungle sunrise, let it come, let me be found worthy, CHOW! Two hundred rifle butts smash upon the asphalt to shake every screw and slam the barrels out of alignment, but Jesus, what a lovely noise! Moustached lieutenants from the University of Toronto quiver like Damascene blades. *Slllope AH!* The rifles jerk to two hundred shoulders, but we have swallowed two hundred swords, our necks do not twitch. *Byrrryhflank, flank, flank,* the echoes fly over, *MAAH! Boom, boom, boom.* Rifles laid upon our left shoulders, graceful, relaxed, superior, our fists rise and fall thumbnails skyward, black boots fly out, our brains shrink to chicken size, hearts fill with happy idiocy, with a *tow-row-row-row* of the British grenadier. Forgotten the Fascist beast, but all the beautiful dead life remains of barracks squares from Calcutta to Stirling Castle: wax on the sergeant major's moustache, beer-dimmed eyes of privates, gonorrhea, caps tipped to the rim of the head—a hair further and they would drop off—lieutenants finely bred as prize spaniels, prayers for the royal family at church parade. Bulky packages of prayers arrive at heaven's gate at different hours all Sunday long due to the time difference between Hong Kong, Malta, and Vancouver and, spaced out in this way, cannot be easily ignored by those in authority. Proud the old corporal at bayonet drill: keep moving at a steady walk, rifles held breast high, the morning sun sparkles off the steel, yes, Father William, and moaning with fear the German machine gunners wring their hands and run away.

But why does the brain hum with this northern nonsense? Ah yes, orderly corporal, arms swinging, up and down, up and down, *pound pound* (also *slish slish*—Petawawa was a camp built on sand, risky for the walls of Jerusalem but solid enough for our tar-papered buildings) to the gates of the disciplinary barracks. *Rat-a-tap-tap.* Who can doubt a chest so swollen with love and authority, and brown eyes that stare so confidently straight ahead? F battery claims its prisoner for court-martial. The messenger is passed in, through the barbed-wire enclosure, into the reception hall of the wooden buildings. There. That was it. The leopard-skinned lady had brought me back across fifteen years, cloudy and half-fulfilled, to my youth—happiest days of our lives—to the cleanest place I ever knew. How many battles lost because the doctrine of perfection begins and ends at the well-polished boot? Cleanliness overpowering, frightening, obscene, the walls still moist, the floors with a texture of felt from scrubbing, cleaned with toothbrushes, fingernails, tears. The strutting guards, thick of pink neck, with the small peaked red-topped cap of the MPs, turkey cocks, scrubbed by the prisoners, too, after the floors and the urinals.

F battery's prisoner. Through a wire grill gate, down a hall snugly carpentered and surgically clean, with an eye slot in each wooden door, I am led to Allouette's door. When we enter he stands at attention, or almost so, head twisted a bit to one side and tilted back, as if he were surprised at what he saw. He is short, dark haired, with the clumsy body of these French Canadian conscripts. A whisper of a frightened smile lies on his face trying to please us; nothing at all can be read in the round protruding eyes. He too is clean. His boots glow like lumps of anthracite, his face is shaved as smooth as a baby's, dotted all over with the little red spots that come from shaving hard and fast without soap. He has a waxen skin, scrubbed too, a corpse handled by an over-conscientious mortician. There is a gentle look to his face. All roughness has been smoothed away, and he is malleable as cooked asparagus. A bench, a blanket, on the shelf a Bible for the stern but comforting words of the Regimental Ser-geant Major of us all.

"All right, march, Allouette," the sergeant says. He is comforting too, a father, of sorts, to these unhappy prisoners. "Don't think you can smuggle anything back in."

Out we go. *Pound pound.* It is hard for him to keep up. His eyes swivel at the richness he has not been seeing. A truck, three soldiers walking together and laughing. *Slish slish.* The sand spreads a thin scarf upon his glowing boots. He glances worriedly at this and tries to polish the boots again by rubbing them against his pant legs. Better him than me, better him than me. "Corporal, not so fast." The words are said to the air, quietly. If I hear them it is not his respon-sibility. We stand behind a corner of one of the barracks, where I light him a cigarette. He draws as deeply as he can, sucks the smoke into every corner of his lungs, forces it down his nose, fills his entire body with smoke. Each drag is made the same way. He smokes the cigarette down until the ashes burn his lips, then throws it reluctantly away, and we march across the parade ground to F battery. He looks about him nervously. There he ate his meals, there he slept and suffered, and there he could not bring himself to return from his leave, but what freedom and humanity those buildings seem to possess now.

"Hello, Allouette, come to pay us a visit, eh?" the orderly sergeant says. "Straighten up now," mutters the sergeant major from Quebec, who walks with something of a camel's rocking because of his flat feet, not a sadistic man but so merciless in his devotion to military correctness that never in my life have I met a man who frightened me as he used to, and how could Allouette leave his mother and his sweetheart to return to the sound of the sergeant major's voice? We make a little parade: I, Allouette (without his cap, to show that he is even lower than a soldier) then the sergeant major, who wheels his tiny troop around in front of the major's desk. Nor is the major evil. Manager of a department store in Montreal, he runs his battery conscientiously and will listen to his men when they have a trouble. But Allouette's trouble cannot be made good by any officer. In bad French the major asks how long Allouette overstayed his leave. He already knows: thirty-four days. A lieutenant, our defense counsel, asks Allouette if he kept his uniform in his closet. Yes, sir.

Poor Allouette. Where was his home? One of the ugly mill towns along the St. Lawrence with the outside stairway going up to the second floor. Church, Sunday dinner cooked by his mother, movies with Anne-Marie, but the two of them don't know what is happening on the screen when every ten minutes he glances at his watch. How can he leave the penny-caramel sweetness of life in St. Oradour? He cannot explain to Anne-Marie what the army is like. She does not know what frightens him but it is terrible; when they are alone for a little after the movies she lets him put his hand under her dress. He will not return. Not today. It doesn't matter. Now the camp becomes even more frightening. He will stay away longer and live in fear, sitting by the radio in the living room, afraid to go out. Can his mother drive him away, or poor Anne-Marie? She must grant him a little more, he is so miserable. On the kitchen table, on the couch, in the hallway. The first time the MPs pay their call he is away from home, in civilian clothes, though some last call of sense or thrift keeps him from throwing his uniform away. He weeps. He cannot answer when the priest scolds him. What more can Anne-Marie give him? She will have her own fear now. It is a relief when the man in the black coat stops him outside the church and tells him to step into the car.

The major asks questions, so does the lieutenant. There is nothing either to ask or to reply. I stand to attention. I am good. I am a prop to the empire and the struggle against fascism. Allouette is just waste. The sergeant major calls his little parade to order and out we march from the major's room. "Back you go, Allouette," says the sergeant major. It is not an unkind voice. Who could be unkind to a man returning where Allouette will go? In the Canadian disciplinary barracks, the prisoners do not have their fingernails torn off, they are not savaged by dogs, not burned with cigarette butts.

We march away. The stockade is eight minutes' march. Allouette has eight minutes to look at the sky and the trucks and the pine trees. Suddenly I am ashamed. The MPs expected to be cheated a bit. They are that human. "What would you like to do?" He looks startled. No one has asked him that question for a long time and he does not know what to answer. I wheel him around and we walk past the edge of the parade ground, through the thin screen of pines until we stand on the bluff overlooking the river. It is amazing how close the sight of the river is to us, only the thinnest wall of trees cuts it off, but no one looks, no one bothers. The water of the Ottawa is always the darkest, steeliest blue. In September, however, the banks and the islands are splotched with yellow from the birches and red from the maples against the dark green of the pines and firs. On the Quebec side the forest stretches, paler and paler, almost twenty miles to the blue roll of the Laurentians. Allouette and I smoke our cigarettes and watch the river and the woods. In early April we were grubbing out birch stumps at another section of the bluff, our faces muddy where we had wiped away the sweat—slaves not badly treated, paid, well fed, never whipped, but slaves—when we heard a metallic sound coming from above and we looked up from our mattoxes at a flight of geese, all calling, flying north. They were near enough for us to see their markings and hear the steady beat of their wings. "Wish I had my gun," one man said. I don't know whether he meant it, maybe he did. Killing is easy, and those same soldiers were shot at enough in Italy and Holland when their time came. But what longing came over our faces as we gazed after those honking geese on their journey up to Hudson's Bay.

Allouette and I turn around and march back to the parade ground. A few minutes still exist that we can steal from the MPs. In the canteen he points to a chocolate bar and some salted nuts, a bottle of orange pop. (It is too early for a beer at the wet canteen.) He cannot speak, he can only point to what he wants. He is so very clean and silent, any soldier would pick him out for a prisoner. We march back slowly. I hear him sigh when we glimpse the wire of the stockade. Too late I remember that he might have written a note to Anne-Marie. Through the gates again, into the orderly room where the sergeant goes through his pockets and make him slip down his trousers in case he has hidden anything—the prisoners know how to split a match in four lengths and get a light from each one. He gives his wondering half-smile to the sergeant, head cocked back and eyes wide open, and he is marched away down the clean wooden hallway.

VIII

RETURN AND TIME

"WE WON'T HAVE TO struggle with French any more," Marilyn Haas said, but her husband was so strangely moved by the sight of the green-jacketed guards at the far end of the bridge that he did not answer. Out in the control hut one official stamped the Renault's tryptych, another barely glanced at their passports. Larry set the car moving again. After her five months in France Marilyn bubbled with new enthusiasm. The stop signs excited her, and the girls with their long braids, and when they left the border she exclaimed over the hayracks lined along the fields like children at calisthenics. "It looks as though it's grown right up out of the ground," she said of the first village they came to. The heavy timbered houses, the red and gold dahlias, the dung heaps, the chickens, the long, narrow spoked carts, the men and women and children, all grew of one piece. "In Iowa the houses are built on top of the ground. Here I bet they send down roots a hundred feet deep." A tightness in his chest kept her husband silent, and he spoke only when Marilyn asked him to pronounce a name or translate one of the signs.

Soon they left the vegetable abundance of the Rhine valley—like driving through a salad, Marilyn said—and climbed over the first barriers of the Black Forest to a plateau of upland meadows. The road held little traffic. The car traveled rapidly past the fields where whole families were raking and stacking hay, past the orchards, and through the idle towns.

The low forested hills, the creamy mountains of cumulus rising ahead of them were all sharp and new to their eyes. It was only the French soldiers who did not fit. Sunday afternoon in an occupied country and they earned fifteen francs a day. They slouched against the wall of a church or squatted on the curb and stared at the girls, the hay carts, and the automobiles. When they saw the French car and the French license, their faces brightened and sometimes they waved. "Here they like us," Marilyn said in surprise, and each time she waved back.

Because she was tired they did not drive as far as Ulm, but stopped instead at Tübingen, at a new Gasthaus designed, it seemed, by a twelve-year-old who had been handed a ruler and a sharp pencil. Where shall I put the car? Please take the suitcases to the room. We don't want a heavy dinner. Larry could speak again and not fumble around like a fool or pronounce his words loudly and slowly for those who wanted his money to understand.

"Yes, Lieutenant Haas, we have very nice roast chicken this evening."

They were hungrier than they thought. They finished one carafe of wine and ordered another until Marilyn said she felt fine and thought it would be fun to look around. Tübingen was a pretty town, built on both sides of a swiftly flowing, green-brown river. Where the buildings thinned out, willow trees hung over the water, and there was a park through which the young couple walked past the neat grass and beds of geraniums and a small lake containing a pair of swans. The slow twilight had brought out other couples who found pleasure in each other's company, strolling or seated side by side beneath the chestnut trees. It was offensive, ridiculous, to see the little patrol of French soldiers wearing white gloves and submachine guns. At a bride's pace, with their eyes straight front, the officer and his two men paraded past the geranium beds.

The store windows, however, were the glory of Tübingen,

stocked with electrical machines and gadgets shining in nickel plate. And the Germans who were comparing differences of quality and price in these same windows obviously possessed the money to buy these handsome articles. The drifting French soldiers had nothing to spend even if the stores had been open. They were a minor nuisance the town had learned to ignore.

The Haases left Tübingen early next morning though Marilyn did not feel particularly well. After an hour of hill and valley driving they got on the autobahn and traveled as swiftly as the Renault's wheels would turn. The highway, however, turned the country on either side into an abstraction. Woods, stubble fields, church towers glided past as if someone were cranking them by on a painted backdrop. The speed was abstract too—objects off the road were too far away to measure it, and vehicles moving almost as fast neared and distanced themselves gradually. Only the figures on the signs sweeping by told them they were going someplace, getting closer to Augsburg, to Dachau, to Munich. "Dachau"—printed like any other town name. At the cutoff Larry read the sign, *Dachau Ordnance Depot*-5 kilometers.

On the far side of Munich they caught their first view of the Alps, and Marilyn recovered her enthusiasm of the day before. "I can't believe they're real. At least I can't believe it's me who's seeing them." Forest stretches became heavier. The church towers were topped by onion domes. In the middle of the afternoon they crossed the Austrian frontier. "You're out of Germany now. See, that wasn't so bad, was it?" she said comfortingly.

Marilyn had been thrilled the first day she stood in the middle of Place Stanislas in Nancy and turned herself around to see the dignified gray palaces on all four sides. That was the beauty and tradition of Europe. Also, as close as she ever got. The ghetto walls held her tightly. The French had not the slightest inclination to accept an outsider, and the other army wives were indignant that she should even want to go outside. Larry, who had no interest in France and considered one army post about the same as another, wasn't much help. The Haases, like everyone else, played a lot of bridge. But music was Marilyn's love. Mozart's music was the nearest approximation to pure beauty that she ever hoped to find. In Salzburg she would not be an American or a soldier's wife. She would be a pilgrim.

"What do you remember about it?" she demanded again.

"Not very much," he confesssed. "There was a tunnel that went through a mountain."

Marilyn had looked forward so intensely to this city that he was even more alarmed than she as they drove by blocks of stuccoed villas. Then they turned a corner. The domes and turrets of the cathedral rose before them and the festival flags of every nation fluttered in front of the opera house. "That's it!" Larry said, stopping the car. "And there's the tunnel, right through the mountain. We couldn't see where it came out and it seemed funny to have a road disappear into a mountain right in the middle of a city." A policeman gestured for him to move on.

The Haases spent three days in Salzburg. They went to three operas. Larry became accustomed to speaking German and began to accept Marilyn's view that the music was one token of the German spirit. He found himself enjoying this solid dose of opera, partly because of the change the music worked upon his wife. Sitting in a café, after Marilyn could walk no longer, they would order coffee and whipped cream and she would tell him the story of that evening's performance. As she went on, eyes sparkling, about Mozart's life or the development of his music; without thinking she shoved her glasses up on her forehead the way she used to in college. Her cheeks flushed. She spoke with authority and conviction. Larry had dated other vivacious coeds in Iowa City, but this generous devotion had placed her above them and above himself and he had resolved to win her. Life in Georgia and in Lorraine had dulled this spontaneous, disinterested enthusiasm. It was worth driving across Germany ten times. They had paid no small price for their marriage. Marilyn's parents had readily accepted Larry, as a person. He was smart, he had good manners, he worked harder—Mr. Lundgren delighted to observe—than any of their friends' sons. But the label "Hungarian-Jewish son-in-law" had locked the old man up in a long stubborn anger. For this boy to marry a gentile was a bitter blow to George Weinberg. He had accepted this unknown charge from a refugee agency nine years earlier, out of compassion and also, Larry came to believe, though he was genuinely fond of his awkward, inarticulate foster father, because such an act gave George Weinberg stature in Jewry and in life itself that otherwise he did not enjoy. George had wanted—what he wanted was always perfectly clear, though it was impossible for him to state a direct fact—his Lazar (George was the only one who used Larry's old name) to become a rabbi, to take over the drugstore, or to marry one of his daughters, none of which came to pass. Larry, who had held back in high school, blossomed at the university; he gained honors in engineering and worked during the summer at the Lundgren Gear Works in Council Bluffs. Mr. Lundgren's daughter he had won and Mr. Lundgren's plant he would some day manage and his old age he would gladden. Lazar, whose mother's father had been a rabbi in Szeged, had been tempted away into the bright gentile world. George did not realize that the boy, even before he learned how to speak English properly, had decided that the shadowy remains of Judaism followed by the Weinbergs contained no meaning for him. Not that the Christians obeyed anything more vital—their goals were the same—but they moved freely. There was no limit to what could be obtained. Larry had had enough of limits. He would always be grateful and dutiful to the Weinbergs; nevertheless he was not on this earth to give George Weinberg the re-assurance he had not found through his own life.

Now Marilyn wanted to continue her pilgrimage on to Vienna, and they set out on the highway toward Linz. For lunch they would stop at St. Florian, the abbey where Anton Bruckner had lived and composed. To be on the road again excited them both. The overcast day heightened the meadows and forests' greens on either side, the flowers' reds, the hay-stacks' yellow browns, and the mountains' gray to the south as if the two travelers were wearing colored glasses.

"It isn't a question merely of traveling across country. You get the sense of traveling in time too," Marilyn said. "My great-grandparents in Sweden must have farmed pretty much the same way these people do here."

"You should have seen my village."

The smells in Salzburg had made him think of Kaposvar again. Out of the open doors came the same smell of beer, vinegar, and meat cooked with paprika and caraway, and at the tables the men made the same gesture to wipe their moustaches with the back of their hands. On Saturday after-noons the peasants used to tie up their carts and buggies in a long row outside the White Falcon and go inside to get themselves drunk. Wiser Jews took their Sabbath walks in another direction, but Lazar Haas liked to walk past the open door. A wind of apricot brandy, beer, sweat, urine, the dangerous voices, an accordion, and at the doorway a peas-ant wiping both sides of his moustache with the back of his hand and swaying a bit backward and forward. If he man-aged to focus his eyes on the boy walking down the middle of the street he drew a breath and yelled, "Hey, Jew, beat it!" Lazar set out on a run, with two or three gentile boys at his heels. The danger was enticing and a legalistic scrap of his mind asked why didn't he have the right to walk past the White Falcon if he wanted to. In the late summer the barn behind their house rang with the laughter and gossip of peasant girls shelling the nuts his father bought and sold. Other peasants came to the house with great crocks of honey that his mother strained into glass jars. In wintertime the yard was full of birds hopping and pecking about the mounds of nutshells. When the weather was bad he and Janos lined up all the chairs one behind the other and played train. Larry did not speak often of that world. To claim that boy's life as his own seemed false, as if trying to claim a title he had no right to any more. But these past days he had spoken about it a number of times.

Rain blurred the windshield. Marilyn was studying the map. "Look here's Mauthausen, the other side of the river after Linz. Is that the same place?"

"Yes."

After some reflection she said, "What would it be like to see it again?"

"I was thinking of finding out," he replied with careful casualness.

She thought again. "Then you've been on this same road?"

"Yes. The convoy came this way, then it turned south at Salzburg. If I'm not wrong we may already have passed Gusen. That was my home too."

"I thought you were just at Mauthausen."

"That was better known," he said. "Only the Jews were sent off to Gusen. It was stuck away in the forest, even more hidden than Mauthausen, and I think the plan was to get rid of us all there, but something happened to the orders. Not that enough people didn't die. At the end everything was falling apart. They actually stretched out the corpses as boundary markings inside the barracks. Then the Germans got panicky because the Americans were coming, and they decided to take us back to Mauthausen. We were so weak we could hardly walk, but they marched us twenty-five kilometers a day,"

"You must have marched through this town?" she asked with a sort of childlike literalness. The road had passed

into his room to comfort him and to share the terrible experience. The gray wooden barracks were still there, some of them. The sky was the same, the same threads of rain slanting down at his face. The puddles on the ground were the same. He held his breath as he walked, almost on tiptoe, across the terrace.

A new slab of polished granite had been set beside the stone gate, lettered in Russian at the top, German below, in memory of the 122,328 victims of Nazi savagery: Russians in the position of honor, then Poles, then Hungarians—it didn't say Jews—Romanians and French and everyone else, Germans too, and fifty-six Americans, Jews probably, ex-immigrants whose green passports hadn't protected them. Little plaques and monuments were set all around the terrace—to the citizens of Yugoslavia, to the Jews of the community of Vienna, to heroic Colonel General Bessarabov. Larry read the German text: on the night of February 12, 1945, Colonel General Bessarabov was chained naked to this wall, and while dogs tore at his flesh his captors hurled buckets of water upon him until he turned into a pillar of ice, a hero of the Red Army, steadfastly refusing to reveal the information demanded by the Nazi sadists.

He hadn't forgotten that night completely. Somehow the rumor got around, a Russian general was being tortured, they had killed him, but they didn't get what they wanted. All right, by God, they can't always get what they want. Even little Lazar Haas had felt that. The signs said that here captives had been held in chains, here was the path to the rock quarry, here the path to the gas ovens.

Monuments. Glass cases held faded photographs with French captions, which Marilyn was reading. In the soggy field beyond the terrace stood four granite columns inscribed with words in Polish, a marble shaft bearing the cross of Lorraine, an ugly semicircle of white stone with star and pillars, all honor to the 40,000 heroic etc. etc. Rain. And no one. The Russians had taken great pains with these memorials. No one came. The kapo of his own barracks had been a Ukrainian who made two Polish Jews whip each other because they were friends. All honor to the Red Army. At the far end of the barracks he saw a figure bent over in a raincoat walk across the yard and disappear. One other.

The rain beat harder. Marilyn stood under the eave of a barracks, he could see her raincoat was soaked through. She was looking at the ground. He should not let her get chilled, but he did not know what to do. A boy with dark sunken eyes, ears jutting out from his skull, a tough little animal watching for a piece of food or a blow. And he had escaped. He had broken free, he grew up, and his wife was carrying his child.

The story was false. That wild little creature had been left behind. It was false to claim any relationship. All this had never existed. It never was, it never had been, not to good people of Linz or Salzburg or Council Bluffs. He was protected, safe, soft, thinking only about himself and maybe his wife. Nor had his mother existed, nor his father, nor Janos who had cried when they climbed out of the cattle train in Poland. His mother said, "Don't cry. It will mean hard work but we're not afraid of hard work. We'll get through. Don't cry." Women were marched one direction for their showers, men and boys another. Smaller children were told they would receive a special ration of fruit, and all of them, Janos too, were taken away. A crowd of wild men with shaven heads and black-and-white pajama suits dashed by, yelling in an unknown language, and ran between Lazar and his father, who never saw each other again. Later on he knew that he would not live to be free, but he still resolved to keep alive as long as he could, almost out of curiosity, to see what would happen, what new adventures would befall Lazar Haas before his unimportant life was ended.

What was he looking for? What kept him here? The rain ran down his hair and under his collar. It had soaked through the shoulders of his raincoat and through his shoes. Whom was he expecting to find?

"Hallo!"

He turned, Marilyn raised her head, to see an excited man standing on the terrace by the steps from the parking lot. The man walked toward them, holding his useless raincoat against his chest with one hand, the other vibrating agitatedly. When he came closer he cried out again in French.

"No. We're not French, we're Americans," Marilyn said to him. Larry could understand her French.

"Americans?" the man exclaimed with an outburst of disappointment, and said something else.

"He says the place is forgotten. No one cares," she explained to her husband, though she did not look directly at him. Her voice was tired, it trembled with cold. "He's very worked up about it."

Hunched over, still clutching the front of his raincoat, the man turned back to Larry. His flat-topped hat, brim turned up all around, the way Frenchmen like to wear them, was ridiculous, and it didn't suit his anguished face. He asked another question, still refusing to believe that Larry couldn't understand him.

"My husband was here once. That's why we came," Marilyn's tired voice explained.

"Gefangener?" shouted the Frenchman.

"Ja. Ungarn."

The Frenchman's German was exhausted. He said something about *garçon* and held out his hand to show small size.

"Yes. Thirteen. I came from Auschwitz, in September, in '44," Larry said in German.

"Lager Nummer?"

"Nine."

"Fifteen. Two years." The Frenchman held up two fingers and peered at him, seeking some proof for these facts. His own face had not changed much in eleven years. "But everything is forgotten. Alles vergessen," he repeated. "A tourist?"

"Not exactly. Soldier, American army, Nancy."

Reluctantly, the Frenchman turned to make a remark to Marilyn in a cynical voice.

"We're arming the Germans now. Are you pleased about that?" she translated. Larry didn't answer. The Frenchman spoke, she translated again, her eyes fixed on her shoes. "Are you pleased? Is this the sort of world you hoped to see?"

"All my family was killed," Larry said. "I went to America. I've made a new life for myself."

The Frenchman jerked his head. "Are you a Jew?" That word Larry understood in every language. "Is she Jewish? What does she think of it?" he asked about Marilyn without looking at her.

"I'm not a Jew," Marilyn answered in her slow, painstaking way. "What do I think of this? I didn't think of it very much before today. But isn't it better perhaps to forget? I mean, where do we go if all we can do is hate?"

"It isn't only that," Larry said, almost to himself.

The Frenchman asked a question of Marilyn directly.

"I don't know. I never thought," she said slowly. Her damp face was white and her shoulders trembled. "Perhaps we have lost more than we knew."

"My wife is very cold," Larry said. The Frenchman looked at her again and nodded. The three of them went down the steps together, Marilyn leaning on Larry's arm, and stopped by the two cars.

"Where are you going now?" the Frenchman asked in German.

"To Vienna. My wife is interested in Mozart."

The Frenchman nodded, rubbed his hands together to warm them.

"Children?"

"February."

He glanced at Marilyn, then patted her on the arm and shook her hand, and held out his hand to shake Larry's hand. He spoke once more to Marilyn. She smiled at his words.

"Yes, I am." She translated for her husband. "He said I was fortunate that you lived."

"Good-bye," the Frenchman said. "Good luck."

Larry opened the door and helped his wife into their car.

IX

THE VORTEX

The snow swirled fiercely above the roof of the steel works.
Norris sighed and went on to the next sentence. *From far
north of the Arctic Circle it had come, and the wind that
had rushed over the frozen Yenisei and the Ob, over the
tundra and the naked birch forests without end, over the
taiga of a lonely slant-eyed trapper and the lean white fox
to be his prey, now swooped upon the Krasnoyarsk Steel
Works and sent a great sheet of orange flame into the tur-
bulent sky.*

Norris raised his eyes, watering after seven lines of cloudy
type, to the figure in the double-breasted gray suit at the far
side of the waiting room. Despite the newspaper before him,
the other man was interested only in what Norris was doing,
and the latter politely smiled and held the book up in the air
before he returned again to *The Best Is Not Good Enough.*

*"Fire and ice—thats' our land!" grimly ejaculated Engineer
Greboyedov, fists doubled up in his pockets.*

The literary snow was matched by a temperature of ninety-
one degrees at the Hyderabad airport, and the sweat from
Norris's hands was already making the edges of the volume
(a product of Liberty House, Ltd., New Delhi,) wilt gluily.
The plane from Mysore has been so badly pressurized that
slow worms of pain still crawled through his sinuses. His
brain shrank away from the hot bones of his forehead; his
stomach (the little hostess had passed around a tray of shrimp

mayonnaise and honey cakes) toiled forebodingly. Engineer Greboyedov knocked the caked snow from his boots and strode on toward the steel works. Author Gletkin, *Bombay Times* stuck in his pocket, was standing beside Norris' chair, looking, however, at the showcase of dolls in regional costume so that his presence need not annoy the other.

"Page two," Norris reported.

"Paid too?"

"No, no, I'm on the second page."

Mr. Gletkin moved closer to the showcase, trying to decide between a water carrier in coarse cotton dhoti and a little nautch dancer thinly veiled by her pink and orange muslins, but nevertheless anxious about the reader's opinion.

"It has a strong opening," Norris reassured him.

"It tells the truth as it is. Like Dreiser."

"Like Jack London, too."

"We'll have to do better than that," Engineer Greboyedov told himself resolutely. The sacrifices of his people, the backbreaking toil of the puddlers, even the dim dreams of the Kirghiz fox trappers——

"You reading Gletkin's thing?" said a cross voice at Norris' elbow. "Any good?" loud enough to be heard by the author bending over his dolls. But Mr. Callison was interested in philosophy, not literature. "It must be terrible to have to write without freedom to say what you believe. You're a writer. You know that. Maybe they're just too conditioned," Mr. Callison concluded scornfully, "to know what the word Freedom means."

Hugh Norris' ability to judge anything was shrinking from the heat that had lain and trembled around him for the past two weeks. It beat upon him like a flail, it squeezed him like a fist. His efforts to reach beyond the alabaster Taj Mahals in these showcases, to go deeper than the earnest half-truths of Indians he met, had ended while his brain shriveled up like a biscuit left in the oven. "The heaven over thy head shall be brass and the earth under thee shall be iron"—that line from somewhere in the Old Testament had fastened itself upon him. He could think of nothing else while he wandered about under the brass bowl. If Mr. Callison was not noticed perhaps he would go away. Norris returned to Siberia.

The resolute little figure in the heavy work trousers turned and faced him. The face was marked, perhaps permanently, by fatigue and strain, but it had accepted unflinchingly the destiny that history had assigned her generation. Brother fallen before Stalingrad, sister had picked up the rifle and turned it to a draughtsman's pencil. Her determined eye met Engineer Greboyedov's, yet the gesture of her hand pushing away a look of flaxen hair . . .

"There's more in that showcase than in his whole damn country!" Mr. Callison couldn't help himself. He had been playing on the team for too long. The temperature, his maimed digestive system, the defeat at Mysore were all connected in his aching mind with the Russians, and Gletkin was the only Russian in sight. "I'd give a month's pay to know what was going through his mind right now."

"He has a ten-year-old daughter back in Moscow. Probably he's wondering what doll would please her most," Norris answered. Mr. Callison shot him a look of distrust.

"I bet he buys her a steelworker. If he brings home a dancing girl there'll be trouble down at the Writers' Club."

Norris had seen the other dolls in Mr. Gletkin's raffia bag: herdsmen, rug weavers, peasants from the airports at Karachi, Bombay, Damacus, Baghdad. He crossed his fingers and hoped that Mr. Gletkin would choose a nautch dancer.

No, a steelworker, complete with goggles and slag rod. Mr. Gletkin showed it to Norris, straining his eyes to see what page the reader was on now.

"Nice?"

"Very. I'm sure your girl will like it."

"What did I tell you!" Mr. Callison's whisper trembled with victory. They watched Mr. Gletkin and his little proletarian drift to the next counter. "He's looking for a scarf with a hydroelectric plant embroidered on it."

One month more and the cultural attaché would be ready for a padded cell. At first glance he was a pleasant enough man, with inoffensive peanut-colored hair and an intelligent, somewhat cramped face: eyes, nose, and mouth wedged together from some misapplied idea of neatness. The thumb of his left hand, however, twitched back and forth ceaselessly against his fingertips. The beat of the thoughts in his head made his eyes alternately narrow and distend. At ninety degrees Mr. Callison had to be polite with brown people whom he disliked and who disliked him. He could not strike the beggars, he could not break a chair over Mr. Muratchee when the latter smiled and enunciated, "America possesses a thousand bombing planes, but it does not have India's sense of moral values." The discipline that directed him could not be a German's, it had to be American, with the good-natured tolerance and respect for human values typical of America. The relaxed pattern of his argument—"There's a lot to what you say, but you may have overlooked these points"—was, however, as rigid as a Jesuit's.

At another time Norris would have been led to look deeper into the furnace of Mr. Callison's spirit—a writer cannot deal only in people stuffed with custard or nutshells—but today he wanted all human contact to remain as impersonal as possible, limiting himself to Mr. Gletkin's prize-winning novel presented to the world by its Indian typesetters.

The gray-blue eyes examined Engineer Greboyedov without flinching. Nothing but the absolute truth would ever pass their fiery scrutiny.

Mr. Callison had run across Norris in New Delhi and virtually kidnapped him for the Mysore Writers' Congress, not as a star like the famous California playwright, or a voice of America's future like the young Nashville poet, but as a unit of what embassy jargon would term the nation's literary infrastructure. Two novels, seven magazine articles, one poem: spokesman for the second-string of the American culture team. "This will give you lots of new material," Mr. Callison assured him. "And we don't want to leave the field free for the Russians." He was to shake hands and talk with Burmese novelists and Syrian essayists and be a tangible American, brother to Walt Whitman and Truman Capote.

Actually, the man he saw most was Anatoli Gletkin. "I trust this does not embarrass you, Mr. Norris," murmured smiling Mr. Muratchee at the first dinner, pointing to a vacant chair beside the person in black-rimmed spectacles and ill-fitting gray suit, "but in India spiritual values are of more importance than power politics." He and Mr. Gletkin passed the chutney back and forth as they conversed about literature; that is, Norris paraded out a stable of names to which Gletkin allotted a line of praise or blame. "No, we do not care too much for Dostoevski, he is so introspective," and they went on to Chekhov while Mr. Muratchee and his colleagues smiled and nodded at each other.

Talking to Gletkin was like whittling willow whistles—a tedious job and when you were finished you didn't have much, but it could be done. They fabricated these units of conversation at every meal where they were placed to- gether—their war service against the Germans, their children, the books they had read—until Norris marveled at the mir- acles of modern transport that allowed him to make small talk in Mysore with such a piece of wood. Gletkin, of course, was strictly an infrastructure man also. Nikolai Priluki was the Soviet star, a handsome, ivory-skinned, prematurely bald artist who spoke an elegant English, remembered all the delegates' names, and quoted their epic poets. Words about spiritual depth and esthetic leadership slipped like golden coins from his lips. He smiled deeply into each man he addressed, even the Americans. What nonsense all this rivalry is, the smile might say, or, altered the slightest way for some- one else, what twaddle that ponderous fellow is speaking.

That smile disoriented the American delegation. The famous California playwright fought back with confused scraps of invective about kulaks and Lithuanians. The young Nashville poet was entranced to have met his first Russian. That Priluki should have two hands and ten fingers was proof of amazing humanity. He pushed aside the Indians to stand even closer to the great man. With a look, with a smile, he would penetrate to the Russian soul and exorcise the cold war by a mystical transcendentalism. "Don't give me instructions. I obey a higher loyalty than patriotic servility," the poet rebuffed Mr. Callison, who as a mere official could not enter the meeting rooms and paced the lobby of the Hotel Edward VII like a coach on the day of the big game. Trembling, the cultural attaché turned to the playwright. "Get in there, damn it!" he barked. "Tell 'em about the ILGWU art classes! Tell 'em——" He reeled and would have fallen had not Norris caught his arm.

Even though participation at an international writers' congress had for him the intellectual seriousness of picture postcards, Norris was dismayed to see this one end up as one more Russo-American contest of value neither to literature nor to man. Nevertheless, he threw himself into his infrastructure responsibilities and sought out other grade B men to talk about translation rights, serialization, and publishing contracts, bones and sinews of literature. But then Mr. Muratchee would show up, reluctant Gletkin in tow, with a "Here is your new friend, Mr. Norris," someone would pull out a camera, and the delegates would pile up around the Russian and the American for another photograph. The Mysore Congress had been no victory for the Stars and Stripes.

"Come on, Norris, let's all eat together."

Norris glanced up in surprise from *The Best Is Not Good Enough*. Hatred rather than food kept Mr. Callison going, it had seemed, but the cultural attaché now turned to a large black woman, fanning away as she worked on the crossword puzzle in her lap. "Come join us, Mrs. Spottswood. Norris and I are going for a bite of lunch."

"Thank you, Mr. Callison," she replied politely. "I'm quite comfortable."

Mr. Callison twisted his exasperation into a taut graciousness.

"They have a nice restaurant here, Mrs. Spottswood. It'll be three-thirty before the Delhi plane takes off."

"This Indian food doesn't agree with me, Mr. Callison. I've had gas all morning."

She dismissed him with a nod and turned back to her puzzle. Callison almost stamped his foot. It wasn't a matter of her wretched digestion. It was her duty to have lunch with them. Gletkin must not be allowed to observe that representatives of the American state and culture were eating alone because they considered Mrs. Spottswood racially inferior.

"A little yoghurt perhaps, Mrs. Spottswood, would make you feel jim dandy," he urged her. He smiled until his gums showed but his anguished eyes flickered over Norris, who would not help him, and Gletkin in that wrinkled gray suit and the whole hostile world of the Hyderabad airport waiting to be convinced of the sincerity of American ideals.

"Well, if you insist, Mr. Callison," Mrs. Spottswood sighed, sticking the crossword puzzle book into her handbag. "A bite won't do me any harm."

They sat down at a table in the fly-humming restaurant and gave their orders. Mrs. Spottswood commented on the way her travel with the State Department paid off richly in new words she picked up for her puzzles, but Callison had no further desire to talk to her. He kept glancing at the entrance for Gletkin to appear. The waiter set down the plates before the wrong people; Callison's spoon was marked with a fat thumbprint. His hand began to shake. Norris made conversation with Mrs. Spottswood. She had started her mission from Liberia, lecturing in Monrovia and Khartoum and Mysore on YWCA techniques, games that encourage cooperation, games that encourage leadership, with no visible awareness that Khartoum might be different from Chicago or Mysore from Monrovia but in the simplicity of a true missionary, sent into a troubled world by John Foster Dulles with her black leatherette handbag and her placid, heavy step.

Callison let his breath out sharply. Gletkin had entered the restaurant and chosen a place two tables away. He carried all his gear with him, not trusting the checkroom attendants, and set himself the task of placing certain articles on the chair and certain other ones on the table and folding his raincoat over the chair back. Such precision whipped Mr. Callison into fury.

"They're hardly human," he whispered loud enough for the whole restaurant to hear. "I just wonder what goes through their heads."

"Maybe what he's going to have for lunch," Mrs. Spottswood suggested. She and Norris exchanged naughty smiles.

"They've had no experience of normal human relationships. If he'd grown up in a town like Danbury he wouldn't be able to endure such a life."

Suddenly Norris felt a deep sorrow for the cultural attaché. Danbury was a town he knew also. Green Connecticut hills, maple trees red in autumn, the brick high school where laughing boys and girls elected the president of the Stamp Club, inns that served fried chicken and cottage cheese, hat factories with their self-respecting, car-driving workers—the Russians didn't know about Danbury. They were willing to destroy the whole state of Connecticut. It meant nothing to them. It meant nothing to the Indians. No one in all of Hyderabad knew the things that the Rotary Club did for the people of Danbury.

The waiter brought Gletkin a dish he hadn't ordered. The Russian shook his finger crossly. Mr. Callison almost sobbed with joy.

"See, they don't have the slightest comprehension of what

democracy means. It doesn't make any difference what Marx says."

Gletkin had heard. He looked over at the Americans' table, his stolid face creasing in a frown.

"Ha, ha, he's losing control of himself! That cast-iron discipline cracks when it meets a new strain."

"Mr. Callison, you shouldn't get yourself so upset," Mrs. Spottswood murmured.

"They're not hemmed in by the NKVD here. They have to face reality the way it is!"

A number of Indians were beginning to turn around too, in alarm, or with the faintest pleasure at sight of the wild eyes in that cramped, trembling face. Norris put a hand on his arm.

"Easy does it, old man."

But Callison jerked his arm away and pointed directly at the enemy.

"Hungary showed how the Red Army defends the international proletariat, didn't it?" he shouted.

"Mr. Callison," warned Mrs. Spottswood.

With dignity Mr. Gletkin began to butter his roll.

"Karaganda! Vorkuta! Katyn!" Callison had thrown Norris's hand and wrenched himself to his feet. "You don't like to hear these names, do you? Or maybe no one ever let you find out what they mean!" he shouted at the silent figure chewing on his roll.

The headwaiter scurried up and then halted and wrung his hands. Callison knocked his chair over but could not free himself from Mrs. Spottswood's arm around his shoulder. Norris grabbed his wrist. Indians and Europeans had jumped up to see what was happening, but Mr. Gletkin took another bite of his roll and refilled his glass with mineral water.

"You're afraid to face the truth! You won't see the contradictions of your own system!" the anguished little man howled, twisting toward the door. He stumbled and wrestled, but then he suddenly quieted and let himself be guided by

Mrs. Spottswood's huge arm. Only at the very door of the restaurant, where a turbaned Sikh colonel, beard tucked away in a chiffon cloth, was seated beside a tiny wife, did Mr. Callison halt. With a patient courtesy he smiled and said, "You see, in America we no longer draw any distinctions whatsoever because of race."

X

THE STONE GUEST

I

THE SUN, WHICH HAD LONG SINCE RISEN to the east of
Salzburg and Seville, gilded Napoleon's statue atop the column in the Place Vendome, awakened the chambermaids of
Grosvenor Place and sped across the Atlantic far swifter than
the elegant *Ile-de-France* steaming in the same direction, had
touched the easternmost tip of Long Island and was rolling
up on one after another of the famous watering places on
the South Shore like some silent, special-fare express train.
Now it lighted the most famous of all, and out from the
cloak of night became evident the outlines of the elm trees
and white clapboard houses and the formality of the boxwood hedges, sweet smelling in the windless summer dawn.

The dew glistened on the white picket fences and the
hydrangea blossoms. The shimmering light awakened the
robins, thrushes, orioles, and in the pond marshes the red-
winged blackbirds, to cheerful calls and trills, and the English
sparrows to noisy complaint. Out upon the misty lawns
ventured the cottontails, nibbling at the grass and every so
often standing on their hind legs to scout for enemies. In the
potato fields of the Polish farmers that surrounded the summer colony the cocks crowed. No other sounds but nature's
had broken the morning's calm when suddenly a piercing

shriek silenced the birds and made the little rabbits jerk up their ears in alarm.

It came, and again it came, from a large, handsome white house where lived old Commander Frobisher and his daughter Ann. It came from the hallway of the second floor. A slender girl in a nightgown, her long dark hair awry and her face twisted with passion, clung to a man in a navy blue blazer and white flannels, who roughly plucked her hands from his arms and pushed her away.

"We're both civilized people. Let us know when it's time to say au revoir," he enunciated coldly through the foulard that masked his face.

"Monster!" she screamed again, and in exasperation he tried to put his hand over her face.

The door of another bedroom opened and the situation became more confused as a powerful old man, vigorous and dangerous still despite his white hair, burst out upon the landing.

"What's going on here! Who are you, sir? What are you doing in my house?" he roared at the masked intruder. And at sight of his daughter, his anger compounded itself with fear. "Are you all right, Ann?" he cried, and again at the intruder: "By, God, sir, what have you done?"

"There is no need for melodrama," sneered the masked man with a clipped, metallic intonation. "We can all behave like civilized human beings."

Again the old man glanced at his daughter, her face now buried in her hands.

"You scoundrel!" he exclaimed and hurled himself upon the intruder.

"Let's think matters out clearly," the stranger began, but the Commander was too powerful to be held at bay, and he reached for the stranger's neck with his heavy old hands. The stranger pivoted, one leg still extended along the edge of the landing, and with a thrust of his arm impelled the old man further upon his lunge. Tripping over the outstretched leg, hitting the stairs head first and then catapulting in a wide somersault, his bathrobe flung out like the wings of a bat, the Commander smashed his forehead against a wooden spoke where the stairs turned, and slipped sideways. Arms and legs flopped upon the treads. Then the heavy old body lost its motion and lay like an overturned piece of furniture. The stranger sprang down the stairs to peer under the bathrobe.

"This need never have happened at all, I assure you," he said through his mask to the girl, who had staggered to the edge of the landing.

"You killed him!"

"Bad-tempered old man, hysterical daughter," he commented.

Stepping carefully to avoid the outsprawled pajama-clad limbs, he descended the rest of the stairs. The girl clung to the railing, but suddenly her face changed. The front door was flung open just before the stranger reached it, and there stood the figure of a slight young man.

"Octavius!"

"Good morning to you, young man," the stranger said contemptuously, extending an arm to brush the newcomer aside.

"Octavius!" the girl cried again. He reached out tentatively to seize the stranger's shoulder. "Stop!" he commanded shrilly. The stranger pulled himself free and knocked the youth to the floor. Then he stepped out the door and slammed it behind him. The girl ran down the steps, holding the nightgown to herself as best she could, but was unable to pass the body of her father and halted irresolutely as Octavius picked himself up.

"Ann, are you all right?"

"Catch him! He's killed Father!"

Octavius ran out of the house in pursuit just as Bridget emerged from the pantry. She screamed. Eileen and old

Moira followed her and they screamed too, throwing their arms in the air and rocking back on their heels, and Ann had to forget the awful shape sprawled on the stairs and send Bridget for Thomas the gardener and help Moira control Eileen, who tossed in hysterics on the couch.

"'Tis the hand of death that has touched my young life," shrieked Eileen. "His bony fingers quell the best of my strong heart."

"A nice hot cup of tea, dearie, will set you to rights."

"Like the black storm cloud over the headland of Connemara Bay he rushed down upon us!"

"Breakfast time soon, dearie, hot crumpets with melting golden butter," crooned old Moira, wiping the froth from the girl's lips.

Thomas limped in breathlessly behind Bridget, but Eileen's wails together with the necessity of averting his eyes to avoid seeing young mistress in her nightgown made it hard for him to take in what the trouble actually was. Octavius Iredell returned also.

"Did you catch him?" Ann whispered harshly.

"No. He ran through the Cooneys' hedge."

"You didn't follow him?"

"We've never gotten along with the Cooneys," he explained lamely, avoiding the burning brown eyes. She sighed.

"Help Thomas carry Father to his room."

The two men, with help from Moira and Bridget—Eileen had turned her face to the back of the couch and was sobbing quietly—picked up the poor old man with his dented forehead and carried him to his bed.

"I'll phone the FBI!" announced Bridget, but Ann stopped her and made the disappointed woman phone Dr. Nugent instead.

"Life, ma'm," said old Thomas, "is like a basket of summer fruit, a lily whose blossom lies shriveled and fallen by eventide."

"A handsome man he was in his uniform," old Moira said.

"The sparkle upon his dress sword warmed your heart. 'I feel fine, Moira,' he said to me only yesterday, 'I feel strong as a young horse.' The longest life indeed is a drop of water in the river of eternity."

Octavius regarded the remains of his prospective father-in-law's energy and courtliness, fine clothes and ambition, dignity in Wall Street and presidency of the Tennis Club. Mixing daiquiris with a raspberry beaten up in each so the pink shade would please the ladies, and now what? The women in their bathrobes, a chorus of ancient Mycenae, telling the ancient changes on life and death, the visitors to us all. Weary of weeping alone, Eileen appeared at the doorway, her hair falling over her damp and senseless face, and stared with admiration into the Commander's bedroom, which she had never seen before.

"Don't you think we ought to get the FBI, Mr. Octavius?" whispered Bridget. "They'll need a habeas corpus for the coroner's inquest."

This insistent whisper was as futile as the furniture itself, the monogrammed sheets and the canopied bedstead purchased in Edinburgh, before the path of death. And the shocking violence of the stranger had really done no more than accentuate, speed, vulgarize the inevitable coming. Ann returned in her dressing gown, a ribbon binding her hair.

"Can't I phone the FBI, miss?" Bridget pleaded.

"No," came the curt reply.

"Are you sure you're doing the right thing, miss?"

"He would have wanted it this way," Ann said and walked out of the room.

"I couldn't sleep. I had the feeling something was wrong," Octavius explained on the landing. "I kept walking back and forth in the orchard, trying to work out a line. Then I heard your scream."

"And you don't have any idea who he was?" she asked him.

"Don't you?"

"He had that scarf around his face. I couldn't tell."

"Did he"—Octavius choked on his question, confused between the horror of the word he might use and Ann's calm—"Did he get into your room?"

She averted her face.

"He came in the window. It was too dark to see who he was."

"Why didn't you scream when he entered?"

"I thought it was you. Then it was too late."

He saw his own figure stealing up the rose trellises—the thorns pricked his fingers—and silently slipping his leg over the sill, listening to her sleeping breath as he stood looking down on the slender shape, dark hair spread out upon the pillow, one arm flung gracefully back. A sharply drawn breath tells that she is awake and the room is shaken by a tremor of maidenliness, but the warm sheets are opened and the slender arms raised.

"I wouldn't have done that," he said, reality stopping his dream of a dream.

"Maybe you should have!"

He wandered down the stairs slowly, uselessly. By the door he stopped.

It had no longer been dark, and no possible similarity existed between his slender figure and the stranger's powerful one.

The doorbell rang and he opened it to admit old Dr. Nugent with his black bag, Mr. Floyd the undertaker, and stout Captain Donohue with three other policemen, poor Bridget's substitute for the FBI. The policemen busied themselves with the measurement of the stairs and the picture frames, the snipping away of bits of carpet to be dipped in chemicals. Captain Donohue, a friend of the family to people like the Frobishers and Iredells, took Octavius' story.

"I think he fell," Octavius said.

"Like this, like this?" demanded Captain Donohue's son, who was learning the trade. He somersaulted down the stairs, rolled, tumbled, and did dangerous back flips until Eileen screamed in excitement.

Ann appeared from her room fully clothed and the police captain snapped his fingers to halt his son.

"I appreciate your care, Captain Donohue," she said firmly, "but I do not think it is necessary. My poor father slipped and fell."

"A strange accident, Miss Frobisher," Captain Donohue began. "He hit his head against the banister with a terrific force. He didn't just slip."

Ann sighed. "I'm afraid he was . . ."

She couldn't finish. Captain Donohue took her little hand in his great red ones.

"I'm sorry, miss. I understand the way you feel."

With families like hers there was much he had no right to know. She raised her eyes bravely.

"He would have wanted it this way."

The police captain bowed gravely and then they all tiptoed down the stairs and out the entrance. Bridget watched them go with chagrin on her round modern face, but a flashing glance from Ann told her that gentlefolk are accustomed to direct their affairs in a different way than the movies say, and she retreated to the pantry.

"You handled them magnificently, Ann," Octavius said.

"It's not something for outsiders to concern themselves with," she replied with dignity. "That is *your* duty. You have until midnight to find that man. And to kill him."

And with that she drew herself up straight and walked proudly to her room and locked the door behind her.

II

"Dead?"

"Quite."

"You sure?"

The man on the bed did not reply but his stare made the short fat man shift his weight restlessly.

"Honest, boss, someone's going to complain."

"We're dealing with gentlefolk, Leo. This isn't Kansas City.

"Even on Long Island you can't kill a man and not expect someone to do something about it."

The fat man's plaint rose and fell monotonously. The man on the bed closed his eyes.

"He fell." The supine figure glanced at his companion fidgeting while he sought courage to complain again. "When I want you to worry, I'll tell you."

The fat man gave up. "Okay, boss."

"Now I'd like to sleep a bit. We're due on the beach at eleven-thirty, there's the match coming up, and lots of things to be ready for. And I didn't get much rest last night."

"I'll bet you didn't," the fat man sniggered, trying to be friends again. The man on the bed was already asleep. Leo tiptoed out of the room and sank unhappily into an armchair. From his pocket he took a damp and stained bundle wrapped in a handkerchief, dainties foraged from last night's party: a squashed caviar sandwich, cheese puffs, a little pasty shell impaled on a wobbly stalk of asparagus, a strawberry tart, some chocolate peppermints, all wedged together. He picked them apart and began his breakfast. In Dallas they had eaten steaks as big as soup plates, and in Atlanta Leo had gobbled ten drumsticks in a row, reciting verses from Gilbert and Sullivan in between to hold attention while Don stole away with the hostess. But here the food wasn't anything special and the worries came in jumbo size.

It had been nice in New Orleans; the classic approach, Leo with the maid, Don upstairs with the mistress, champagne on both floors, a traditional evening ending with a sentimental kiss and no hard feelings or hasty exits. In San Francisco the track twisted—some college boy had fallen for Don, and Leo had to decoy him away and spend two hours discussing Baroque art so that Don could be alone with his sister—but at least they had eaten well. What salad bowls! And little fried shrimp with mustard sauce.

In Chattanooga they were revivalist ministers. Leo became dean of admissions at a Bible training college and had done pretty well himself with the homely sister who had flunked her exam on minor prophets and feared she'd never get anywhere now. In Wichita they introduced themselves as staff officers straight from Detroit. The boys at the truck assembly plant had involved themselves in funny bookkeeping, and their wives were touchingly anxious to smooth things over.

Don always wanted change. One evening Mother, two daughters, and the cook; next a rice pudding of a girl whom he saw as a challenge. Lady wrestlers, the alumnae picnic of the Vassar Club, the softball team they managed for a week, the spiritualist séance in Boston where Don entered as the spirit of Lord Byron—the past ran together in Leo's mind. He shared the surplus. He didn't mind. The homely sister is often jollier. There were tense moments also, split-second getaways, nervous dialogues with fathers and husbands: "No, you can't see him now, he's working on tomorrow's sermon." "He's kneeling beside his mother's grave." "He's having an epileptic fit." Money came in irregularly, but Don didn't worry. A widow in Tulsa had deeded him half-a-dozen oil wells. They drove a Cadillac because Don had made friends with the lady who ran the raffle. Now they were settled on Long Island for the summer because Don was curious about those leather-faced dames in their cashmere sweaters and wanted to raise his social standing. And already he had killed an irate father. He'd tell Leo when to start worrying. But when he did, Leo had better have some mighty good ideas on tap.

He finished the caviar and the chocolates and pushed himself out of his chair to hunt up a bottle of ginger ale before he turned in too for an hour of shut-eye, but looking out the window, he saw a woman peering around the hydrangea bushes, trying to see in the house without being noticed. Leo couldn't see her face, but the standing orders were, without exception—and you could underline that and write it in capitals—to report any female on the premises.

He opened the bedroom door. Don was immediately awake. "The Frobisher girl?"

"No, taller and heavier. Older."

Don sprang up and ran noiselessly down the stairs and stuck his head out a window. Sure enough, a woman wrapped in an evening cape, a white scarf loosely covering her face, was stepping stealthily through the grass.

"May I be of assistance to you?" he called in a cordial voice. She turned but the scarf still hid her identity. "Does that look like anyone we've known recently?" he whispered to Leo.

Leo's brain shuffled rapidly through the past twenty women.

"Can't place her."

"I'm looking for a Mr. Johns," came back the cultured, definite tones.

"Who shall I say is calling?" Don inquired, satisfied by the line of the hip.

"Just an old friend." The figure started up the path toward the road. "I may be by again."

"Not so cold and unfriendly now," laughed Don, leaping out the window. "Drop in for a little bite of breakfast. Do."

She turned and let the white veil fall. Don halted.

"Ah, Donald," the woman exclaimed. "How long I've been waiting to have a good talk with you."

"Elvira, what a pleasure to see you again," he said, re-gaining composure.

"I've read the most spiritual book by Norman Vincent Peale recently, and when I set it down I knew I had to see you and have a serious talk about changing your ways."

"You've got a generous heart, Elvira," he said with a winning smile.

"You still have your silver tongue, Donald." She shook her head sadly. "I've worried so much about you."

"That's awfully nice. Say, Leo," he called over his shoulder, "see if you can rustle us up a couple of sidecars."

The lady smiled.

"Really, Donald, you should learn some new routines. What does a sidecar mean—time for your riding lesson, or an appointment with your psychiatrist?"

"Ah, Elvira, we can't fool you can we?" and when Leo opened the front door and announced: "We're fresh out of Cointreau, boss, but there's a long-distance call from San Francisco on the upstairs phone," he was surprised by the laughter from both of the gentry.

"Come on in for breakfast, Elvira. Leo will whip us up one of his cheese omelets." He gave his arm to his ex-wife and conducted her inside. "You're looking just fine, my dear," he said, pouring her out a small glass of brandy. "That desert air does wonders for you."

"I've been living in Duluth, Donald. And I've had a lot of chance to think——.

"Those long winters are just grand for thinking." He filled and raised his own glass. "Cheers. Or na zdrowie, as the Polish farmers around here still like to say, a fine hardworking race, a credit to the land of opportunity."

He smiled carelessly at the earnest woman before him. That tea-rose pattern suited her vague perfume, the way her eyes wandered even when she was speaking most seriously, the shoulder straps peeping around her neckline.

"After I had finished that wonderful book, Donald, I came right down here. Then I saw you at the Tennis Club last night——"

"I suppose you've read Reinhold Niebuhr too. It's a provocative challenge he poses the modern liberal, who must find salvation outside the frame of historical development, and at the same time avoid using this awareness as an excuse for social passivity."

"The false pleasures you find in the life around you, Don-

ald," she began when he had finished, "are meaningless if
you think of the eternity that awaits your soul."

"I know." He nodded. "Neo-orthodoxy is trying to rein-
state hell. I have nothing against that at all."

"Don't play with me, Donald. You're still a young man.
You still have a chance to make a real change."

He took her hand.

"Elvira, if I had met you in time my whole life would have
been different. Beauty and moral fervor. I've never met another woman"—and he gave her hand a squeeze that brought
a strange look of confusion to her eyes—"and I've met too
many, I'm not proud of my life—but there's a spark burning
left by the one true woman I've known." The door from the
pantry opened and Leo stamped in with a covered dish on a
tray. "Here's our omelet, piping hot," Donald announced.
serving the lady. "Just a little more salt, please, I think, Leo
old man." He poured the coffee and pressed the toast upon
her. "Just like old times, eh? Leo's a wonderful cook."

Elvira sighed.

"We're chopping a little bit of green pepper in with the
cheese. now. That's something we picked up out in Frisco.
Have you ever tried a Popular Front? I met some old-fashioned Reds out there and they make a jam omelet for breakfast and pour vodka on it——"

The pantry door swung open again. Leo, his shoulders
slumped forward, two marks of soot on his forehead, sighed
heavily.

"Well?"

"Boss, that stove's shorted. Blew out. Zowie."

"Damnation! Fix it."

"You took the course in electronics, not me."

"Still the same lovable incompetent," he said to Elvira and
threw down his napkin. "I'll be back in a second, my dear."
He went up the back stairs to his room, lay himself on the
bed and immediately fell asleep.

"The mountain air makes you look younger and prettier than ever, Miss Elvira," said Leo.

III

Octavius stepped thoughtfully over the hot soft sand. Navy blue blazer and cultivated voice had proclaimed the attacker a gentleman, and almost all the gentlefolk appeared at the Beach Club between eleven and one.

As a little boy wearing a sunsuit and a floppy hat Octavius had come here every morning with his French nurse and dug in the sand with his bucket and his shovel. The young women he stepped past now with their unstrapped bathing suits held against their chests and their own chubby children digging soberly in the sand had been the little girls with whom he had erected great sprawling Arab tents out of the beach umbrellas and canvas chairs. They had married and become very thin and the beach sun gave them hard brown faces. "Good morning, Octavius," or "Hi, Tavy," they called him.

Between the bathhouse wings lay an oven-hot stretch of sand where it had always been the custom for adolescent girls to bake themselves and which he called the Market Place. They lay in rows, little paper cones protecting their noses, white ointment smeared over their cheekbones, elbows dug against their sides and palms turned out so that the inner sides of their arms would be browned, chattering and calling out, "Hi, Terry, hi, Larry," in surprised tones at the boys who came by, as if never in the world had they expected these cavaliers to appear at eleven o'clock each morning.

Octavius had never made the transition from Arab tents to Market Place. He had been unnerved by the jungle rivalries behind that friendliness, he lacked popular skills, and other things interested him more. After a time he found himself a stranger in his own town. Maxfield Iredell was the richest man of the community and Octavius was his only son, but the girls were too foolish to realize what a catch he was.

Now he was engaged to Ann Frobisher, partly because their
fathers had lived next to each other for thirty years, partly
because her astringent brown eyes that told men and women
alike exactly what she thought of them had caused her too
to fail in the Market Place.

Nevertheless, the beach was the source of much of his
poetic imagery: the sand castles he had never built strong
enough to stand against one incoming tide; the castles he
had built when the tide was going out, when the wisest
system of canals never brought the water back and the bat-
tlements dried and crumbled.

He inspected the poolside and then returned to the beach.
Beyond the mothers and children he spied the handsome
figure of Donald Johns, who had rented a house here two
weeks ago and could do everything. Last night he had danced
with Ann at the Tennis Club, and with him she had become
graceful and charming. Octavius moved slowly toward him.
The build was similar perhaps (though Octavius, sensitive to
the onion-skin gradations of the spirit—affability, philan-
thropy, anxiety and greed—was apt to be vague about ex-
ternals); maybe the hair too? Johns was laughing with Pam
Fairbrother, swollen up in her beach costume with seven
months of child. She had been one of the older girls he had
silently worshiped and with whom he used to people the
fantasy islands where their steamers foundered.

"Morning, Octavius. A bracing westerly breeze," Johns
greeted him. A towel slung over one shoulder gave a Greek
or Spanish touch to his naked chest.

"Good morning, Mr. Johns."

"Isn't it terrible about Commander Frobisher?" Pam said.

"Tell us what happened," the stranger demanded.

Octavius stared at the black eyes, at the mockery glinting
through the concern. Had the eyes been black?

"Octavius was there when it occurred," Pam explained.

"I came just afterward. It was hard for Ann to describe
the events clearly."

"The poor girl!"

"You can't expect a poet to be alert to practical details like policemen," Pam apologized for him.

"On the contrary, a poet with the insight of Octavius possesses the exact qualities of a detective."

"You've read my poems?" asked Octavius. He received praise from people who never read further than the first two lines, and yet he never quite lost hope. When they judged him in his own trade he was any man's equal.

"Of course. They are a part of the cultural furnishings— if I may use a poor word—of our time." Johns smiled warmly. "I know they are part of my own."

"Really?" He could not help himself. "Which one in particular?"

"I've forgotten the name, but the lines I know. Often, often I've gone back to them when I've felt walled in by the vulgarities of contemporary journalism."

Eyes shut, he paused, then raised his hand and began to chant:

> The reticent carrot buries its gold—
> > Montezuma, why are you weeping?—
> > in the sullen earth.
> Nanny wheels the go-cart, but she forgot the spade,
> > > forgot the spade.
> Slim hieratic princess borne by youth's pulpy pleasure
> > in formal ceremonial sunburn oil.
> Laughter falls from the lion-headed fountain—
> > Laughter
> > Laughter
> > Tears?

Octavius breathed deeply.

"Is that the way it goes? I'd give everything to hear you read it yourself, but those lines I've tried to store away."

Without a word Octavius bowed to the stranger and walked away. The beach umbrellas exploded out of the glaring sand like pinwheels. Black as Spanish grandees marched the chauffeurs behind the solemn children going home for lunch.

"My God, Donald, have you actually read his poems?" Pam demanded.

"Of course not. They all write the same thing."

"Oh, Don, you're a dangerous man!" She shook her finger at him. "If I didn't have my little chaperone along . . ." She patted her swollen front.

"Don't lull yourself into false security, provoking girl," he exclaimed gallantly.

She laughed again and said good-bye—her legs were killing her—and he continued his stroll. His cleverness left a warm curve upon his lips. And he had not been merely flattering Pam Fairbrother. A pregnant woman shines with musky femininity, timeless, freed of personality and fashion. She brings with her memories of the teeming cities of sun-drenched Sumeria and the strange snake goddess of Khmer. Besides, she is touchingly grateful for attention.

Johns stopped to watch a little girl of six or seven who was digging in the sand with a slightly younger boy. He scooped out the wet sand at the bottom of their hole for her to pile and pat together into a tower. She demanded his shovel to smooth its top. He wouldn't give it up, so she grabbed it. He hit her, she cried, the nurse confiscated the shovel and banished the boy. Now the girl needed him no longer. First he threw sand at her. Then he went away and returned with some shells taken from another child's castle. Still she wasn't interested, and he kicked the sand foundation.

Johns smiled at this early victory of the feminine. For those with eyes to see, the world was a rich place.

He came to the Market Place. "Hi, Mr. Johns, hi, Don," the immature voices piped. Immediately half the girls sat up and covered themselves while the other half stretched their limbs out further upon the hot sand and twisted beneath his eyes. His smile broadened. It amused him to observe to what extremes jealousy and desire might impel this pack of unconscious little animals. Not womanhood at its most charming, yet this seedbed was the future, an intimation of nature always changing and always the same, like the moon which waxes and wanes with woman's rhythm.

"That's a flattering bathing suit indeed, Cheryl," he complimented the plainest of the girls, "though I hardly think you need its help." Cheryl writhed under the unfamiliarity of the praise. "How did you acquire such a beautiful shade of brown?" Cheryl appeared to have stopped breathing. The other girls' smiles tightened like scars. "Will you be coming to the match this afternoon?" The tortured girl to Cheryl's left lifted an arm in protest, but he had eyes only for his wordless nymph. "Cross your fingers for luck for me, will. you? Don't forget," and he bent down and patted her foot while a sob strangled in the throat of the blonde on her right, pretty and naked as a magazine cover.

He left his little laboratory. He did not blame them in any way. He accepted them as the sea accepts the rivers. They knew it, even these unripe girls; they knew it even when they screamed and cursed at him—a woman not seen in anger is a book half read—for no other man could love them as he did. Will, force, conviction, in a world of the timid and stale who repeat to each other what they read in magazines. He did not ask that people like him. His was not a personality like warm wet soap that will accept every thumbmark.

Suddenly he halted. Coming down the boardwalk was Zerlina Floris, to ordinary eyes a pretty young woman carrying a rubber surf mattress but for him a flame of strange, gallant, pathetic beauty that seared his heart.

"Ah, Zerlina," he sighed, grasping her hand before a dozen pairs of angry eyes at the Market Place. "I've been waiting in misery all morning for you."

"Donald, how can you possibly expect me to believe a word you say?" she laughed, and her laugh reaffirmed the whole heartbreaking intensity of her beauty.

For what is life's one enemy but time and what is time's one check but beauty? In the luna moth slipping across the swamp, the lady's slipper, the hummingbird, life says that time has no meaning. Tomorrow's death cannot debase the golden coinage of today.

"Zerlina, your beauty makes you heartless."

"My beauty has made me wise, Donald."

"You waste it upon those who cannot possibly know its value."

No one else knew the pinnacle to which life had raised her, nor how short a while time would leave her there. Tomorrow her gardenia thighs would show their first pulpy blemish. His hand trembled as he put it on her waist. The eyes at the Market Place turned to little green slits.

"Masetto will be cross, you unprincipled man. And about five hundred people will be made very curious," she said, lightly removing his fingers.

"I see the sun where Phoebus drives his team across the heavens' zenith, the sea where Triton rises to blow his conch, and the sand where Venus has thrown her used-up diamonds. I see those and I see you," he crooned into her ear. "Nothing more."

"The cautions of my rational mind are blurred by your teasing words," she murmured dreamily.

"Reason's first duty is to teach us which harmonies are fitting to our own spirits, and yours, dear girl, are lyric, not didactic."

Gently he led her along the row of half-open beach pavilions.

"My feet are no longer headed toward the foaming surf," she observed.

"Your feet fall upon the sand as softly as blossoms from a plum tree."

They reached his own cabin and he thrust back the curtain shading its porch. She stopped in indecision.

"I may have seriously compromised myself. My fiance is to play you this afternoon for the finals of the tennis tournament."

His laugh gurgled like a mountain waterfall.

"Let us drink to his good fortune."

From an ice bucket in the corner of the pavilion he drew a small bottle of champagne. Bemused, she watched his fingers fluttering over the crimson foil, and the wire, and then the slow irresistible force of his thumbs as they forced out the cork.

"Pop! Like childish fears when the sun comes from behind the clouds. Bubble! Like the laughter of golden girls."

She giggled despite herself. He drew the striped curtain to shield them from the glare.

"To Masetto's good fortune," he whispered, and their eyes met through the bubbles springing from the champagne.

Then the curtain was rudely flung back and there stood Elvira Johns in pastel-colored beach outfit, carrying a large rubber ball, while behind her whispered and giggled the entire seraglio from the Market Place.

"I'm so glad to find you, Donald," she exclaimed. "These youngsters say you promised to play ball with them. That was awfully generous. Put your glass down now and come along." And as her ex-husband emerged blinking into the rapidly formed circle of oily, sandy adolescents, Elvira turned to Zerlina and with her most winning smile said: "Would you care to join us, young lady?"

IV

The Tennis Club bleachers were full. Among the madras shorts and garish Italian trousers there were enough white flannels and blue blazers, flowered chiffon afternoon dresses and picture hats, for the older generation to look at the crowd and reflect that here, at least, nothing had changed. Octavius and Ann arrived after the match had begun. To reach their places was a painful process for everyone must seize her hand and murmur, "What a terrible blow, Ann dear," followed by, "I'm sure he would have wanted it this way." The club flag was flying at half mast, and that this tragedy should have occurred on the last day of the tournament, with Commander Frobisher's spirit presumably looking down upon the final match between Donald Johns and Masetto, the young visitor from Tulsa, gave a solemn air to the afternoon. If his daughter attended as her father's representative, bearing witness to the whole tradition of sportsmanship, it was the duty of all the rest to be no less brave.

Octavius and Ann took their seats, in a corner where they could see the largest number of people. In fact a large number presented themselves to pay condolences, including young men who had suddenly realized that Ann was heiress to a large fortune, which should not be wasted on a man as wealthy and as unexciting as Octavius Iredell.

The first set was in its seventh game, the younger player clearly winning. His rifled serves and volleys hurtled the net so furiously that Johns had almost to dodge them. Masetto charged about his court like a bullock, exulting in his youth and strength, and showing by flashes of a scornful smile— whenever sportsmanship permitted it to appear—what he thought of this overrated old man. The second set went on in the same way. Johns picked up a few points only when a smashing volley seemed to bounce off his racket back over the net and die before the bullock force could adapt itself to this puny shot.

Masetto was sweating coarsely by the third set, but the healthy grins he threw to his friends in the bleachers expressed his will to finish off his despised opponent. With furious energy he won four straight games. Oddly, however, one could suddenly almost see Johns pick up strength. The smile on his lips did not change, but every ball sent over by the slightly flagging enemy found him in the right place, and he shot them back with geometrical precision. Masetto, mag-

nificent in victory, appeared frantic under pressure. Even a
terrific spurt at the end of the set did not win it for him.

The fourth set was long spoken of at the club; aging
players who saw themselves defeated by their sons and junior
partners invited down for the weekend dreamed of duplicat-
ing it. Johns was merciless. Grim as a samurai, he chopped
the ball with such a spin that it bounced back toward the
net or merely whirled on the ground like a top. At the net,
ten feet high it seemed, he spun like a Catherine wheel, or
stood with his back to Masetto and simply flicked out his
racket, or with the mannered grace of a temple dancer gently
returned the wild balls to the one spot where Masetto was
not. Again the simile of a bullock fit Masetto, for his bulging
eyes and lolling tongue, the sway of his thick neck as he ran
led those spectators who had gone to Madrid to buy gab-
ardines and needlepoint rugs to exchange whispered com-
parisons to the dreadful end of a bullfight.

Finally, when Masetto had strained to retrieve a volley
into a corner, alarming white splotches appearing along his
jowls, Johns lightly tossed his racquet from right hand to left
and lightly tapped the ball over the net, where it rolled
between Masetto's feet. A ripple of laughter came from the
ladies, and the aristocratic figure, racquet still in his left hand
and his right resting upon his hip, pivoted to the applause
as a geranium turns toward the sun.

"That's he."

"Are you sure?" Octavius whispered back, although he
had reached the same conviction that it could be no one else.

She did not reply. Her hands clenched together as her eyes
followed every movement of her attacker, now humiliating
the helpless Masetto further with easy shots that he couldn't
possibly miss, reviving his hope, and then as soon as he had
recovered a little, racing him raggedly about the court again.
Octavius didn't know if he felt sorry for him. The Masettos
of the world had always cut him the most painful wounds.

"You have until midnight," Ann repeated. Though Octavius had been raised in an environment where laughter was the retort to melodrama, he could not afford, after glancing at Ann's face, to take her words lightly. Suicide he had planned a hundred times, murder never. The simplest method, to return home for his father's pistol and then to go and shoot Johns in the middle of a crowded room, had the merit of closing once and for all the question of what he should do with his life. He wished he could be sure of that, and of no courtroom, no dealings with practical people— and no prison, worse even than prep school.

The match ended. Ladies hastened out on the court, ahead of the club officials with the silver cup, to congratulate the victor. As Ann and Octavius walked silently along the porch of the club house, an imposing woman in her late thirties, in gray chiffon, with effusive face, hastened toward them and they stopped, set to receive one more commiseration for brave suffering.

"My dear, you're poor Ann Frobisher, are you not?" she demanded, her eyes shifting from one face to the other. "I'm Elvira Johns, Donald's first wife," she hurried on. "I couldn't be expected to know all the details and indeed perhaps I shouldn't, but I have an intimation that my unprincipled ex-husband may have been involved in your misfortune." She took their silence for agreement. "Donald is giving a victory party this afternoon—how like him to assume he would win—but the real purpose of it is his designs on that Zerlina girl. People don't take those things seriously any more, but I don't think it's right when she's already the fiancée of poor Mr. Masetto."

"I can't work up much sympathy for Zerlina," Octavius remarked.

"A feather-headed little thing, I'll grant you that, but it's time we tried to halt him. You two are serious, principled young people, and I thought you might be willing to help me."

"We might," said Ann thoughtfully.

V

The glasses paraded across the table like an old-fashioned regiment in full dress. Proudly Leo reviewed the shining columns. Like an old general, he was stirred by their bright, icicle glitter and by awareness of the service they would perform. He looked forward with relish to a war in which he was confident of his supplies, the bowls of jewellike cherries and pearl onions and sullen olives, the bottles in the icebox, the tun of coal-black caviar. Caviar must be fresh; Leo tested it with a large spoon. He shut his eyes and for a moment he did not even chew, relishing the cold opulence against the backs of his teeth and the roof of his mouth. In black silence the heavy taste imbedded itself in his tongue and crept up into his nasal passages and out to the tips of his fingers. The day's worries slipped from him.

Like a roll on a kettledrum came footsteps along the hallway. Leo jerked his hand away from the cracker plate and stood at attention. Don strode into the room, beating his hands together to some silent tune that rushed through his brain. The silver hair at his temples was brushed into wild little horns, and the excitement and vigor of his body throbbed through the dark red raw silk of his jacket.

"Is the caviar absolutely fresh, Leo? Is there enough vermouth? Look at the petal on the orange gladiolus," he warned, marching in front of the table.

The commands were not necessary. Leo never forgot. He had left the wilted petal on the orange gladiolus expressly to please his master's keenness.

"And the refreshments in the other rooms?"

A little to eat, a little to drink had been placed in every room so that guests would freely wander about the big hospitable house.

"Remember the party in Phoenix when we were talent scouts for that Las Vegas nightclub? You suggested the girls would dance better with their dresses off. Remember?" Leo suggested, brightening his master with the lamp of reminiscence.

"Leo," cried Johns, "all over Long Island pretty women are changing from afternoon dresses to cocktail gowns, bending and twisting as they slip them on, wrinkling up their pretty noses when the zipper sticks. Leo, I know every one of their little mysteries—the touch of perfume behind each ear, the final look to see if their stocking seams are straight— put them all together and the word is magic and I'm as breathless now as I was a boy of thirteen. We did have a time in Phoenix. That was six years ago and now a whole new generation of girls has grown up and is waiting for us back there. The world is turning, turning, turning, and we turn and whirl unceasingly with it."

He spun in a pair of waltz steps and snapped his fingers in the air.

"We're growing older too, boss," Leo burst out before he even knew he had opened his mouth. The great black eyebrows rushed together like storm clouds.

"Leo, there'll be twenty women here this afternoon I've never met before and each one entirely different from all the others."

"Yes, boss."

"Zerlina will be here, inflamed by our disappointment of this morning, guilty and nervous, and if you'll just keep Masetto occupied——"

"Masetto's a clod!"

"Promise him a job. Fix him up a place in the Paris office. But keep the drinks pouring out, keep the music going, get 'em laughing and arguing, get 'em all worked up: the elections, racial equality, religion in the modern world. Roil 'em all up."

During this declamation a short, smiling violinist entered the room from the far side, followed by three waiters in scarlet coats, and the four paraded measuredly up to their employer. The waiters' faces had been rubbed smooth as the stones of the sea. The musician was more clearly a human being, though decades of fiddle playing had left his neck warped permanently to one side. His smile shoved out at the same angle and so did his walk, which proceeded like a crab's.

"Good afternoon, sir," he announced in a thick Danubian accent, bowing a bit crookedly until his violin almost touched the floor. "It's time."

"Zehul, good afternoon indeed! I'm relying upon you!"

"Standard progression?"

"Stricter than ever." He held up a finger: "One?"

"Conformity. Gems from *Brigadoon*."

"Two?"

"Intellectual distinction. Bach?"

"No, Bartok. This is no ordinary cocktail party, they are not ordinary people." He held up three fingers.

"Sentiment. Gypsy tunes."

"The heart. Make them cry, make them yearn for the unattainable. Four?"

Zahul's wide grin widened further. "Frenzy."

"The ultimate."

The musician bowed again. The doorbell rang. The party had begun.

The first guest was Veronica Hamish, who had also been the first out on the court after the match. Zahul played "My Wild Irish Rose." Nothing could have been more correct. Don turned away toward newer arrivals, warmed up rapidly by the scarlet-coated waiters who moved about like flames, but he had not forgotten her. "Fill her up," he murmured to a stone-smooth waiter. Sunshine, good health and clothes and idleness had given Veronica a passive, impersonal appearance, like a tastefully decorated hotel room. She wore her white linen dress with the pale blue cashmere sweater thrown over her shoulders like a uniform. For twenty years she had been satisfied to eat from the same dish but now she wanted sharper seasoning. Don glanced at his watch. Twenty minutes.

A lilting voice sounded behind him and Don swung around gaily to clasp Lorraine Tillotson, unobtrusively holding out two fingers to Zahul. Without seeming to move his feet Zahul drew near them and shifted from "Old Man River" to a tuneless serenade by Bartok. Lorraine was a tall broad-shouldered woman whose intelligence had made her miserable in this pretty town. She had a habit of stooping so as not to stand taller than other women. With his eyes he sought to draw her straight and set her shoulders proudly back.

The two Hillary sisters, whom he had neglected this morning at the Market Place, drifted up, thin and refreshing as salads.

"No, my dears," he scolded gently, replacing the cokes they held with martinis. They looked timidly at the gin, but his bow of absolute courtesy assumed that they were masters of the situation and very mature. Perhaps their mother would allow his invitation to a picnic Wednesday if their cousin Eric went along, a sleepy youth who was crazy about tokay after a heavy lunch. Foolish mother and the girls themselves would trust in numbers, when numbers—with the simplest gambit out of the eighteenth century; which of you two lovely girls has prettier thighs?—could be a positive advantage. Three fingers held out surreptitiously and Zabul's violin became a gypsy's fiddle, weaving a sugary, moaning Polish waltz. Phase three. He winked and each sister thought the rakish look was for her alone.

Still no sign of Zerlina. He checked his watch and turned to Veronica Hamish. A glow spread over her face as he pressed her hand. No explanation, no apology, the pressure upon her hand told her anything she wanted to believe.

"Oh, Donald, you have such a charming house! Wherever did you find one as lovely as this?"

Her glass jiggled a bit. He gazed into her moist eyes.

"It's very amusing. Why, only yesterday, I found a tiny door in the cupboard of the upstairs bathroom that opens right on the stairway to my study."

"That sounds awfully quaint."

He looked deep into her eyes and squeezed her hand so hard this time that he knew it hurt. A flash of a smile and he was gone.

Now he addressed himself to Mabel Thurston, avoided by other men for her slack limbs and torpid spirit. Back and forth they handed soft phrases while his imagination offered him Veronica, so brown and, where the sun didn't reach, so white, as if she wore a droll sort of harlequin suit. Five minutes passed. With a formality resting upon infinite leisure he took a wordy farewell of sweet flattered Mrs. Thurston and ran upstairs.

Five minutes more and he strolled back down. The party was roaring like a zoo. He saw the smoky faces of Ann Frobisher and her poet fixed upon him. Was that Elvira with them? That put pepper in the soup.

But then in the doorway appeared the sweet shape of the woman he had been waiting for. Tomorrow, light as a spider's thread, the first line would etch itself upon Zerlina's throat. For her today would never return. He hastened to her side.

"That was certainly handsome of you to come, old man," he exclaimed sincerely as he grasped Masetto's hand. "You don't know how much it means to me."

"Sorry we're late."

They had been quarreling. Her eyes sparkled, his were surly—she had won. In fact she was still breathing heavily, and the swell of her flower-soft bosom left Donald near to swooning.

"How about some caviar, old man?"

That set them moving to the refreshment table where Veronica was placidly chewing from sandwiches held in both hands, and movement might divert Masetto. Don had built

up a number of collections for just such purpose: German
model railroads, Persian miniatures, an old illustrated edition
of the Decameron. Match a man with the right attraction
and he would be safe for an hour. But what might interest
Masetto he did not know, and this movement had pocketed
Zerlina with a crop-haired youngster from Yale still carrying
a tennis racquet who was refilling her glass and making her
laugh at his stupid jokes. If Donald was that careless Masetto
had no reason at all to be jealous.

"You'll be staying in New York for some time?" Donald
asked while they both watched the animated Yale student.

"I oughta be gettin' back to Tulsa," Masetto grumbled,
defending himself against these Easterners.

"You'll enjoy that. I can see your job means a lot to you."
Their eyes flickered irritatedly over each other and over
the seething swarm. Ann came back into view in her black-
trimmed cocktail dress.

"It ain't so damn much. I'm in an investment company,
but all the good jobs are filled by a bunch of chair warmers."

"It's not what you know, it's who you know, is that it?
That's the way of the world." Donald sighed too. "What is
your speciality?"

"I wrote a thesis on dollar convertibility. Isn't that a hell
of a subject?"

"Young man, you don't belong in Tulsa," Donald stated.
Leo had just put his arm about Mabel Thurston's shapeless
waist, but his master's eyebrows recalled him to duty. "Leo,
I think I've found the man we've been hunting for. This is
my associate, Mr. Porello," he explained. "He handles all
our European relations. I rely on his judgement absolutely."

Leo and the younger man looked at each other with distrust.

"Leo, Radiquet is being transferred to Vienna next month.
isn't he?"

"Yes, sir."

"That just leaves old Cunigonde in Paris."

"Looks that way."

"Maybe we're in luck. Masetto here is an authority on international currency. He may be tied up under a stiff contract but you try and make him change his mind."

Donald flung an arm briefly over Masetto's shoulders. "You just don't know how hard it is to find qualified executive personnel. A bunch of fast-talking Yale men who never did a day's work in their lives. Leo, treat him carefully!" And he laughed and vanished.

Leo shifted a bit so that the other's back was turned to Zerlina and began stolidly: "Paris is a very significant city . . ."

Don circled quickly around the edge of the room, flashing four fingers at Zahul, who sprang from the quavering minor, the methodically maudlin, to the frenzied. He shoved his fiddle against his chest and whipped the bow back and forth: csardas, hora, kolo, trepak, all the booted oafishness of Wallachia and the Bukowina whirled out from his fiddle, rhythms these gentry were not used to, and there would be gin spilt and blouses torn, but Mr. Johns, when he was pleased, paid far above the scale of the musicians' union. For a moment Donald studied the twitching of his guests' slack shoulders. Then he made his way swiftly to Zerlina, stepped on her immature escort's foot, and while he was objecting, put his arm about her waist and led her to a corner of the room.

"But isn't Paris awfully expensive?" Octavius caught the shout above the screech of the violin.

"At the salary you'd be making——" was all that came to his ears for the guests were beginning to stamp their feet and to bang their fists on the table tops.

Ann was drinking tomato juice. It was the first time Octavius had ever been cold sober at a cocktail party. The bellowing and smoke transformed the room into a branding corral at roundup or a Congo village at full moon as the merrymakers trembled together belly to belly. Zahul had stuck a foot up on one of the chairs and was jerking his bow wildly across his violin. The woman next to Octavius was tossing her head in happy imbecility, carried back to girlhood days at the mouth of the Danube. One by one her hairpins emerged like worms and dropped upon the carpet.

"See her now?" Ann asked him.

"You could lose an Alaska grizzly in this room," Octavius shouted crossly. Zerlina had been caught up in Johns' last parabola, and to make a stand on Zerlina's virtue, as that foolish Mrs. Johns had persuaded Ann, was batting at a sticky wicket.

"Find out where he's taken her."

"Where are the snows of yesteryear?"

"But is Paree like what they say it's like?" the flat voice ground its way mercilessly over the cries and mumblings about it.

"Young man," groaned Leo, clinging to Masetto's coat collar with the doggedness of the Dutch boy at the dike. "You may have seen shows in Tulsa but the shows there——"

He never finished. Zahul was concluding a Moldavian hora with a wild succession of arpeggios. For a split second he paused before touching that highest note. The note was reached, not by him, but by a piercing scream. All noise ceased. Octavius leapt to a door leading off the living room and threw it open, to reveal a disheveled Zerlina in the act of tearing herself free from her host.

"Monster!" she shrieked.

Johns' senseless face stared at them.

"You've shown again your complete lack of moral control!" cried the tremulous contralto of his ex-wife.

Zerlina had freed herself and tottered to Octavius' protection, but Donald seized the poet's arm and would have broken it into kindling had not the burly figure of Masetto interposed itself.

"How dare you lay hands on my girl!"

The crowd muttered and Zahul, forgetting whose interests

he was supposed to serve, accentuated the ugly mood by fiddling low storm music. Donald drew himself up haughtily.

"Yapping curs!" he threw at them. The mob blinked its bloodshot eyes. "Ha ha, to force this girl you'd have to act swifter than an old man like me."

The Yale man shook his tennis racquet. Then Veronica Hamish silenced the nagging little voices inside of her by sailing a crystal ashtray through the air. It dug a gash into the wall twenty feet away from Johns, but there were a lot of those ashtrays, razor sharp, heavy as manhole covers. A dozen people could have been slain if the wobbly individuals who grabbed for them had let fly.

But Leo kept his head. He jumped on a chair.

"Hey Ludwig," he shouted, "where's that other case of caviar?" The mob turned its head. "Where you been keeping that champagne?" he shouted at the waiters. Unsure of themselves, a couple of men set down their ashtrays. Two shots rang out, half the women in the room let out screams—but it was Leo, who ran past, foaming bottles held high for all to see.

"Champagne out on the lawn, folks! Ludwig, get a move on with that caviar!"

A couple of ashtrays, a couple of oaths still flew through the air. But already Zahul had begun a rhumba and Veronica Hamish was shaking her bracelets like maracas. Donald stood with his arms folded across his chest and did not stir.

"You'll never set foot in the Tennis Club again!" old Conrad Cumberland bellowed from the doorway.

"The swimming pool is closed to you too, sir!" Mr. Van Torley cried.

He did not stir. Leo carried the champagne far out on the lawn and farther, and then the guests decided to go home and spun their cars through the bushes and cracked the fenders into the elm trees at the other side of the road. Leo saw the last go before he returned to the house. For a moment he thought his master had fled until he saw the feet sticking out at the end of a great armchair by the fireplace and the hand holding the empty wine glass.

"Boss, that was some close shave."

The only reply was a dry click as the stem snapped in two.

VI

Leo swept up the broken glass and righted the vases, picked up the cigarette butts from the rug, while Donald slumped in front of the fireplace. He had tried to free her for love. He had tried to cleanse her spirit of half a decade of nastiness in parked cars, but something had gone wrong. Some nuance of emotion had soured and that flirt had been allowed to recollect her code of partial virtue. His judgment had failed: he had made his move half a minute before he should—that damned fiddler had confused him. He had made a mistake.

"We all make mistakes, boss. That's why they put erasers on pencils," Leo had attempted. "Maybe it's a warning, boss. Maybe it's time to change. You could go into the ministry. They make lots of dough. Buy a ranch. Settle down. We'll blow this burg. Them skinny women aren't your type. Let's go back to New Orleans. We were happy there."

Donald held up his hand and the faithful servant fell silent. He took the glasses and plates out to the kitchen and began to wash up. The room was completely dark when he had finished, but his master was still sitting in the chair. Leo made a fire. The flames darted up and threw the deep eyes into blacker shadow. Leo returned with one of his master's favorite cheese omelets and a glass of Armagnac. Timidly he looked for a sign of life. Not a glance or a motion of the hand. Only as Leo tiptoed out of the room once more did he hear a heartbreaking sigh.

An hour later glass and omelet stood untouched.

"Remember when we were traveling for the Ford Foundation and interviewing those Wellesley girls? Remember the

Democratic picnic in Columbus?" Leo whispered. "Tomorrow we'll leave this town and we'll make ourselves a new life. Why don't you go to that dance after all? Show them they're all wrong if they think they got you on your back. I bet Zerlina is eating her heart out."

And gradually Leo's words insinuated themselves into his heart and kindled there a little of the old blaze. He left the living room—observed by Octavius, standing irresolutely in the underbrush with his father's automatic in his pocket. Half an hour later Donald stepped into his huge convertible and was driven by Leo over to the Beach Club.

A hundred Japanese lanterns outlined the loggias and the brick walls and towers. It was a fancy dress ball to mark the season's end, and though a few provincials had put on bunny costumes and clown suits, the gentry wore evening clothes and eye masks and perhaps a feather to indicate an Indian princess or a scarlet ribbon across the chest for the Prince of Monaco. Donald's great height and patrician bearing, the faultless tailcoat when most of the men were indulging the slackness of white jackets ironclad his refusal to admit any possible fuss about his right to go where he pleased. The guards admitted him without a word. The guests who recognized him despite the small mask—who else would apppear in such black pride?—marveled at his presumption, but buzzed impotently. Shouldn't the committee do something?

They shrank back as he came up the steps. He ignored old conquests like Veronica Hamish, who thought with terror and thrill that he had come to reclaim her, and even Zerlina, who was drinking punch in the corner. The orchestra was playing a Vienna waltz. Ottilie Rathbone, the most beautiful, refined, and wealthy woman of the South Shore, clutched grotesquely in her husband's pudgy arms, was pushed soggily around the floor. Donald touched Rathbone's shoulder and without a word removed Ottilie from his unworthy arms. I should stop it, I should have him forcefully removed, I should call the police, Rathbone groaned to himself, but some quality of objective respect, stronger than mere morality, held him like everybody else silent as the evil man spun around the floor with his prize. His tails whirled like scythes. Swan-necked Ottilie Rathbone, for the first time in her life held by a man worthy of her, resolved not to think. Eventually the dance would end. Then steps would be taken to adjust the situation, but now she was a part of the music, swaying and twirling to the poor "Blue Danube," this evening stripped of all staleness of beer gardens and ferry boats and revealed in the pure spirit of elegance, of gaity, and of the haunting melancholy that comes as we observe all beauty and know that it will pass. The orchestra leader, who had studied the Mendelssohn concerto at fourteen and realized at sixteen that it did not pay, cleansed himself of twenty years of compromise, and crooned at his musicians to play as they had never played before. A whirlwind at the coda and Donald clicked his heels to Ottilie and again to her anxious husband, and strode haughtily from the floor.

Even Octavius, his fingers clutching the hard ugly object in his pocket, felt himself lower middle class because he was venturing to cause trouble. It was already past eleven. Ann had raised her eyes significantly to the clock, whose servant he had become. Wearily he headed toward the archway where Johns had disapppeared.

To dance with the most unapproachable woman of all had shown the invincibility of Donald's spirit before those sheep. He could depart, victor again. He and Leo would travel to some humbler place and perhaps after all it might be time to take up a trade—he had always been attracted by the ministry—and marry some worthy girl and raise a family. But the plaudits had come too easily, the servility of that pack had been too evident. Why should he not humiliate them in his usual fashion, and prance like Pan between the heiresses and the hatcheck girl until at dawn he should hold unscathed Ottilie Rathbone herself? Then they would not forget him. Zerlina could be picked up too on the way.

Out on the moonlit boardwalk along the beach came the rustle of immature giggling from the couches and covered chairs. Irritably he considered packing off this callow venery, but he had more serious matters on his mind. Just inside the entrance he ran into Lorraine Tillotson.

He looked down at her, into her eyes behind the red sequin mask, at the mouth which could do other things than talk, and at her brown shoulders merrily freckled. The currents of the life force swirled murkily around them. The shimmer of his eyes showed her that he was not implacable and he observed how that bare bosom began to rise and fall perceptibly, the ordinary little smile faded from the lips, which opened against her will.

He counted five. Then he raised his hand and with languid helplessness she dropped her own into it. He turned to lead her out to the beach when who should turn up, to his disgust, but the poet.

"Run along, you wretched puppy," Donald snapped. Lorraine moaned.

"My apologies to you and Mrs. Tillotson for his interruption," Octavius said with heavy sarcasm, but then he didn't seem to know what to do next. He was afraid of his adversary, but not afraid enough to run away, and he showed his crooked, chalky teeth in a pointless grin. Donald grabbed him by the shoulder and shook him.

A swish of chiffon from the boardwalk announced the arrival of Elvira and Ann. What could he have possibly seen in that girl? And some grotesque dwarf wrapped to the eyes in sheets and bathtowels popped into the entranceway and popped out again. A damnable clutter.

"The posse had pulled up, has it?" he tried to address them debonairly. "A good psychoanalyst might help free you folks from these compulsions."

Ann looked at her fiancé. "Well?"

Wisdom said to leave. Luck was running out. But around the corner the face of the ladies' cloakroom girl suddenly stopped him. It was a pale, tough little face, unsoftened by education. She smiled as he went by and his troubled heart became free.

"What's your name, my little beauty?"

"Clothilde, monsieur."

He heard the click of high-heeled shoes coming down the stairs, the noise Elvira made, always in a hurry and trying to step firmly so she wouldn't trip, holding up her skirt and peering nearsightedly at the steps and the people she met.

There beside her dullard stood Zerlina, and again he thought of a gardenia, soft and velvety, ripe and swelling. God would cast her aside, but he had made her beautiful for a moment.

"If I found him again I'd crumple that stuck-up face like an accordian." Masetto was threatening in his peasant accent, chewing up the syllables like potatoes. Then the little round eyes focused on the figure in the tailcoat and the words ceased coming out of the purple face.

"Zerlina, what a beautiful gown you chose tonight." Donald bowed. "Come, I have important things to tell you," and he took her hand.

"Hey," bellowed Masetto. "Whoodya think——"

Donald laid his hand upon the angry chest and glared into the hot confused eyes, and Masetto stood with mouth open as Donald left the bar.

"Say, big boy, this is going a bit far," she gasped as they ran up the stairs.

"It is no time for words."

"You must think you own me," she complained, excited despite herself.

"I do. Despite everything, tonight you belong to me and to no one else."

"Gosh!"

His hands held her by her arms and slipped over her shoulders and up her beautiful plump neck and the sides of her cheeks. He held her face so he might kiss it and then ran his hands through her hair till her head was forced back and he kissed her again on the lips.

"I'm telling you," she murmured, "Masetto's going to be mighty sore."

"Agh!" he cried angrily, jerking her head back by the hair and kissing the plump brown throat. Let her be his once and then break her neck. He pulled her to him. All the soft swelling of life was pressed against him. Her face opened like a flower beneath his lips.

"I'll be damned! The dog returns to its vomit."

The poet again, his thin unhappy face blotchy with passion, stood in the doorway. Donald dug his fingers into the soft back as he pulled the helpless girl away.

"I've listened to my last stale literary quotation."

"It's not literature that concerns us, it's death," and Octavius tugged from his pocket a monstrous automatic.

Donald looked at the gun and the exalted face. Hurl Zerlina against the gun and death would be her lover, the only rival he would bow to. He saw the shocking beauty of blood against that white gown.

"Ha!" he spat. He raised his fists in protest. Zerlina was grabbed from his side, and he saw his ex-wife, her hair mussed and her shoulder straps twisted, who had pulled the girl from him.

"The police are on their way and whether they will find you dead or alive, I couldn't say," exclaimed the poet.

The bouncing rhythms of a samba came from the ballroom.

"Don't waste time, Octavius," commanded Ann.

But that same little Arab in sheets and bathtowels slipped between the figures of the crowd, struck the pistol out of Octavius' hand and then whirled through the door to the beach. Donald sprang lightly across the intervening space,

slapped Octavius' face with the back of his hand, tripped up
Masetto, then cleared the steps in one leap. Around the
corner the French cloakroom girl leaned her elbows wearily
against the counter. Her face brightened as she saw him and
she did not seem startled as he vaulted over her counter.

"Ah, Clothilde," he whispered in her ear, "how tiresome
these rich American women become." He kissed her and
squatted down behind the partition as pursuers' feet clattered
along the corridor.

"Which way did he go? Did you see him go by?" Donald
slipped his hand under Clothilde's skirt and caressed the
smooth hard inside of her knee.

"Up those stairs, monsieur! You'll catch him if you hurry."
His hand passed down over the swelling calf. The little
foot kicked him gently.

It is wisdom to recognize the humble exterior that true
wealth wears. He shut his eyes and let his hand climb like a
gentle vine up that smooth firm trunk.

"Are you planning to spend the night here?" the cool voice
sounded. He gave her a little squeeze. "That's very delightful
but now I am on duty."

As he started to rise she placed her hand on his head.

"No, madame, I have none now but my assistant will bring
a new package in five minutes. Thank you, madame." The
footsteps went away. "Okay, now leave. Go through the
pantry—they'll all be drunk—and up the back stairs to the
manager's room. The door's unlocked. When they stop looking you can climb out the window.

"And where shall I find you, Clothilde?" he whispered.

"I don't go very far. But now, vite, vite—they'll be back
again."

He kissed the little lips and vaulted back over the barrier.
She fluttered her fingers in farewell. He slipped through the
service door. A cook in a soiled undershirt was giving the
finishing shapes to an ice-cream mold with his thumb, licking
it to keep it warm. A couple of assistants were playing cards.

No one noticed him. He climbed the stairs and went through a door marked PRIVATE. Donald smiled at the two empty champagne glasses and the stocking lying at the foot of the couch. From an onyx box upon the desk he took an Egyptian cigarette and lit it wearily. He would be glad to go to bed. The door opened suddenly, however, and there once more stood Octavius. They looked at each other without surprise.

"You are persistent."

"They're organizing a treasure hunt downstairs. I thought I might as well check this stairway."

"No gun? No friends? Just outraged honor as your companion?"

"Just outraged honor."

Much of Octavius' life had been lost in talk and to turn from one more nighttime chat to Ann's stringent command would not be easy. Nor was the decision entirely his as he judged himself and then the panther sitting loosely upon the desk. From below came the orchestra and the crowd noise and the clatter out of the kitchen and serving pantries. And despite all his efforts of will to fasten his mind upon the duty at hand, it wandered off irresponsibly.

"Night. Cocoon of darkness wherein the worm of life stilly stirs," he said sadly, looking down at the desk with the manager's heavy playthings.

"And spins, knowing not, matter of distant dawns," Donald picked up with a smile.

"And we are left, yawning like weary waiters, life's soiled napkin limp upon our arms. Is there yet time?"

"To seize and grow while fireworks burst like evanescent breasts upon the sky."

Octavius raised his eyes.

"Oh Octavius, you will be grateful to me—not merely for having removed a cantankerous father-in-law and taught a partially reluctant girl some of the sweets of love. Desire, anger, honor, there is the matter for poetry, not the stringing of words together like brightly colored beads for children in progressive kindergartens. Go, take your Ann with you along the beach, with the wet sand underfoot and the ocean hissing sweet as death upon the sands, hold her arm firmly and climb to the topmost dune, under the moon, over the ocean. Hold her to you, make her know your will till the grayness over the distant ocean sends a spark, a flood of sunlight to you, and then you will be a poet, fertilized by sorrow and longing, your words pouring forth like cries from the heart——"

He paused to watch the effect of his words. A thin smile had come to Octavius' mouth. He had taken a bottle of cognac from the sideboard and was filling the two champagne glasses upon the desk.

"My boy, I wish you well," Donald said. "So much of life waits before you! A trembling girl, and it is for you to lift the veil."

Octavius raised his face sideways, the thin smile still resting upon half of it.

"My boy, those aren't the correct glasses for cognac," said Donald. "But never mind, when one drinks to friendship, the glass is the punctuation of the sonnet. What a wonderful trade you have. Tongue-tied as I am, how I envy you."

He picked up his glass and waited as Octavius took his and came around to the other side of the desk. But the disciplined, elegant face contorted as Octavius threw the contents of his glass into his eyes. He doubled up, his head a perfect target for the bottle in Octavius' hand. Like a cracking melon his skull broke and he fell without a sound to the floor.

The door flew open and in rushed the manager and Mr. Van Torley, policemen, Masetto, and a dozen confused forms.

"There, he is, there!" cried out the manager hoarsely.

"Ah, my boy, you have defeated him," said Mr. Van Torley. "Are you all right? You can see," he turned to the policemen and explained, "this brave boy, a poet you might be surprised to know, the son of Maxfield Iredell, confronted the monster, who immediately attacked him, and in self-defense against tremendous odds this boy was able to beat him off."

More people pressed into the room. A scream came from Elvira Johns, who cast herself on her knees beside the dead body. Octavius saw a dazed, twisted figure wrapped up in a sheet—faithful Leo.

"However did you do it?" crossly demanded Masetto of the poet.

"I threw a glass of brandy in his face. That blinded him and I hit him over the head with a bottle."

Other women appeared and stared with fascination and disbelief at the crumpled body and the unhappy young man who had killed him. Zerlina's face was puffy and creased. Midnight had passed. She had crossed the line, and dawn, to a skilled eye, though the finest eye of all was closed forever, would find her beauty irrevocably tarnished.

"Well, young man," the burly police chief said, "we usually don't like the idea of you gentlefolk taking the law into your own hands, but that man there was clearly a bad sort——"

"I'll talk things over with your father tomorrow," Captain Donohue finished sympathetically.

"Let's all get back to the dance," suggested the manager. "There's a lot of good champagne going dead in the bottles. There's a lot of good music still left in Silvano's saxophone."

"I'm owed a lot of back salary," came a wail from the bedsheet. "Where am I going to get my money?"

"You come along with me, you scoundrel," the policeman said.

"You'd better take Miss Frobisher home. This has been a tiring day for her," Mr. Van Torley cautioned Octavius.

They all descended the stairs, Octavius holding firmly on to Ann's thin arm, but instead of turning back toward the dance floor or even the exit where the cars waited, he took her out on the beach and led her across the sand to the distant hummocks of the dunes beneath the moonlight.

XI

PARIS IN THE SPRING

SPRING HAD COME, or in fact early summer, and had brought with it the almost jungle richness of the chestnuts' foliage, flowers in the Luxembourg and the Tuileries like petunias and snapdragons that Caroline had forgotten grew in France, café tables set out upon the sidewalks, and American tourists. Already in April, when she went outside her own narrow pattern of streets, she had heard their voices and seen them in tailored navy blue dresses looking into the shop windows along the Rue de Rivoli. Now students, teachers, and families whose vacation times were governed by the school year were beginning to arrive, even in Caroline's part of town, dressed in nylon fabrics, draped with cameras, light meters, and heavy shoulder bags, like explorers of the Upper Niger. During the past weeks Caroline had received a number of visitors, friends of the family from St. Louis, parents of girls she had known at college, and her standard of living had risen perceptibly, in the restaurants where she ate and the seats at the opera.

This did not suit her need to study for the final examinations at the university, nor her decision that these examinations were important. It confused her, too, that the year should end in the way it had begun, talking about good lingerie stores or the qualities of French character shown by hotel employees.

Yet at the same time she was glad to see someone like

Mrs. Groves, whom she had known since she was a little girl, and to sit in the dining room of the Hotel Bristol and order anything she wanted without looking at the price. Mrs. Groves and her friend Mrs. Compton had come up from Italy and seemed to have enjoyed every part of their trip. Whatever they had eaten or seen or heard had been delightful, and the enthusiasm and interest of these two middle-aged ladies apparently brought them only courtesy and friendliness wherever they had gone. Even a spell of grippe in Zurich that confined Mrs. Groves to bed for three days had been put to good advantage, for illness in a foreign city had allowed her the luxury of sustained reflection about herself and her world that the mistress of a large house in suburban St. Louis rarely enjoys.

"I suppose it teaches you how little you actually know, Caroline," Mrs. Groves concluded. "I'll go home and turn myself into a real European authority to anyone who'll listen, but if I met someone who spent a month in the States and had never talked to anyone except salesgirls and desk clerks, I wouldn't give two pins for all he'd learned. You're the first person we've met who's really lived here the way you ought to. What's France like, anyway?" And she went on: "What have you done? What sort of friends have you made? What have you learned?"

Then she laughed at her own inquisitiveness and the demands she was putting on this polite redheaded girl who had left her family and her college for a year to study in Paris and find out what the world was like. Caroline had always liked Mrs. Groves. The questions were reasonable ones—Mrs. Groves had bought all the leather goods and lingerie she needed in Florence and now was interested in other things—but what could she answer?

"It's the coldest city in the world." And she began to tell some anecdotes of the terrible weeks in February. "It's the most expensive, too."

But that didn't answer Mrs. Groves' questions. And it was

not only courteous but politic to answer them frankly, for Caroline imagined what sort of conversation her mother had had with Mrs. Groves. If the visitor could take back home some factually reassuring news about the wandering girl, Caroline's own return would be easier.

"I'd appreciate very much the chance of meeting some of your friends, Caroline. Margie and I don't speak a word of French, but we'd try to listen intelligently."

Bring Brigitte, who hardly opened her mouth with a stranger? Or Dominique, whose reaction toward Americans was that of nice St. Louis people toward Jews? Or Sophie, who looked as if she slept in her clothes? Her friends, won with difficulty, were the most personal means by which she understood France. But this knowledge couldn't be handed to a stranger on a platter. Each person had to make his own discoveries. Caroline could only point out the surface characteristics: beauty in Paris, for example the view down the Seine to Notre Dame, rests primarily upon dimensions of age and distance.

"They're awfully busy now with their examinations," she answered, and started a funny description of her apartment and the ailing copper octopus that heated water for the tub. The two ladies invited her to a musical comedy the next evening, but she was already going to *The Magic Flute* with a friend.

"It's the lower-middle-class ideal of heaven. Promenade under these crystal chandeliers in a new tuxedo and stop at the bar for a glass of champagne—by gosh, it's worth being good."

Caroline laughed at her companion's glancing at herself as they passed one of the mirrors, for a moment very pleased with her reflection in the apple-green dress and the contrast of her bright coloring with that of her handsome brown escort in his dark gray suit.

"And when the buzzer rings," Chris elaborated, "one

throws away one's fifty-cent cigar and slowly, slowly strolls back to the red velvet chair. Then the curtain goes up and once again you have the Lord God and the angel chorus singing the Toreador Song."

When the last examination for them both, on Racine, came in three days, the opera was probably self-indulgence, at least for Chris Smallwood, who needed a good grade, but right afterward he'd take the night train for Spain and they would not see each other again. Caroline also didn't know whether she could have stood one more evening at the miniscule desk designed for notes to another woman's husband, listening for the final nighttime noise, the grind of the key in the bedroom doors of Madame Lhoullier and her daughter. On the other hand, she wasn't sure whether she liked the performance or not. Its unrelenting splendor, with the Queen of the Night descending out of the heavens in a shower of stars, was paid for not merely by the hammering backstage while Sarastro sang his hymn to rational sobriety, nor by her concern, as her father's daughter, as to just what sort of a bill someone would have to pick up for the costumes and extras, but by the confusion wherein all this kaleidoscope whirled together into a muddy brown. A little condescending, insulting, in the assumption that the audience wanted nothing better than a gorgeous box of chocolates.

"You don't understand how precious those chocolates are, Caroline," Chris had checked her. "I'll be eating them for the rest of my life when I get back to Nashville. Last fall I used to get all exercised about the women in mink coats who came just for the spectacle, and then I suddenly thought what a slam-bang spectacle it was. Even the mink coats can fill up their suitcases with it and go home better and richer women."

"Is that man filling up his suitcase with beauty?" Caroline asked, nodding at a swollen creature whose small eyes bulged unseeing from a purple face and who seemed aware only of the churn of duck and cognac in his stomach.

"He doesn't have to. He's more important than the so-prano herself," Chris gaily replied.

"He buys the most expensive seats."

"That's only half of it. The real pleasure of people like that girl over there"—he directed her glance toward a sallow, bony young woman in a mauve dress buttoned up to a worn little white collar, her lips, hands, heels pressed together and only her eyes alive, peering out of an existence consecrated to saving things and to weighing one duty against another—"lies in being able to stare at the beautiful clothes of the rich steak-and-chop man's wife and to despise their stupid faces and to feel that she alone has the depth to appreciate Mozart. If everyone came here just because they loved music, where would be the stimulus?"

"Not her, Chris. She's one of those French girls who have never laughed in their whole lives. If she found a bit of happiness she'd never recognize it."

The two of them spoke almost feverishly, exicted by the lights, the people, and the awareness that this was their final evening together. A year in Paris, however, had taught Caroline too vividly how it was possible for human beings to keep alive without in any way actually living for her to pass off the girl in mauve as an item of conversation.

But there were other chocolates for them to gather. What Chris called the steak-and-chop men from Chicago and Düsseldorf. A pair of Indo-Chinese women wearing embroidered silk gowns slit below the knee, who came by them gesturing like butterflies and conversing in a frail insect language. A coal-black African, his cheeks hachured with scars, frightened wife clutching his arm, was backed against a pillar and stared in a sort of frozen rage at the shock of lights and colors trembling before him. The guards in dark beautiful jackets and kepis wore the dignity and medals of old heroes as they patrolled to see that people did not smoke in the wrong place.

"All this I'm putting away," Chris said to her, "just the way my mother does her canned peaches."

They also passed two heavy-jawed women, speaking with flat, slurred American accents, whose eyes' cold flash told that this sight of the redheaded girl and the young colored man together was to be inserted into their own album of Paris souvenirs.

Those eyes angered her. Caroline couldn't forget them during the next act, for they reminded her that Chris might view the opera differently from the way she did. When the villainous Monostatos appeared on the stage, he was presented as ludicrous by Mozart, lecherous and cowardly, the natural character of a blackamoor. Sarastro's priests might be rationally philanthropic because the dirty jobs in their kingdom were carried out by dusky underlings.

"A half-dozen more good bonbons and our chocolate box will be full," Chris said as they came again into the long mirrored hall for the second intermission.

They were both attracted by a stately woman, erect in the slow current like a boulder encircled by driftwood, who was declaiming in shrill crackling French to her followers, snapping her wrists with the force of wit until her rings and nails flashed like fireflies. Each passing woman turned, as Caroline did, to observe the sables and brocade, but she had been in Paris too long to be unaware of the infinity of microscopic stitches sewed upon the gown by bent and squinting girls. The money, art, and spirit insisting that the clock had been stopped proclaimed the fact so proudly that one peered and discerned the network of little scars upon the throat.

"They can't let go," said Caroline, turning for another glance. That also gave her the profile of a face she knew. She might still find her way back to their seats without being noticed; nevertheless, she touched her escort's arm.

"There's an old friend of my mother's I'd like you to meet." And after she had greeted Mrs. Groves, she made her introductions: "This is Mr. Smallwood. He is a student here. He comes from Nashville."

"My mother was born in Nashville," said Mrs. Groves with a lady's graciousness, though Mrs. Compton kept a very still face. "I know it well."

They hadn't been able to get tickets for their original show and now were glad they hadn't. Wasn't the performance marvelous? Yes, but she should see what they did with *Faust*. Mrs. Groves and Chris maintained such an easy pattern of conversation until the buzzer began to ring that Caroline wondered if the world had suddenly changed without her being aware of it—not true, Mrs. Compton's face told her— or if words had ceased to have meaning and people handed them back and forth like painted chips. She felt closer even to somber Mrs. Compton.

"Shall we see you again, dear, before we leave?" Mrs. Groves asked as they separated. "We'll be here until Thursday."

"I think I'd better put all my time into study. This evening has been a luxury, I'm afraid," Caroline apologized.

She couldn't meet Mrs. Groves again. Every word and look, every silence had acquired a double meaning.

"It's been wonderful to see you, Caroline. I'll have to ring up your mother as soon as I get home and tell her all about her fine daughter."

Caroline's smile froze as they turned away. She was glad she couldn't observe Mrs. Groves' face now. She watched Papageno's pains to find another highly sexed parrot for a mate and the nobler ordeals of fire and ice that Tamino and Pamina underwent protected by the magic flute and their love for each other, but not much came through. What she heard was the silence between herself and Chris. The opera ended. A few words of thanks for the invitation and, crossing the street outside, of warning about traffic, but without needing to consult each other they had buried themselves in the thickest streams of people leaving the building, and they walked rapidly away from the blue-white lights of the Place de L'Opéra still in silence.

"You look tired. Shall I hunt up a taxi?" he suggested.

"No. I'm fine," she answered tartly and immediately regretted not having accepted his offer. Then he did speak, with an effort to be casual.

"Our mutual contacts in Nashville did not give Mrs. Groves and myself as much in common as you might expect. Maybe we didn't move in the same circles."

"She's a very nice person. I've known her for a long time," Caroline remarked lamely, to be able to say something. The next time he spoke seriously and she knew that she had not misjudged him.

"What will she say to your mother about her daughter's life in this wicked city?"

"She's a reasonable woman, Chris."

"She couldn't have acted nicer. I was proud of her. But I know Nashville better than you do, Caroline."

She sighed. "To hell with it."

"I'm sorry, Caroline," he said. "I never would have asked you if I had had any idea——"

She stopped and face him angrily.

"Do we know each other? Do we have any idea of what the other person is like?"

"I think we do."

"Then don't say foolish things."

A half-smile appeared on his face. At the next street crossing he gripped her arm firmly and she knew the air had cleared, whether Mrs. Groves carried her guilty secret to the grave or phoned St. Louis for Mrs. Maltby to rush her daughter home before it was too late. Or did anything in fact except understand matters the way they were.

The two were entering the Place Vendôme now, illuminated for the summer visitors at the Ritz, and they stopped to gaze up at the silvery shadowy column and at the black-

and-silver façades curving back at either flank. It was a part of Paris she rarely saw. She had accepted her friends' judgment that it was as improper, from the thick smell of money around it, as Montmartre with its nightclubs and naked girls. Now she was sorry.

"What a beautiful city," she exclaimed softly.

"No more beautiful, no more ugly, no freer, no more wretched, no more wonderful—all around me, everything, and I was a little drudge conjugating the verb *connaître* and knowing nothing!" he burst out. "I'm going down to Badajoz and sit in the sun—I'll get warm for once—and try to figure out . . ."

He didn't finish. She smiled at the mention of Badajoz. He had found a new name. He had been drugged with names when she first met him: Emma Bovary, Phèdre, Place des Vosges, the Schumann Plan, has Vouvray more fragrance than Côtes du Saumur? And she had thought him an impossible snob until she realized that names were the currency in which he was repaid for loneliness and an overwhelming sense of ignorance. Raised in Nashville, attending college in Atlanta, paying a visit to his cousins in St. Louis, but for one year all the names of the great globe itself were his.

"I'll go to Badajoz and Burgos and León and Salamanca, and then I'll go back to Nashville."

He laughed, she laughed with him, and they both were about as ready to cry. They continued along under the arcades of the Rue de Castiglione, stopping once to look at a window filled with bright yellow summer dresses, once in front of a bookstore.

"If I owned every book I've wanted to buy this year, what a marvelous library I would possess," he said.

"But see how lightly you can travel."

They walked through the arched passageway beneath the Louvre and on their left was the palace's great square stone horseshoe and on their right the gardens of the Tuileries. Taking the next passageway, they reached the Seine. There was a light mist and no moon, but the embankment lights shining in the water made a hundred. They passed a pair of lovers embracing by the parapet and an old woman with too much lipstick who was a prostitute, which always frightened Caroline.

"During the worst of the winter," she said, "I used to dream of coming here for a week as a tourist. I'd stay at the Ritz and go shopping every morning, and I'd take long naps and walk around the streets in the twilight."

"That would be somebody else, Caroline. It wouldn't be you."

"Oh, yes, it would," she insisted. "And I'd have two hot baths a day."

"You were delirious."

"Then one could pretend it was a magical city for sure."

"You'd come down with indigestion from eating too much. You'd be worrying how to smuggle those new clothes past the customs."

They were walking, slowly, in their own part of town. Chris was escorting her to Madame Lhoullier's building before he turned toward his own quarters in the Boulevard Raspail.

"Two solid days for Racine. We should get to know each other well."

"What will you be looking for?" he asked.

"Passion. Honor. The contempt for happiness. What we Americans don't understand."

They had reached her door. He took her key and unlocked it for her.

Come and see me the next time you visit your cousins in St. Louis. Phone and take a taxi and have dinner with my parents. She kept silent. So did he. With all his talkativeness he had always been able to keep silent when there was nothing to say.

"Take a little exercise. Don't read all the time or your eyes will go bad. Those French kids don't understand that," he said.

"No, they don't."

He held out his hand. She took it, and then she leaned forward and kissed him before she shut the door and with her last remaining energy ran up the stairs.

XII

THE PROPHET

FOR A NUMBER OF YEARS I lived in a pleasant and prosperous suburb of St. Louis where the lawns were always neatly kept and at least one auto stood in front of every house. Under such conditions it is hard to tell whether another man is wicked or a fool. What is the purpose, where is the opportunity even, for being wicked, unless you throw stones at your neighbor's dog or deliberately set out to seduce his wife? Times were good. You could be pretty stupid and still share in the slices of cake. It was a world where moderate virtue and moderate intelligence brought nice rewards. At the same time, a man who was dissatisfied with the ideas or standards of his street felt that he was punching smoke or swimming with his shoes on. He seemed cranky, a nuisance to his wife and his neighbors, and in the midst of his prosperity he might hunger for some clear sign of right and wrong and some clear demand to act upon it. In wartime, of course, evil and stupidity are less disguised, though most men are still not much bothered so long as they themselves are untouched, and very few indeed will ever cause trouble.

I did know one such troublemaker, Private First Class Olon Cleves, a typewriter repairman of a big headquarters unit between Naples and Monte Cassino where we both served minor roles during the winter of 1944, shivering, damp, and gnawed by the feeling that war calls up sharper than any other, exasperation. We weren't afraid for our lives, we weren't impelled by hate or love, but we were exasperated: by the mud, by the ceaseless cold that twisted a man up like an olive tree, by the tent ropes over which we tripped in the dark, by the monotone, self-pitying creatures who were our tentmates, and by the sheer meaningless drip of time before the war should end. On the other hand, we were pretty well fed. The food was hot and usually more than sufficient, and much as we grumbled about spam and powdered eggs, our three meals were, after mail call, the most welcome events of the day.

Just to the east of our bivouac area rose a hungry war-broken hill town named Presenzano, from which, at each mealtime, appeared twenty or thirty children to collect our leftover food. They waited between the garbage pit and the washtubs with their empty cans and cracked china bowls for us to empty out the beans, bread and pancake scraps, soup, coffee, and fat. Mothers and grandmothers would reheat the slop back home and that would be the family's meal. "Hey Joe, please, hey, hey Joe?" called the quick boys with their wise grown-up voices, elbowing, smiling, their sharp eyes calculating who had a good messtin, who looked generous— real little businessmen. The little ones, holding the cans over their heads, struggled to keep their footing in the tussle. The shy ones stood in the rear and you had to push through the pack if you wanted to make sure they had something to carry home. It was a nuisance, in a way it was humiliating, and some of the soldiers were irritated enough to prefer throwing their garbage into the big pit. Still, we were grown men in boots and a dozen different pieces of wool clothing, and many of the little girls were just wearing dresses and sandals without socks, with shorts and a ragged sweater for the boys and maybe an old army cap pulled down over the ears.

The hubbub offended the company's administrative officer, Captain Sutro, and one morning an order was posted on the bulletin board by the chow line saying that henceforth, in the interests of sanitation and discipline, leftover food was not to be given to unauthorized civilian personnel. I'm glad to say no one paid any attention to this. After breakfast we doled out the same cheap charity of oatmeal slops and half-eaten French toast. An MP stood guard by the washtubs at lunchtime, a serious, stupid young man, but who cares what an MP thinks? The children were agile, and if he attempted to enforce law and order at one spot, we could scatter a bit further and he was left to complain, "Hey fellas, don't do that," and be laughed at. Only the littlest and timidest children, whom even he could frighten, lost out.

But by suppertime Captain Sutro had fixed up the system. Three strands of barbed wire, thirty yards long, had been strung behind the washtubs. Two MPs with tommy guns had been set on guard. The boys and girls and one old woman stood on the other side of the wire with their empty tin cans and watched us throw our food into the garbage pit.

We were angry, we were ashamed before those silent children, and we grumbled about this swollen example of discipline. But that was all. No one spoke to Captain Sutro about it, no one complained to the other officers. A soldier is accustomed to injustice and each man occupies himself only with his own cares. At breakfast the next day, when about half the usual number of children showed up, unable to believe that the order would stand or fascinated by the sight of food being tossed into a hole in the ground, we looked in the other direction.

Here begins the story of Pfc. Olon Cleves. Noon came and my colleague Sergeant Juraschek and I set out for chow, jangling our messtins cheerfully. But passing a pyramidal work tent we noticed that a sheet of paper, with a red border put on in grease pencil to attract attention, was tacked to the Typewriter Repair sign. We stopped to read it—everybody read everything—and neatly written in capital letters was the following:

But whoso shall offend one of these little ones who believe in me, it were better for him that a millstone were hanged about his neck and that he were drowned in the depth of the sea.

Matthew 18:6

To the point, and yet safe: a man can't be court-martialed for posting a verse from the Good Book. A sobering message, a reminder of the moral seriousness of what had been done, and many soldiers, seeing the children still waiting, without hope, beyond the barbed wire, stopped again to reread it after lunch.

In the discussion Juraschek and I had at table, one item we were sure of was that Captain Sutro would see the sign. Bustling around the camp all day, he put on a show of iron efficiency. If someone emptied a handful of cigarette butts outside a tent door, Sutro would see him and mark the offense by an angry command upon the bulletin board. Anything more complicated than cigarette butts rattled him, but for small things he was everywhere. He'd see the sign. Another question: just who was the typewriter repairman? I knew him by sight, though his cloudy, featureless face was easy to forget. He was a short, thin, slightly stooped fellow in his middle thirties who set his cap right on the middle of his head, the permanent private first class, the sort of character for whom two pinball games and a glass of beer on Saturday night would be a week's recreation. He ate with other small tradesmen like mimeographers and paymaster's clerks, but no one we knew even knew his name.

Out of curiosity, therefore, we checked the signboard the following morning. A new message was tacked up, from the Old Testament this time, explaining reasonably why the captain's action was wrong.

And when ye reap the harvest of your land, thou shalt not wholly reap the corners of thy field, neither shalt thou gather the gleanings of thy harvest.

Leviticus 19:9

I suppose it is hard the first time to believe that anything from the Bible has a real application. Religion is wholesome, soft, warm, like custard, good for children and old people. Our chaplain, Captain Poyning, was a harmless man who told Bible stories in army talk ("First Sergeant Goliath,") and who intruded himself upon the unit only in the embarrassed morality talks he was compelled to give, followed by the next officer who said that that was all very well but the only thing he wanted us to keep in mind was that ninety-nine percent of all Dago women had VD.

Why should we be indignant? It is forbidden in army regulations to be indignant about the misfortunes of another. To us the war was exasperation and resentment, both passive emotions. We resented the officers, who treated us with the tolerance of a decent Southerner toward Negroes, our ungrateful allies, the dirty immoral thievish Italians, the folks at home who could go into a bathroom and lock the door behind them anytime they wanted to. Perhaps, though, under this selfishness there lay something of what you might call the hunger for righteousness. Or simply the desire to say that black was black and white was white after the hogwash that composed most of what we were told.

He that hath pity upon the poor lendeth unto the Lord.

Proverbs 19:17

A statement of vague Sunday goodness, and a pretty weak one for that next morning when all the mud ruts were frozen solid and a dust of snow blew against us in the chow line and against the two small boys, huddled together like birds, who still waited for the captain to change his mind. Cleves (we had learned his name by now) must have thought so too, for at noon the sign had been changed, with the borders hachured in red and black so that we would see it was new.

What mean ye that ye beat my people to pieces and grind the faces of the poor?

Isaiah 5:20

The man's anger was worth respecting. In the mess tent Juraschek and I sat ourselves down among the curious who were eating near him. Not that he looked any less insignificant while he hunched over his soup, his cap pulled down firmly in the center of his sandy hair. His skin had an unhealthy violet and yellow tinge to it, his small, nearsighted eyes were more or less blue, and he seemed without interest in what was going on around him, least of all in his new admirers.

"Where do you find all those things you write down?" asked a youngster full of excitement at sitting opposite a celebrity.

"Where do you think?" came the dry answer.

"Is it going to do any good?" I wanted to know. Cleves shrugged his shoulders, and with a hand permanently stained from the carbon off his typewriters took a piece of bread to mop up the soup in his mess tin and then turned to the beans on the lid.

"What are you going to do next?"

The questioning was futile. There was no spark of conceit or levity in the man that would let him expose himself. He shrugged his shoulders again—his mouth was full—but when he had swallowed he answered with the same noncommittal aridity: "I'll wait and see."

"You'll get yourself in trouble, Cleves," Sergeant Juraschek warned in his best fatherly manner, though he was at least a dozen years younger than the pfc. "Don't fool around too far."

"You think I'm fooling?"

The flat Midwestern voice (he came from some town in downstate Illinois) and the pale blue eyes were so uncompromising that Juraschek made no reply. "He looks like an angry log of wood," the sergeant said later.

This crusade added some novelty to each mealtime, one verse tacked on top of the next so that you could check on the ones you had missed.

For it must needs be that offences come; but woe to that man by
whom the offence cometh.

Matthew 18:7

Sometimes with a literary flavor:

As the partridge sitteth on eggs and hatcheth them not, so he that
getteth riches and not by right, shall leave them in the midst of his
days and at his end shall be a fool.

Jeremiah 17:11

In wealth and power Captain Sutro was hardly a bank
president, but you could piece out the allusion. What gave
the battle its salt was that every soldier in the company knew
that the captain saw every message. Nosing about the bivouac area for shaves and salutes as he did, he couldn't possibly hold himself away from the signboard. Most officers
are crazy to know what enlisted men think of them, and they
eagerly censored the letters to our wives to read descriptions
of their little foibles and quirks. And we also knew that the
typewriter repairman, who had the tact of a porcupine,
would press Sutro until something blew up.

Cleves shifted to a direct summoning of heaven's fire. The
wretched captain was set up as a symbol of Oriental iniquity.

Cursed shall be the fruit of thy body and the fruit of thy land, the
increase of thy kine and the flocks of thy sheep.

Deuteronomy 28:18

The Pfc. stimulated more Bible reading than a covey of
chaplains. Little apple-cheeked Andy Lewis in our section
had been given a Bible by his mother when he left for overseas (a pretty boy who had learned that if he handed two
cans of beans to a woman he could have sexual intercourse
with her and that if he drank a whole bottle of wine by
himself no one would say a word), and Juraschek borrowed
it to read aloud chapter 28 when none of the officers was in
the work tent. Cleves could stick to that one chapter all
week. We picked out our favorite verses. "And the heaven

over thy head shall be brass, and the earth that is under thee shall be iron" was mine, but the typists preferred "The Lord shall smite thee with the botch of Egypt and with the scab and with the itch."

And every time a soldier passed the captain and saluted him—salutes smartened up, no one risked falling afoul of him now, and when I went up to the orderly room for a pass to Naples the clerks there might have been walking around on eggshells—he would stare with a barely disguised joy into that wrathful face which revealed how the pfc.'s curses were roiling about in his bowels.

And thy carcase shall be meat unto all the fowls of the air and unto the beasts of the earth.

Deuteronomy 28:26

"I saw him! I saw him! The lion's teeth have been blunted!" Juraschek burst into the office, calling exultantly in the Southern accent he affected, in times of emotion. (We had all begun adding a Biblical flavor to our expressions.) "I was passing through the photo recon area and I saw him go by that tent and he turned around to see if anyone was watching, then he read what was on the board and looked around again real quick and then he ripped off the pages and tore 'em all up and kicked down the sign. But I saw him!"

And all the typists and draftsmen whom Juraschek usually bedeviled smiled with the sergeant's delight.

We invented errands to spread the news. I picked up one of the typewriters as an excuse to call upon Cleves. Sure enough the sign was down and those white sheets could be seen scattered against the olive trees and the tent ropes. I came into the tent of sick and wounded machines where Cleves was performing an autopsy on the underside of what looked like a big black crab.

"You've got him wild, old man. Just like stubble in the flames!" I cried out.

"What's wrong with your typewriter, corporal?"

And when some other lighthearted fellow breezed in excitedly with his own quasi-Hebraic line about feeding on wormwood, he was met with a blunt "I'm a busy man." Still, Cleves hadn't finished half of that chapter. By suppertime the sign was up again with a new sheet of paper:

Thou shalt betroth a wife and another man shall lie with her: thou shalt build a house and thou shalt not dwell therein: thou shalt plant a vineyard and shalt not gather the grapes thereof.

Deuteronomy 28:30

That was Saturday. Now, what notice would Captain Poyning have to take of this fire of righteousness lighting up our camp? In a way Cleves had challenged the chaplain as well as Captain Sutro, and Juraschek and I crowded our way into the chapel tent, along with the other godless, to see how the issue would be handled. Olon Cleves was sitting in one of the rear rows, just the sort who went every Sunday. A problem had been posed. On one hand were the hungry Italian children. On the other was Pfc. Cleves muscling in on the chaplain's job and turning the Good Book into a weapon against military authority. I waited for a message in the hymns, in the readings—nothing doing; but it was the first time in my life, I suppose, that I looked forward eagerly to a sermon. Nothing again. Captain Poyning talked about the prophets, about Abraham's recon patrol into Canaan, the logistical problems he had to face, about his faith in the Lord, and closed with the punch line that a good Christian was a good soldier and a good soldier saluted his officers. The worst part was that you couldn't tell what it meant. Maybe this was a rebuke to Cleves. Maybe poor Captain Poyning had let so many years slip by since he had last tied his religion to anything important that he had lost his nerve. Or maybe he just hadn't noticed anything at all.

We passed Cleves on the way out.

"Didn't get much support, did you?" I said.

"Damned Levite. Fooling around the altar with his burnt offerings," was the sour reply.

He didn't give up easily. "Woe unto them that call evil good (Isaiah 5:20)" was the lunchtime quote. Ineffectual as we knew the chaplain to be, in theory at least he was supposed to be on the same team as Cleves. We resented Authority, but we gave no respect to anything which lacked it. By midafternoon, when I had to carry some papers down to the engineers, I saw a new piece of paper in new handwriting tacked to the signpost with this reproof:

Is it any pleasure to the Almighty that thou art righteous?

Job 22:3

The counterattack caught on. By evening there were two further notices: that bootlicking remark of St. Paul's, 'The powers that be are ordained of God,' along with 'much learning doth make thee mad,' and on Cleves' own sheet someone had printed "Nuts!"

Monday morning found the board smashed to pieces. Bits of wood lay on the ground before the prophet's tent. A couple of words from the first sergeant to some hophead would have been enough. For after all, Cleves' fight, though we were apt to forget this, was in behalf of the Italian children and too many of our men simply hated all Wops. If they suffered they deserved it, a holdover from good old orthodox Calvinism.

Cleves found an apple crate which he stood up outside his door, and if you bent down you could read:

Woe unto you that are full! for ye shall hunger.
Woe unto you that laugh now! for ye shall mourn and weep.

Luke 6:25

But on our return from lunch the paper had been torn off. Our prophet began to look ridiculous, like the bearded cranks back home who carry signs saying "Are you ready to meet God?" The children had disappeared. We threw our garbage into the big pit every day. Captain Sutro's authority, supported by church and state and red-blooded public opinion, stood untouched. Should Cleves have gone on a hunger strike, for instance? It was hard to tell what he was thinking, for his face was as shut in now as it had been when the attack was going well. Yet, after all, the Bible is a big book, he had a lot of material to draw upon.

Therefore I am full of the fury of the Lord:
I am weary with holding in.

Jeremiah 6:11

He was calling down destruction upon us all. Then you caught sight of the poor fellow sitting by himself over his food, his cap still pulled down over the center of his forehead.

Now Captain Sutro could afford to take his long-awaited revenge. Cleves showed up at the messhall with the sleeve of his jacket bare. He wasn't so small that he couldn't be made smaller. The signboard was gone too, permanently, though to a flap of canvas by his door a small filing card was fixed by a paper clip:

And they departed from the presence of the Council, rejoicing that they were counted worthy to suffer shame for his name.

Acts 5:41

And what of Presenzano in the winter and the people who lived there? We hiked up to the town with our dirty clothes and some scoured it for women. Apple-cheeked Andy Lewis had a mistress ten years older than he, with two children. We paid for our laundry with the lire that the army printed and with food, candy, cigarettes, and sometimes a piece of clothing. I wonder now what those people lived on and what they fed their children with, but that is because I have children of my own. At that time, as I have said, I was occupied with my own troubles. A telephone line ran up to the police station, and my own laundress, who had spent eleven years in Boston and spoke with a genuine New England accent, owned a bathtub, though no water ran in it. Except for that the town had been untouched for a hundred years. The animals had always lived in the houses (the street was everyone's toilet—in hot weather the smell must have been fantastic). There had always been too many babies, even if a lot died. There had never been enough rain (when it was needed), enough food, enough jobs. Living in Presenzano was like living under a flail that beat upon each generation from childhood to old age and death. And during these years the war scraped over Italy like an iron rake.

I was always glad to start off on the laundry trips—I used to carry our major's bundle along to make it easier to get away—to leave the tents and see human life again: houses and animals, women and children; but I always came back heavyhearted.

Juraschek and I had dropped off our laundry with the lady from North Boston (we used to repeat street names to each other and she'd tell me the buses she took) and with the sacks of clean clothes under our arms were going downhill again when we saw Private Cleves climbing up the steep cobbled road. His breath came out in little puffs, and as he drew near the bare hands purple with cold showed against his laundry bundle and those violet and yellow patches upon his face. It was hard to imagine that this man had been convinced that by pinning up Bible verses on a signboard he could halt the march of injustice.

"Not much has come of the crusade, has it?" I said when we met, not meaning to be unkind, but still trying to learn what had turned him onto this path.

"No, I didn't handle that right," he said.

"What made you think you could?" Juraschek asked.

"I've read the Bible all my life, every evening. I underline the parts that seem important. And when that fool put up his damn barbed wire, I had a call," he explained in a level, expressionless voice, though he was still breathing hard from the climb. "I knew what I ought to do. For the first time in

my life I had a call. I live in Cobalt, Illinois. That's not far
from Mattoon. I never had a call there."

"What are you going to do?" I kept at him. "Have you
spoken to the chaplain? He might speak to Sutro, or he might
even see the general."

"He knows what he should do as well as me," the thin
man said in contempt.

"Are you going to give up?" Juraschek asked.

"I don't know," he answered. "It seems like the call sort
of died away."

We separated then and the two of us continued silently
down the road back to the bivouac area whose pyramidal
tents and optimistic nets of camouflage rose up between the
crooked olive trees. We didn't say anything, rare enough, for
Alex Juraschek had a comment on the economy, psychology,
or sociology of just about anything you could name.

When we had finished supper that evening—the days were
longer now, it was as light then, though the ground was still
frozen instead of muddy—Juraschek and I were headed for
the garbage pit with our spam scraps and bread crusts, when
Alex caught sight of a couple of kids with their empty tins
coming along the cart road from Presenzano, maybe on a
trip to one of the New Zealand units camped below us in
the valley. It would have been a long walk.

"Hey, paisan," he called and they came up to the wire,
staring suspiciously. Juraschek poured what was left in his
messtin into the can of the smaller and then gave him his
bar of chocolate—we had been issued a candy ration that
evening—and what else could I do but follow suit with the
second boy? As we turned away I noticed a couple of other
men taking their messtins up to the fence.

The next morning about a dozen kids were waiting again
for their slops, more came at lunch, and it continued that
way for the rest of the time we were stationed at Presenzano.
Two or three times the MPs showed up to safeguard Authority by driving the kids off, but at the following meal no

obstruction would be set up and I suppose that all in all our unit did its fair share of this sort of cheap charity. Sutro never appeared at mess time. No messages came down from the orderly room. Of course you couldn't tell by looking at Olon Cleves whether he was pleased or not. He ate by himself and he nursed his ailing typewriters, and perhaps the card clipped to his tent door had been there some time before I noticed it and came up close to read what it said:

What doth the Lord require of thee but to do justly, and to have mercy, and to walk humbly with thy God.

Micah 6:8

XIII

THE HONOR OF THE HOME

THE TYPE OF SUBURB represented by Prairie Dales calls forth a particularly repellent style of analysis. Scratch an American and you reveal a sociologist, as the proverb goes, and any half-educated individual who takes one look at Prairie Dales is convinced that if he examines any single home or housewife, he will understand mid-century America, from infant care to theology. And sex. Everyone likes sex. Perhaps the simple monotony of the lawns, driveways, mailboxes, and picture windows evokes lurid thoughts about the claims adjuster on Woodmere and the accountant's wife on Meadowbrook lusting for each other, which can be extrapolated to reveal the woes of all middle-class America. Which can be said to have involved Willa Burrage with Henry Cabot Lodge and Nikita Krushchev on their trip across Iowa in the late 1950s.

On this morning in July Willa had kissed her husband off to his job at a farm machinery corporation in Des Moines, had kissed Ronny and Kenny off to the swimming pool, had washed the dishes and made the beds, tidied the magazines and dusted the tables, when the front door chimed. This surprised her. It was too early for Doreen's coffee visit, too early for salesmen. She checked her hair in the hall mirror and opened the door.

The man in the blue suit smiled. He had put on weight, there was gray in his hair, but that face could not be mistaken.

"Emory Novak!"

"Willa, hello there!" he said, heartily but a little uncertainly. "I was in Des Moines. I couldn't meet this fellow until lunch. So I said to myself, I'll go see Willa Burrage."

She was not prepared. She did not respond as he expected and his smile faded.

"Emory," she repeated. He was obviously waiting. "Well, come in."

She pointed to the couch, carefully taking the chair.

"You're prettier than ever, Willa."

She couldn't say that of him.

"What are you doing now, Emory?"

"I'm still in cans." He laughed. "I'm pushing our new cans for industrial wastes. I'm having lunch with this fellow but I said to myself, I gotta see Willa again."

A silence came upon them.

"How is Cheryl? How are the girls?"

"They're fine. How are the boys? How's Joe doing?"

She offered him coffee. He followed her out to the kitchen while she turned up the heat under the pot. Her nervous walking about upset her as much as when he leaned against the door to smile at her. Back in the living room she tried to be sure that he was the only one on the sofa, but when she made the mistake of sitting a moment to pour the cream, he put his arm around her and kissed her.

"No, Emory, no!"

"You've stopped smoking, haven't you?" he remarked. "I've always said the only sure way to stop a woman smoking was to kiss her enough."

"Well, last year——" The unexpected approach confused her. "Joe thought——"

He kissed her again.

"Emory, this is all behind us." She pushed him away. "It's done with. I told Joe——"

He put his arms around her and kissed her mouth, her eyes, her neck beneath her jaw. He began to unbutton her blouse. She sighed.

The unusual noise of many cars and even motorcycles coming nearer had made itself heard the last minute or two, but really the whole morning had lost its focus. She removed his hand. He put his arm around her waist. But then the tempo of all the details accelerated, for the cars and motorcycles stopped in the street outside, and she heard doors opening and shutting, shouts, the crisp sound of feet on the driveway. Emory's face froze even more fearfully as they both stood up.

"In there," she gasped, pointing to the bedroom, but he had already vanished. Staring, aghast, out the window while she mechanically rebuttoned her blouse, she saw police and men with cameras and men in dark suits and the burly man with the bald head and half-familiar face all getting off motorcycles and out of cars and converging on her house, when the doorbell chimed.

She opened the door halfway. A man knelt before her, his camera pointed at her face. "Hold it, Mrs. Burrage!"

She reeled back from the flash, which allowed a motorcycle policeman and two young men in dark suits to brush past her. Despairingly she turned her head and caught the mute witness of the two cups on the coffee table. The yard was already filled with strangers and beyond them she glimpsed the startled faces of her neighbors and the excited running children.

"Mrs. Burrage, your mailbox said. If you would be so gracious . . ." A tall man in expensive clothes was speaking to her. He possessed an air that showed, as Joe Burrage would say, that he was used to giving orders, but also at this moment oddly out of command with the aggressive figure of the bald-headed man behind him, and behind *him* a group of other men with ill-fitting suits and ugly hats who did not look in place at all.

"Hey, Mrs. Burrage, what's your husband do? How many kids do you have?" rasped a harsh voice at her elbow. A tide of men were pushing into her living room carrying notebooks and cameras, some taking up a silent, vaguely threatening stance in the corners as if someone might do something he shouldn't, and she was buffeted by random commotion until the tall man brought order back with a gesture of his arm.

"Mr. Krushchev, I'd like to present to you a real American housewife, Mrs. Joseph Burrage."

One of the clumsily suited men muttered a sentence of strange words, and Willa just had time to tell herself, "He's speaking Russian, in my living room. This is Krushchev," when the burly bald man with the little eyes grabbed her hand. He look tired and exasperated but his face also had a look of surly enjoyment at all the commotion.

"I'm Henry Cabot Lodge, Mrs. Burrage," the tall man stated. "We apologize for bursting in like this."

"I'm David Carmichael, State Department." Another man with silvery hair and the most beautiful gray silk tie she had ever seen hurriedly introduced himself and with a glance at his watch turned to the Russians. "This, Mr. Krushchev, is a typical American home," he said, speaking loudly and enunciating each word precisely as if he were speaking to his grandfather.

"Hey, Mrs. Burrage, what's your first name? How old are you? Where are the kids?"

"This is it, Mr. Krushchev," Mr. Lodge stated with an air of triumph despite the glaze of fatigue he shared with the Russian. "This is the American home," and the wave of his hand presented them Willa's couch and chairs and television set and the table with the two coffee cups still on it, although there were now so many people in the room—all men except for one lady reporter in a flowered hat—that it was hard to see the furniture. "There are twenty million homes just like this all over the United States," he concluded. "Solid, new, clean."

Clean, thank God, but she resented it that Mr. Lodge had not noticed anything special. Like the striped curtains. Where was Emory?

Krushchev spoke to her. The interpreter repeated: "What does your husband do? How much money does he earn?"

"He's in the advertising department in Warren Harvesters. He makes eighty-five hundred dollars, before taxes."

"We Americans are proud to pay our taxes, Mr. Krushchev," stated Mr. Lodge.

"Hey, lady, you a Democrat or a Republican?"

"Mr. Burrage is a Democrat. We both voted for Stevenson," she added a little diffidently.

Mrs. Burrage, that's wonderful!" Mr. Lodge turned his grand smile upon her. "That's nothing to be ashamed about. It takes two great political parties to make American democracy!" He put his arm around her shoulder while the cameras flashed. "You see, Mr. Krushchev, the details that separate Mrs. Burrage and myself mean nothing before the fundamental beliefs that unite us!"

Krushchev dabbed at the sweat on his forehead. "Da, da."

He had said *da*. That meant yes! The dictator of Russia was speaking in her own home, and she could understand him.

The unity of the group, however, fell apart and they scattered, Russians and Americans together, peering into the kitchen cupboards, opening the medicine cabinet above the bathroom sink, writing down the names of the comic books on the boys' floor—she hadn't picked up the comic books, and where was Emory? The exploration also disturbed Mr. Carmichael, whose hand was twitching from the times he kept checking his watch.

"Mrs. Burrage, what did you like best at school? What are your favorite books?" asked a reporter with horn-rimmed glasses and a gentle voice. Willa wondered whether he worked for one of the big newsmagazines in New York.

"Do you use mixes when you bake a cake?" This was the lady reporter in the flowered hat. "Did you breast-feed your babies?"

And who——" attempted Mr. Lodge.

he must carry on. And in a quiet, steady voice Willa
rrage said, "Mr. Lodge, I'd like you to meet an old friend
mine, Mr. Novak. Emory, this is the American Ambassa-
r to the United Nations, Henry Cabot Lodge, and Premier
rushchev, the Dictator of Russia."

Emory did not move. He remained in his apelike posture,
ngertips dangling by his bent knees, his lifeless face staring
at them. Had shock killed him? Would the slightest tremor
cause his body to collapse among the shoes at the bottom of
the closet? His eyes blinked. And Willa caught a glimpse of
a wide, awful grin spreading slowly across the face of the
Communist leader.

"Ho, ho," he chuckled. "*Stary droog*, old friend."

The spell broke. A dozen cameras sprang into the air.

"Please!"

An anguished cry burst from the throat of the ambassador.
The wretched official who had pulled open the closet door
flung himself before it, to shield with his own body Emory's
poor crouching form.

"Emory, come out! I'd like you to shake hands with Mr.
Lodge," Willa commanded, her voice still under control from
the last reserves of moral strength she did not know she
possessed.

There came a rustling of clothes and Emory appeared
around the State Department man, still crouching, his eyes
blinking in total incomprehension.

"How do," he whispered, extending his hand to the minor
official. Willa's flashing eyes revealed his mistake. Silently he
shuffled across the bedroom rug to Ambassador Lodge, gradually raising himself to his full height. "How do you do? I'm
Em Novak. I work for Illinois Can." Uncertainly he turned
to the dictator. "How do you do," he repeated, unsure in
this case whether he should offer to shake hands.

"Ho, ho, old friend, Mr. Novak, old friend," Krushchev
roared and seized Emory's hand so vigorously that the poor
man shook.

"Pliz, lady." An ugly Russian with fa\ lenses placed his face up to hers. "How o with husband?"

His companion, winking at her, whispe\ tion.

"Nyet, Dimitri," the first man snapped.

That meant no. But her pleasure at underst everything the Russians said was shaken by t. disorder of her guests. Hot and cross, they pul, dresser drawers and slammed them shut. In th cameraman was handing out beer from the icebo\ reporter was running her finger over the picture to ing Mr. Carmichael's watch, Henry Cabot Lodge pu, the cover of their bed.

"Look, Premier Krushchev, look at the quality of \ linen in this perfectly ordinary American home."

"And here, Mr. Gorochenko, you will the Burrages' \ robe, inexpensive but adequate and in good taste."

These clear words from a modest State Department offi standing beside the bedroom closet held some premoniti to Willa's ear. This was the one door in the house no on, had opened. She was too late.

"Two suits and a sports jacket," the State Department man was explaining to his Russian colleagues, but as he pulled back the sports jacket, his words died. There, with no hope of becoming anything else until the end of time, his blue suit blending with her husband's suits and his shoes blending with the shoes on the closet floor, was Emory. His face, which had been hidden behind the jacket because his knees were bent, stared out at them from the back of the closet like a great round plate.

Silence swept over the people in the bedroom, a silence so intense that it sucked in the probers and pryers from all the other rooms. A Secret Service man had pulled his automatic halfway from his shoulder holster.

The same grin had spread to the faces of all the Russians. By the naked anguish they shared with Mr. Lodge one could tell who were the State Department men and the nicer American journalists. But the photographers, ready to do anything in pursuit of their trade, again raised their cameras.

"No, please!" the ambassador cried again.

"Mr. Novak dropped by for coffee," Willa explained, her voice fading. "He's shy. That's why he hid."

"Of course. He's shy!" ejaculated Mr. Lodge. "This has been a very traumatic experience for you both."

"Shy?" The dictator queried. His interpreter whispered a word. Krushchev laughed and all the Russians grinned even more broadly.

"Guy de Maupassant, eh," said the shameless Russian with the thick lenses and dug his elbow into Mr. Carmichael.

"I think we should leave Mrs. Burrage's lovely home," began Mr. Lodge in a dignified tone. "Thanking her for her gracious welcome, apologizing for all the confusion we have caused . . ." The State Department men and the more responsible reporters nodded their heads warmly and smiled at Willa. "And perhaps there is no need for any of us to take any further pictures or write anything about Mr. Novak, who feels so ill at ease among strangers. For it is a matter of the honor of the home."

A somber man whom Willa had not noticed before stopped to Mr. Lodge's side and repeated his last words in slow and firmly enunciated Russian. Even the cameramen seemed to absorb their gravity. But not the foreigners. The bald-headed dictator and all his cronies with their floppy pants and big cheap shoes were having a fine time.

"Mr. Novak," asked the obnoxious Russian with the dirty mind, "how long you and Mrs. Burrage old friends?"

Wordlessly Emory's mouth opened and shut.

"Mr. Lodge is right. We must all be going," Mr. Carmichael said briskly. "We've got a busy day ahead of us. We want Mr. Krushchev to see that stockfeeding demonstration."

"Mrs. Burrage, you've been more than hospitable," said the official who had opened the fateful door, backing the newsmen out of the bedroom. Willa looked supplicatingly into the eyes of the Russian dictator, his face swimming through her tears. The grin softened into a fatherly smile.

"Little lady." He patted her arm. "Lovely home. So nice. We go." But he caught sight of silent, lifeless Emory, and the grin returned. "Ho, ho, old friend!"

"You'll have a lot to talk over with your neighbors, won't you, Mrs. Burrage?" crooned the lady reporter.

Willa reeled at the implication of these words. The front lawn must be solid with all of Prairie Dales.

"We can't leave *him*," Mr. Carmichael said with a nod at her unwanted friend.

A smile lit up the face of the youngest cameraman, a face she had liked at first sight with its snub nose and laughing blue eyes. He took his camera off his shoulder and hung it over Emory. "This is our new photographer, folks. Mr. Novak will come along with us."

His boyish grin spread to other faces around the room. A flicker of hope stirred in Willa's heart.

"Reporter from Tass!" laughed Krushchev, and he in turn removed the camera hanging from his great chest and placed the straps around Emory's neck. And so did the fat-lipped Russian, who clearly relished the foolish way Emory now looked with three cameras dangling frim him.

"We'll take good care of him, don't you worry, Mrs. Burrage," kindly Mr. Carmichael reassured her, his face above the beautiful silk tie alarmed by the sudden tremor she gave. "You just sit down and finish your coffee and pretend we never came."

"Good-bye, Willa," Emory's lips formed soundlessly. The departing visitors bore him and his cameras out the door and she could not reply.

"The American government is very grateful to you, Mrs. Burrage," Mr. Lodge said. Krushchev leaned forward to pinch her cheek. But they all did leave, and almost falling into the couch Willa could refocus her eyes—to the excited faces of Prairie Dales' housewives and children pressing against the windows. The door flung open, Doreen carrying a plate with a huge coffee cake on it, followed by their friends.

"Willa dear, tell us all about the morning you've had!"

CHARLES MERRILL wrote the stories contained in the Great Ukrainian Partisan Movement while living in Paris and Austria during the mid-fifties. They grew out of his experiences as a soldier in Italy, as a teacher for eight years in a tree-lined suburb of St. Louis, and from a wide exposure to the changes of the post-war world, east and west. In 1958 he settled in Boston where he founded the Commonwealth School, of which he was headmaster for twenty-three years. His story of the school, *The Walled Garden,* was published in 1982. He is married and the father of five children.